# "Last Star

## Nicho...

# Copyright © 2018 Nicholas Ryan

Author's note:

*This novel is dedicated to Ebony, who flew to Europe and America with me in 2015 to research this novel, visiting the locations mentioned in the book across several months.*

Also by Nicholas Ryan on Amazon:

**Ground Zero**
**Die Trying**
**Dead Rage**
**Zombie War**
**Brink of Extinction**

The Apocalypse began on a Thursday.
At O'Hare Airport.
Chicago.

# Prologue:

Emily Statham unlocked the door and then paused on the threshold for a long moment. The apartment was darkened, the drapes drawn against the afternoon light, and there seemed no one home. She had expected to find her mother in the kitchen preparing dinner. Emily frowned – and then heard a rustle of sweaty movement and strained impassioned groans coming from behind her mother's bedroom door. Emily narrowed her eyes and sighed. Her mom was with her newest boyfriend. Emily's lip curled into a sordid snarl of disgust. She could imagine what was happening behind that door, and it made her skin crawl with revulsion.

She crept down the hallway to her own bedroom.

The little jewelers box still sat on her bedside table, and she stood staring at it for a long time, filled with a rising sense of monumental anxiety.

She trapped her bottom lip between her teeth and brushed long lank hair away from her eyes. She was a dowdy insignificant person wearing a shabby jacket over a sweater, and a long shapeless skirt, her posture hunched, her shoulders slumped as though to draw attention away from her figure.

She pushed her glasses back up onto the bridge of her nose with the tip of her finger, and squinted shortsightedly around the rest of the room to be certain nothing had been disturbed – and slowly her unease turned, once more, to grim determined resolve.

Without removing her jacket or kicking off the sensible shoes that she wore, Emily perched herself on the edge of the narrow bed and reached tentatively for the little jewelry box.

It was the kind of felt-covered box that diamond rings were presented in; a small cube with a hinged top. Emily prised open the lid and stared down at the capsule, nestled in the bed of red velvet. It looked like a regular cold and flu tablet, completely unremarkable. It might even have been medication for insomnia or high blood pressure.

But it wasn't.

"It's all down to me," Emily muttered out loud to herself. "There's no one left to do God's work. I'm the only hope, and if I don't do this thing…" her voice trailed off as though the consequences were too terrible to consider.

She thought then about Viktor – the first and only man whom she had loved with all her heart. He had come to her when her life had been at its lowest ebb, and had shown her a depth of tenderness that she never thought possible. She remembered his dark blazing eyes and the passion in his voice as he told her about the world and his vision for the future. She listened to him while she lay curled up in his bed, wrung out and exhausted from the intensity of their lovemaking. He had told her that God had visited him, and that the Almighty had shown him a brave new world where there would be peace and harmony.

But not without a price.

Emily remembered the languid feel of his fingers, and the lazy way he trailed his touch along her arms, making

5

her shiver deliciously. She remembered the way he kissed her – the sizzle of his lips and then the deep empty space within her that he filled with thrusting passion and simmering intensity until she knew for sure that she would lay down her very life for him.

Which was why she sat in her tiny bedroom right now, clutching at the jewelry box, the memory of Viktor's smoldering Eastern European accent and his piercing pale blue eyes so vivid in her mind that she felt she could surely reach out her hand and still touch his swarthy face.

But Viktor had disappeared two days ago after armed police had raided his dingy little apartment on the south side of the city. Now, she imagined him being tortured, beaten and brutalized, or maybe even dead.

That sudden thought galvanized her, for life without Viktor would not be worth living. He had become her everything, and if he had died at the ruthless hands of the police, then she too would willingly give up her life for his vision, and for God's sacred work.

She snatched up the capsule from within the little box and slipped it into the pocket of her skirt, then took one last look around the room the way someone does when they are about to set out on a long journey. She caught a glimpse of herself in the full-length mirror and paused.

She didn't look like a revolutionary. She didn't have the restless eyes of a zealot. She looked just like an ordinary, dowdy young woman – a forgettable face that would be unnoticed in a crowd.

Emily smiled cruelly.

She left the room, locked the door carefully behind her, and then went down the hallway and knocked lightly on her mother's bedroom door. A hoarse startled voice called from within.

"Yes? What is it?"

"I want to talk to you, mom."

Emily pressed her ear against the door. She could hear a sudden rustle of urgent movement and voices harsh and suppressed. The bed squeaked and a moment later her mother cracked the door open and her face appeared.

Emily kept her expression impassive. She could smell the odors of stale sweat and seedy sex seeping from the room. Her mother's hair hung awry and her lipstick was smudged around her mouth. Even the soft light was cruel to her, highlighting the wrinkles around her eyes. Beyond her Emily caught a glimpse of the new boyfriend. He was lying naked on top of the soiled rumpled sheets. He had his arms wedged beneath his head, and she could see the spiral of his tattoo across his sweaty chest.

"What is it, honey?" her mother's voice sounded a little wild, a little uncomfortable.

Emily tried to smile. "I just wanted to tell you that I love you, mom."

Her mother pressed at her hair and her expression became confused. She stood naked. The door lay open just enough for Emily to see the pale flesh of her mother's hip.

"I love you too, honey," her mother said. The woman's fingers were trembling, the look in her eyes unfathomable. She cast a quick worried glance over her shoulder and then back to Emily. "Can we talk more about this later?"

Emily shook her head. "No," she said. "That's why I had to interrupt. You see I'm going away for a while – maybe a long time, actually. I might not see you again. I wanted you to know, before I left, that I love you, and I appreciate all you tried to do for me. I know it's been a hard life for you, and I wanted you to know that I am grateful for all your sacrifices."

Emily's mother smiled benevolently, indulgently, and Emily caught a whiff of the rank stench of alcohol on the woman's breath. "I love you too, honey," she tripped on the words and slurred them a little.

Emily nodded. There seemed nothing more to say. She started for the front door and heard her mother push the bedroom door closed, followed by the harsh rattle of a lock being thrown. Loud enough to be heard through the thin walls, the man in the bedroom grumbled, "Little fuckin' bitch. Ain't got no respect for a man's time. Did you tell her to fuck off?"

Emily's mother whispered something placating and then the apartment fell silent again.

Emily pulled the front door shut and went down the steps and out into the Chicago afternoon.

\* \* \*

Emily drove to the domestic terminals at O'Hare Airport and chose terminal 3 on a whim.

She parked her car between two concrete planter boxes in front of the glass doors and left the engine idling. At the far end of the terminal she noticed a woman in a yellow rainproof jacket patrolling the area, waving traffic on and barking instructions to drivers as they ducked and weaved between stagnant rows of stalled cars to drop off luggage and passengers. Emily leaped out of her vehicle and left the driver's door open. It had rained earlier in the day and the blacktop reflected the lights and colors from within the terminal. Emily stood on the yellow line of the curb for a moment. The air felt cool and damp, the late afternoon already darkening beneath a grey sullen sky towards nightfall. The woman in the colored rain jacket came striding briskly towards her. Emily turned her back.

"'Scuse me," the traffic patrol, officer thrust her face close to Emily's. She was a black woman, maybe in her forties, with a weary expression on her face. "Is that your car?"

Emily turned and stared at her little silver hatchback as if she had never seen it before in her life. She shook her head. "No," she said. "It belongs to a guy. He went that way." She pointed to a big blue sign.

The patrol woman widened her eyes a little and tried to peer through the crowd of people that had gathered around the entrances, smoking and chatting on their cell phones, each of them clutching suitcases. She snatched at a walkie-talkie clipped to her belt and went cautiously towards the rear of the vehicle to report the license plate.

Emily walked away. Ahead of her were the doors to the terminal. Displayed on the glass was a sticker with a picture of a handgun and a red line through it. Emily grunted. Airports all around the world had similar stickers for 'No Smoking' and 'No Pets Allowed', but Chicago airport had a reminder for locals not to bring their handguns into the terminal.

Inside the glass doors Emily stopped and took a moment to settle her jangling nerves. Her legs felt rubbery, and the acid burn of nausea in her guts gnawed at her resolve. She thrust her sweaty shaking hands into the pockets of her skirt – and felt the capsule with her fingertips.

"Do it for Viktor," she told herself, chanting the words over and over in her head like a mantra as her feet carried her forward, seemingly of their own volition. "Do it for him and for God."

The terminal was a huge cavernous building of polished floors and banks of fluorescent lighting that stretched in either direction for as far as Emily could see into the press of humanity. The entire terminal seemed filled with milling clusters of travelers who were formed into lines between crowd-control barriers of black and yellow tape. The faces of the people were blank; shuffling bovine queues of people lined up to endure the indignity of airport security checks. Two guards walked past Emily, chatting quietly to each other. They were dressed in blue shirts and black pants, with silver shields on their chest pockets and TSA badges on the sleeves of their shirts. Around their necks were plastic identity cards hung like long necklaces. The men came directly towards Emily, and she lowered her head quickly and averted her eyes. Her mouth turned dry as dust and a hot flush of panicked color bloomed on her cheeks. For a moment she thought she might throw up. A wave of giddy vertigo gripped her and she had to clench her teeth to keep her feet and to fight down her nausea. She saw a woman standing nearby talking on her cell phone. The woman had a suitcase at her side. Emily kept her eyes on the woman's face and shuffled in her direction. The two guards strode on by her without giving her a passing glance.

"You could be first," she thought to herself as the guards went purposefully towards the dark press of waiting people at the nearest security checkpoint. "You, or anyone else who tries to stop me."

There were rows of seats set along the glass wall of the terminal and Emily sat down heavily. She shook with nerves and apprehension. The sudden realization of what she was about to do assailed her conscience in crashing waves of guilt so that her vision filled with beating black bats wings and she thought she might pass out. She blinked away the darkness, feeling the heated flush of her own dread rising hot beneath the collar of her sweater and scalding across her cheeks. She was about to become the world's most notorious mass murderer. Millions were about to die – and she would be the bringer of that death.

*Could she do what Viktor had convinced her was necessary?*

Sitting on the seat beside her was a harried young mother with an infant child on her lap. A nest of luggage surrounded the woman, and her baby lay clutched in one arm. Emily glanced at the young woman surreptitiously from the corner of her eye. She looked pretty, with long brown hair and a slim figure. She hummed a distracted tune and gently bounced the baby in her arm. Emily slowly turned her head and smiled. The woman smiled back.

"You have an adorable child," Emily said kindly. The baby was swathed in a lemon yellow blanket, its eyes milky and unfocused from sleep. Its skin was soft and perfect. "A boy or a girl?"

"A girl," the woman smiled proudly.

"How old is she?"

"Five weeks tomorrow," the woman said and shifted the folds of the soft blanket from around the infant's face so that Emily could see more clearly. "We're on our way to Florida, so she can meet her grandparents."

Emily smiled and then leaned closer to the woman. She lowered her voice to a conspiratorial hush. "Please leave the airport," she said in a chilling whisper.

The woman with the child looked bemused. She frowned at Emily and the smile on her face wavered and then froze. "Pardon me?"

"Please leave the airport," Emily said again, fixing the woman with her gaze, trying through the force of her eyes to make the woman understand that she was serious. "Immediately."

"Why?" the mother asked. She glanced around her, suddenly becoming uncomfortable. She moved the baby into her other arm in an instinctively protective gesture.

"Because something truly terrible is about to happen," Emily's voice became strained. "And I don't want you or your child to be affected. I want you to have a chance to live."

The young mother's eyes grew wide with alarm. Her posture changed. She leaned away from Emily and then came out of the seat, shifting her feet in agitation. She rocked the child in her arm but the movement had become more jerked, more disconcerted.

"Are you serious? If this is some kind of a joke, it's not funny."

"I am serious," Emily said. She took off her glasses and stared at the woman with huge sad eyes. "Please. Take your baby and get out of here."

"*Who the fuck are you?*" the woman's voice rose suddenly and became shrill on the point of hysteria. She looked into the crowd, over the heads of the milling horde of waiting passengers, searching for a security guard.

Emily rose slowly to her feet and as she did, she reached into the pocket of her skirt and her fingers wrapped around the capsule. "I am the bringer of death," she shouted. "I am the Lord's disciple, sent on a sacred mission to free the world from its corruption and evil so that humanity may start again, better, purer, kinder…"

The young mother backed away, clutching her child tightly in her arms, the luggage forgotten. She started screaming, the sound of her voice echoing around the walls of the cavernous terminal. She stood pointing at Emily. Emily felt her cheeks flush. Hundreds of faces turned curiously towards her and then four armed airport security guards came bursting through the crowd, shoving milling bodies aside. Suddenly Emily found herself standing alone and isolated, and around her stood a semi-circle of bodies, their expressions filling with fear and panic as they tried to shrink away. Over their heads, she could see people beginning to run for the terminal's huge glass exit doors.

"Too late," she thought cynically.

Miraculously the nausea, the fear, and the terrible dread all fell away from her. She felt ice cold. She felt detached – as though she were suspended above her own body, removed from the drama and watching the scene play out like a clinical observer. Time broke down into fractured seconds, each one crystal clear, as Emily's senses seemed to overload. She could smell the anxiety in the crowd. It was in their eyes and it was on their skin – a tangible scent that seemed to hang like a cloud in the air. And she could see the alarm in their faces, the wild fear in their expressions, the twisted wrench of their mouths.

A voice seemed to reach out to her from a great distance, and she had to narrow her eyes and concentrate to bring it into focus. It was one of the security guards – a slim man with a boyish face and just the faint wisp of a downy moustache above his lip. He had a gun in his hand, the weapon thrust out at her. His legs were braced wide apart; his body crouched into a shooting stance. The man's face glistened shiny with sweat. He was shouting, and Emily frowned and watched the man's lips moving as though she were deaf and the sound was somehow muffled.

Then at last it all came to her clearly.

"Down on the ground!" the guard kept shouting. Another security guard poised on the edge of the crowd, also had his weapon drawn. Over her shoulder she could see two more blue uniforms. She concentrated on the man closest to her. A trickle of sweat ran from the man's brow, down his cheek, and then got trapped in the edges of his moustache.

"Get on the fucking ground!" he screamed.

Emily slowly pulled her hands from her pockets. In one clenched fist was the capsule Viktor had given her.

"Show me your hands!" the security guard shouted. "Open your hands. Both of them!"

Emily kept slowly raising her arms. Her mouth hung open, the expression on her face almost amused. She felt like she was immortal; like none of this really mattered.

Emily popped the capsule into her mouth and held it on her tongue. She lifted her hands high above her head, palms facing out. The security guard kept shouting at her, his voice becoming strident with his own panic. One of the other guards who stood behind her came forward two paces from out of the crowd as if to seize her from behind but she turned on him, quick as a cobra, and her eyes flashed a wicked warning. The guard backed away nervously and Emily turned round again. She tried to smile at the fearful press of faces in the crowd. She thought that would be a fitting last image for the world to remember; *Emily Statham – the grinning girl who destroyed the world.*

She thought for an instant about her mother, and about the man who had been her father before he had walked out one day and never come back. She thought about the young woman and her baby. And then her mind filled with visions of Viktor. In her imagination he was smiling at her adoringly, reaching his hand out to her, beckoning her to join him. She actually stretched out her hand as if to feel his fingertips… and then she realized it was all an illusion. Viktor wasn't reaching for her. It was the security guard.

Emily's eyes slammed back into hard focus. She snatched her hand away from the guard's grasp and then bit down on the capsule. For a single heartbeat nothing happened… and then a peculiar tang flooded across Emily's tongue and filled her mouth.

Suddenly her lips felt as though they were on fire. She could feel them puffing, swelling out of all proportion. Then her tongue seemed to thicken in her throat. She choked on a gagging breath and her eyes flew wide with abrupt horror. Her nostrils began to burn and a stream of mucus filled her throat and ran from her nose. It drooled down over her lips and hung in long silver strands from her chin. Emily screamed – a fear-filled terrified cry of pain and shock. This wasn't what Viktor had told her would happen. He had promised her she would feel like she was floating, rising slowly and beatifically towards Heaven.

She shook her head and a heaving gout of yellow gore and vomit hurled out of her gasping choking mouth. It spattered the guard and spilled across the polished airport floor. The crowd drew back aghast. Then Emily's bowels voided in a brown stinking liquid spray down her legs. She looked about her wide-eyed and retching with pain. She clawed her fingernails and hooked them into her mouth as if trying to tear out her tongue. Then a trickle of blood spilled from the corner of her eye like a teardrop. She felt it, warm on her hand, and she stared at

15

it in white-knuckled shock. She cried out one last time, and then Emily's eyes rolled up into the roof of her skull, turned yellow and bloodshot. Emily fell to the floor in a wretched stinking puddle of her own excrement and vomit. Her back arched like a bridge, and the crowd heard bones crack with a sound like snapping twigs. Emily's face stretched and swelled, contorting as the cords in her throat bulged from the skin like thick ropes. She drew one final breath, held it for long seconds while her hand reached out in a final desperate plea for help, or maybe salvation.

Then she slumped, dead. The air wheezed from her lungs, and she lay perfectly still.

The crowd gasped in shock, the sound of their moaning and breathless horror undulating as they crept closer, drawn by macabre fascination. The security guard holstered his weapon in white-faced disbelief. He went down onto one knee and reached tentatively towards the dead girl's body.

"Hank!" he looked up into the face of the nearest guard. "Call the paramedics."

The security guard felt under the young woman's jaw for a pulse and found nothing. His fingers were slippery with the dead girl's mucus and vomit. His face scrunched up into a mask of putrid revulsion. He wiped his hand on the leg of his trousers and looked over his shoulder into the faces of the crowd.

"Back up!" he shouted. "Everyone move back behind the security barriers."

The people shuffled away reluctantly, still fixed by their gruesome enthrallment. Then a woman in the crowd screamed a shrill cry of utter horror. The security guard narrowed his eyes, searching. He saw a young woman clutching a baby to her. She was pointing a trembling finger at him, and her eyes were enormous.

The guard didn't see the dead young woman sit upright. He didn't feel the clutch of her clawed hand around his throat. By the time she had come up onto her knees and sunk her teeth into the guard's shoulder, the crowd was running, fleeing in screaming panic.

The security guard fell onto his back, dead, and the thing that had been Emily crouched over the corpse almost protectively. It was panting hoarsely, loathsome yellow eyes rolling demented within the sockets of the skull. It looked around the airport and saw a thousand screaming people fleeing in a wild panicked crush for the doors. Glass shattered and the horrified press of bodies blew out huge plate glass windows.

The thing waited until the security guard's corpse began to twitch into re-animated life… and then it went hunting for fresh blood.

The undead Apocalypse had begun…

\* \* \*

# Part 1:

Steven Tremaine stood on the beach with one hand shading his eyes, and stared out at the blue horizon line where sky and ocean were smudged into an indistinct blur. The Mediterranean was as calm as a lake, the sea seemingly crushed flat by the oppressive afternoon heat. The water glittered like a million sunlit jewels and came lapping up onto the sand around his feet, blood warm.

A hundred yards off shore a suntanned man in a pair of red shorts stood on a long paddleboard, and behind him, like baby ducks in a line, were three women each of them struggling for balance and control of their own boards. They were on their knees, shifting the long paddle from side to side on the rolling wavelets, crying out in fits of panic and laughter.

The instructor turned around and let his board drift.

"Come on, Shelly," he said with a broad English accent, his voice carrying clearly to where Tremaine stood on the beach. "Keep your back straight and your knees parted."

The woman was the last in the line. She was a slim girl with pale skin, wearing a dark bikini. The woman let out a shriek and went tumbling off her paddleboard and into the waist-deep swell.

Tremaine smiled wryly and turned away, his gaze slowly drifting along the horizon until his eyes reached the promontory of the distant headland that jutted like a finger into the sea.

It was a beautiful Spanish afternoon, the long flat strip of Castelldefels beach covered with a thousand sunbaking bodies, their towels and colorful bikinis like bright flowers in a garden bed of sand.

Tremaine sighed. The beach lay forty-five minutes south of Barcelona, and yet it seemed like a world away from the thronging crowds and the bustling frenetic noise of the city. He took a deep breath, watched idly as an aircraft appeared in the distant sky, and then finally – as if he had been savoring the moment – he glanced down at the young woman lying on the beach towel beside where he stood.

Her skin had been tanned to honey brown and her hair lay long and dark across her shoulders. She was lying on her back with her eyes closed, her face lifted up into the afternoon sun like a worshipper. Tremaine's gaze lingered on the young woman's perfect physique, clad in a skimpy white bikini, with a twinge of guilt. She looked disquietingly young – maybe half his age.

He crouched down in the sand and ran his fingers lightly across the girl's shoulder. Her skin felt warm and silken.

"Maria, wake up, honey. I have to get back to the hotel and get ready."

The young woman opened her eyes and then smiled a slow languid invitation. She arched and stretched her back in a voluptuous feline gesture, and wordlessly reached out for Tremaine. Her fingers brushed against the inside of his thigh in a slow cunning caress and he stood up quickly, shaking his head.

"Sorry," he said. "I really am, but I don't have time for any more of that. I need to get back to the hotel and prepare for tonight's presentation."

The young woman pouted theatrically and rolled onto her side. "Then if you have no time for me, I think I will stay here at the beach," she said, her English heavily accented, and her voice throaty.

19

Tremaine nodded. "Do you want to meet again tonight? After the seminar?"

"Sure," she said. "I will be at the same dance club. Stop by if you like, and buy me a drink."

"I'll do that," Tremaine promised.

He picked up his beach towel and pulled his sunglasses from his pocket. He checked his cell phone. He had missed another call from New York. It was the third message he had missed since he had met Maria the night before. He grunted. He knew the number, and for a moment he considered dialing back. Maria kept watching him with dark enigmatic eyes.

"Something is wrong?"

Tremaine shook his head and showed her the phone. "Just my secretary," he smiled. "She likes to keep tabs on me."

"Tabs?" Maria frowned, not understanding.

"She likes to know where I am… and who I am with," his smile lightened playfully.

"You will tell her about us?" Maria asked, openly curious.

"No," Tremaine said. "Some things are best kept secret."

His hotel was a mile along the beach, nestled in the tree line that edged the sand. He waved goodbye to the beautiful young Spanish woman and began slowly walking through the hot sand.

The girl called out to him. "What is your name again?"

"Steven," he called back.

"And you are American, yes?"

"That's right."

"Okay!" she flashed a brilliant white smile. It seemed all she wanted to know. "I will look out for you tonight,

Steven." She waved at him brightly and stayed watching the broad of the Tremaine's back until at last he reached the grassy fringe of the beach and disappeared from her sight.

* * *

Tremaine came down off the stage with the sound of polite applause at his back. He was sweating from standing under the conference room's spotlight, his voice a little raspy, his body just beginning to loosen with relief now that the lecture was over. He ducked behind a plush red velvet curtain and one of the hotel's staff greeted him. She was a tall, elegant looking woman with immaculate make-up. She wore the city hotel's navy blue uniform. Her eyes were bright, the smile almost, but not quite, genuine.

"A glass of water for you, Professor Tremaine," the woman handed him a crystal tumbler. "And there are soft drink refreshments in the mini bar just along the hallway."

Tremaine nodded. He mopped his brow with a handkerchief and swallowed the water in a long appreciative gulp. It was dark and cool in the shadows behind the stage and Tremaine slumped against a wall and loosened his tie. In the auditorium the applause had dwindled and he could hear the murmur of voices and the shuffle of feet as the audience began heading for the conference room exit. He imagined many of them heading to the hotel's bar but the thought of joining them did not appeal – not when compared to the memory of the tall beautiful young Spanish girl waiting for him back in a Castelldefels night club.

21

Tremaine glanced at his watch and made a wry face. He had been on stage for exactly two hours and one minute.

"I know the damned material so well, and I've preached the same message so many times, I've got my lines down to a perfect patter," he thought. The realization gave him no pleasure. He kept repeating the same warnings to the assembled world leaders... and they kept smiling blandly and nodding their heads with inane placations.

No one was listening.

Tremaine let out a long slow breath and was about to follow the backstage hallway towards the exit doors when a short, smartly dressed man suddenly appeared. He wore a hand cut suit of the finest cloth and a silk tie. His face was broad and smiling, his thinning grey hair swept across his brow and curled at the ears and collar. His eyes were bright and twinkling with mischief. The man saw Tremaine and threw his arms wide in a delighted greeting.

"Steven, my old friend!" the man laughed. His accent was French. "How very good to see you again."

"Maxime?" Tremaine's eyes widened with genuine surprise. "What the hell are you doing here?"

Laughing, the Frenchman embraced Tremaine and kissed him on both cheeks, then stood back and shrugged his shoulders in a typical Gallic gesture. He smelled of fine cigars and expensive aftershave. "I came to hear your lecture, Steven."

Tremaine stared at the man, shaking his head slowly. "Maxime, you've heard my lecture. It's the same one I delivered in New York, and in Washington. It's the same speech I gave in Madrid and Amsterdam... and it's the same warning I made in Paris and London. Hell, you know my damned message as well as anybody."

The Frenchman made a contrite face of appeasement and then the smile crept back up onto his lips. "As France's Minister of Health, Steven, it is my duty to keep abreast of all new information," the corners of the man's eyes crinkled into a spider's web of fine wrinkles. "And besides," he lowered his voice conspiratorially and winked, "it is the chance for a brief expenses paid holiday away from Paris with my secretary." He nudged Tremaine's shoulder and then thrust his hands into his pockets, balancing on the balls of his feet. He ran an appraising eye across Tremaine.

"You look good, my friend. Barcelona's sunny weather suits you, eh?"

Tremaine nodded. Maxime Baudin had been a close friend since he had begun his political career at the turn of the century serving as a member of the National Assembly of France. Now the man was the nation's Minister for Health and Social Affairs. "Spain certainly has its natural beauties," Tremaine said abstractly.

Maxime Baudin gave an obligatory wicked little laugh and then sniffed delicately at the air as if to change the subject. Quite suddenly his expression became more like the grave countenance of a politician. He waved one of his hands as if he were conducting a slow passage of music. "This latest news from America..." he paused significantly. "Do you think it in some way begins to validate your theories?"

Tremaine looked surprised. "What news, Maxime... and what theories exactly are you talking about? I've been on a beach for five days with no television and no internet."

"Your overpopulation theory, Steven," the French Minister licked at his lips and his eyes became hooded. Behind the twinkle in the man's gaze there was now some dark cloud of earnest concern. It smeared away the bright glitter of mischief and darkened his eyes so they were almost black. "You have been telling the world for two years that overpopulation was going to bring about the end of mankind one day, yes?"

Tremaine inclined his head cautiously. "Maxime, I'm a Professor of Disease Ecology – that's what we do. We talk about the dramatic rise in the world's populations and how that affects the spread of disease. We talk about how the correlation between the risk of a pandemic and human population density means that *when* the next big pandemic emerges mankind will be unlikely able to isolate it. We're overcrowding the world, my friend," Tremaine tried to lighten his tone a little but the Frenchman did not respond.

Tremaine sighed and then became serious. "Maxime, in the second half of the twentieth century, the world's population grew from 2.5 billion to 6 billion, *in just fifty years*. And by the end of this century, that number could be as high as 11 billion." Tremaine shook his head slowly and frowned, trying not to slip back into the rehearsed language of his seminars. "With so many people on the planet, we are changing the way we interact with animals and our environments. We're living too closely together. Disease in Africa can often be isolated because its origins tend to be in remote communities that can be quarantined. But if those same diseases broke out in the heart of London, or Moscow..." Tremaine shrugged. "It would sweep across the populated centers of the world like a wildfire. It couldn't be isolated. Cities that size could never be quarantined – not with global trade and

24

travel. No, that, my friend, would mark the beginning of the end for mankind."

Tremaine stopped talking for a moment and shuddered involuntarily. He had played out these scenarios in his mind and through sophisticated computer models for several years. It still gave him nightmare chills.

He fixed the French Health Minister with a wary, curious gaze and narrowed his eyes. "What's this all about, Maxime? What aren't you telling me? You've never been this interested in my theories before, and you've never come back stage after one of my seminars."

Maxime Baudin gave a restless glance at the gold Rolex watch on his wrist and then looked furtively over his shoulder. When he turned back to Tremaine, his expression had become more composed. Some of the deep lines of concern that had been etched around the features of his face had softened. "This is not the time, my friend," he clapped Tremaine affectionately on the shoulder. "And I have to return to Paris."

"Tonight?"

"Yes, I'm afraid so."

"Immediately?"

"Yes. I only flew to Barcelona this afternoon to meet with you. I must fly back," the edge of anxiety had crept back into the Frenchman's voice and Tremaine felt himself become troubled.

"What's going on, Maxime?"

The Frenchman shrugged. "I suggest you find a television, Steven. Quickly." Baudin turned to go, and then paused. He glanced back at Tremaine with an expression on his face like a forlorn sad farewell. "You have my number, yes?"

Tremaine nodded. "Yes."

25

"Then call me in Paris tomorrow morning."

Tremaine nodded. He watched the French Minister walk away… and then his cell phone began ringing.

\* \* \*

"Hello?"

*"Where the fuck have you been?"* a young woman's voice bellowed down the line, made sharp by anxiety and panic. "I've been phoning you for two days."

"Hi, Ginny," Tremaine said repentantly. "Sorry I missed your calls."

His secretary, Ginny McClusky panted into the phone, her breathing ragged as if she had run a great distance. Tremaine frowned with an edge of concern.

"Are you okay?"

"No," Ginny's voice dropped to a whisper, and then trailed off into utter silence for long seconds. Tremaine heard the sound of a door opening and then closing. When Ginny spoke again, her voice sounded like an echo. "Steven," she drew a deep breath, "… I think it's really happening."

"Happening? What, Ginny?"

"The end of the world," Ginny whispered. Her voice became hoarse and strained. "I think your predictions are coming true."

Tremaine felt a sudden ice-cold weight settle in the pit of his guts, and then something crept up into his chest and slowly wrapped its tentacles around his heart. He heard his breath catch. "What do you mean?"

"Haven't you been watching the television?"

"No," Tremaine said. "I've been on a beach. I was on vacation, remember."

"Well get to a television, Steven. There must be a television in the hotel, for Christ's sake."

"There is, I'm sure," Tremaine kept his voice steady. "But I'm not staying at this hotel."

"What? Where are you staying?" Ginny's voice became strident.

"In a hotel about forty-five minutes out of the city. A resort town called Castelldefels."

*"Where the fuck is that?"* Ginny snapped. "I booked you a room at the hotel where the lecture was taking place."

"I changed the booking."

Tremaine heard Ginny's deep breaths, simmering with her temper and frustration. She went quiet for a moment and her voice became almost hollow.

"America has been struck down by some kind of a pandemic, Steven. It broke out last Thursday at O'Hare Airport. That was ground zero. Since then it has spread right across the eastern seaboard."

The cold coiling thing in Tremaine's guts slithered. "What kind of pandemic?" he asked slowly.

"No one knows," Ginny said.

"What is the mortality rate?"

"One hundred percent," Ginny said.

Tremaine shook his head. "That's not possible."

"Neither is a contagion that re-animates the dead, Steven. *But that's exactly what's fucking happening.*"

Tremaine pulled the phone sharply away from his ear as Ginny's voice rose to a scream. "Did you say re-animates the dead?"

"Yes!" Ginny had to fight to keep control of her panic. "Everyone who is bitten or scratched by one of the infected dies and then is re-animated as an undead corpse. It all happens within sixty seconds of cardiac arrest. They get up, Steven. They come back to life."

"Ginny, that's not possible."

"Well it's fucking happening, Steven. It's fucking happening. It's on every television news broadcast around the world."

Tremaine felt the whole world tilt off kilter. He clamped a hand to his forehead, his thoughts swirling in chaotic confusion. He closed his eyes and tried to clear his mind – tried to separate the hysteria in Ginny's voice from the few facts she had told him.

"Tell me everything that's known so far."

"There's nothing more to tell, Steven," Ginny cut across him brusquely. "The media are calling it the Raptor virus."

"Raptor virus?"

"That's what the news outlets are using."

"Why?" Tremaine found that his jaws were tightly clenched and that his hands were trembling.

"It's the way the infected act," Ginny's voice dropped as though she were sharing something secret. "They act like raptor dinosaurs. They hunt, Steven. They think on some basic instinctive predatory level. They're cunning…"

"But if they're undead…?"

"For Christ's sake, Steven!" Ginny's voice barked. "Something happens to them. They re-animate, but their senses seemed enhanced. It's like they can smell blood."

"What? Like sharks?"

"Like hunters. Predators. They're killers, Steven. They hunt people down in packs."

"Okay," he said evenly, "What about the first patient? Or any patient struck down by the contagion. Has anyone done blood work?"

Ginny almost laughed, but the sound verged on the edge of morbid madness. "There are no patients, Steven.

Everyone infected is an undead killer. Already the estimates are at four or five million, and that number is increasing exponentially by the hour. In seventy-two hours, America will be a wasteland. No one will be left alive."

Tremaine felt the punch of Ginny's words like physical blows that left him reeling, staggering for balance. He stared into space, his jaw slightly unhinged and the firm thin line of his mouth dropping slack with disbelief. He slumped against a wall and the cold dread in his guts became a fever-like flush across his cheeks. He recalled Maxime Boudin's farewell and the sad expression on the little Frenchman's face. Now the mysterious cryptic questions were beginning to make dreadful sense.

"Ginny, where are you?" Tremaine asked urgently.

"I'm locked in my bathroom," she said, her voice suddenly very quiet.

"Your bathroom? Why?"

"Because they're here, Steven. The contagion has spread to New York. The zombies are roaming the fucking streets," suddenly the last shreds of her composure cracked, like the wall of a dam, and she began to weep softly. "They're killing everyone. Men, women… and children."

Tremaine felt a sob of sickening dread clutch in his throat. "Can you get out of the city, honey? Can you drive to your parents place in Ohio?"

For a long time he heard just the sound of gentle agonized weeping down the line. "Ginny…?"

"They're dead," her voice became small and faltering. "Ohio has been overrun. My mom and dad are dead. The contagion… one of the zombies broke into their house."

29

Without realizing it Tremaine's hands had balled into white-knuckled fists. "I'm sorry..." he whispered impotently.

Ginny sniffed into the phone and her voice shuddered tremulously. "The FFA grounded all flights, domestic and international. They did that yesterday, but it was too late. Japan has already recorded its first cases, and so has Singapore. Steven... the contagion will be in Europe within forty-eight hours. Nothing can stop this thing. It's exactly what you have been predicting. Overpopulation is going to be the death of mankind. It's in the cities and there's no way to isolate those who have become infected..."

Tremaine pushed himself off the wall, his feet carrying him in a numbed daze along the hallway behind the stage, out through an exit door and into the grand foyer of the hotel. The décor was elegant; crystal chandeliers hung from the high ceiling, and the walls were hung with expensive original canvases depicting rural Spanish landscapes. In a darkened corner near the long reception counter there were nests of high-backed chairs around low tables. On the opposite side of the foyer were rows of dining tables where the hotel served complimentary breakfasts to its guests. Mounted on the wall were three television monitors. Somber, fearful crowds of hotel patrons were clustered around each screen, their eyes wide with shock and disbelief. Many were talking on their phones, their faces lifted and lit by the eerie glow of the televisions as they tried to connect with loved ones in far away places. Tremaine stood back from the crowd and looked over their heads at the shocking images that flashed across the nearest television.

"Steven...?"

"Yes," Tremaine said into the phone. "I've just come into the hotel foyer. I'm watching a television right now. It's the BBC's news service."

Suddenly Ginny made a soft stifled sound of horror and then said in a blubbering terrified whisper, *"Oh, God!"*

Tremaine's expression turned sharp and dark. His eyes slammed into focus. He clutched the cell phone tightly in his hand. "What's happening?"

"I think they're here…" Ginny croaked. Her voice wavered and there was an agonizing silence. Then Tremaine heard a sound of shuffling feet. "There's someone bashing on my apartment door," Ginny cried softly.

"Call 911," Tremaine urged.

"It's too late. The emergency service overloaded and shut down."

"Is there a window?"

No answer. Tremaine felt his heart thumping wildly in his chest. He crushed the phone to his ear and listened intently. He could hear muffled movement, indistinguishable, and then short harsh breathing.

"Steven, they're inside the apartment," Ginny wept into the phone. "I can hear them. They're growling, shrieking."

"Ginny, stay with me," Tremaine tightened his voice. "Tell me everything that's happening. What can you hear?"

"Just groaning and shrieking," Ginny's terror was transparent in the croak of her voice. "And footsteps… coming closer."

"Stay calm," Tremaine whispered helplessly. "Is there anything nearby that you can use as a weapon?"

Ginny said nothing and Tremaine felt himself hanging in the silence with the blood pounding at his temples and his hands beginning to shake. "Ginny…?"

"Steven?"

"Yes. I'm here, honey. I'm right here."

"Find somewhere in Europe that will be safe. Find a haven that can be defended. You've got less than forty-eight hours…"

Tremaine was about to reply when suddenly he heard a shockingly loud pounding at a door, and then the blood-curdling scream of Ginny's voice. Tremaine felt the prickling sting of tears in the corners of his eyes.

"Ginny!"

He heard the sound of the phone clatter to the floor and then the splinter of wood as the girl's bathroom door crashed back against the hinges. There was a piercing shriek – the sound inhuman and sinister – and then a gurgling hiss of breath and the distinct shocking sound of bones breaking.

"Ginny!"

The scream in the girl's throat was cut abruptly short and Tremaine stared, horrified, at the phone for long seconds, his body lathered in sweat, his heart thudding frantically in his chest and his hands shaking like a man in the grips of fever.

After a very long time Tremaine shut down his cell phone and turned to stare at the images flashing across the hotel monitors. He felt numb, hollow. Ginny's voice, and the wrenching sound of her dying scream, seemed to echo hauntingly in his mind. Tremaine wondered absently why the television pictures were blurred. He blinked his eyes, and lifting his fingers slowly to his face, he realized without surprise that is own cheek was slick and wet with tears.

* * *

Tremaine did not return to Castelldefels. Instead he sat slumped down into one of the deep foyer chairs, staring out through the hotel's full-length glass windows at the twinkling lights of Barcelona. In the background he could hear the sounds of the televisions, the voices of the news reporters strained as they broadcast each new atrocity of the horror that crept like darkness across the world.

Tremaine did not watch. His mind was seized in a revolving nightmare of memories and imaginations. He recalled the sound of Ginny's terrified screams as she died, and her horrific cries would not leave his mind. The agonized sound of the young woman's voice swirled amongst thoughts about his own predictions – the dire consequences of a contagion spreading like a wildfire as it was fed by densely packed populations. When at last he glanced numbly at his wrist watch, the time showed as 1:35 in the morning.

Tremaine shook himself. He felt physically and emotionally drained to the point of exhaustion. The fatigue weighed him down with an insidious lethargy as though he had drunk from a witch's brew of hopelessness and despair. There simply seemed no escape; no way for the world to survive the global spread of the Raptor contagion.

Tremaine heaved himself out of the chair with an effort and stood, shoulders slumped and his head hanging. It gave him no satisfaction to know that his theories were being validated and that as he did nothing, his dire predictions for the extermination of the human race were being played out around the world in gruesome live broadcasts.

*But what could he possibly do?*

He thrust his hands deep into his pockets and walked slowly out through the hotel's sliding glass doors and into the darkness. The evening was warm and balmy – a night sky filled with stars, and a thick slice of pale yellow moon. Somewhere far off he could hear the wail of a police siren, and on the streets surrounding the hotel people stood in small clusters as though to seek comfort from each other. Tremaine distractedly reached into his pocket and lit a cigarette.

For six years he had fought against the establishment just for the opportunity to have his theories heard, and over the past two years he had travelled the world speaking regularly at world summits and global conferences detailing the very real danger to mankind from an exploding population. The densely packed cities, teeming with humanity, were fuel for the fire of contagion. He had called on governments to stop relying on science to provide vaccines and reactive medical treatments. He had pleaded with them to reconsider urban designs; preventions rather than cures.

No one had listened.

Now it was too late.

The only chance of survival that people had left was to disperse into the countryside – to flee far away from population centers in the hope that the contagion would eventually burn itself out... or to find a city that could be fortified and quarantined... and such a place did not exist.

Tremaine stopped in mid stride with the cigarette smoldering between his fingertips as a new and startling thought suddenly slammed into his mind. He heard

Ginny's voice again – not the dreadful screams at the moment of her death – but her words… her last words.

*"Find somewhere in Europe that will be safe. Find a haven that can be defended. You've got less than forty-eight hours…"*

Suddenly an idea came creeping into his consciousness, tingling along the flesh of his forearms so that his whole body began to itch with exhilaration. The idea hung before him like a ghost of smoke – so tantalizingly close that he closed his eyes and tried to beckon it to him. It formed, then dissolved again. He wrung his hands in frustration and stood very still, willing the idea to materialize. His breathing slowed and his body went perfectly still. He could hear the echo of his blood beating at his temples…

"Jesus Christ!" he exclaimed.

There *was* a place – a city that could be fortified and defended against the contagion. It was the one city in the world he knew of where mankind could make its last stand against the spread of the undead plague.

"Avignon!"

Tremaine crushed the butt of the cigarette under the heel of his shoe and started to run. He could feel the urgent thumping trip of his heart and the adrenalin surge tremble through his fingers. His feet slapped heavily on the cobblestoned walkway, the tails of his suit jacket flapping around his waist like bats wings. He reached the hotel foyer, gasping, panting for breath, still trembling with suppressed excitement; it coursed through his blood, sizzling, as his mind raced ahead over a million contingencies, setbacks, obstacles and possibilities.

He checked his wristwatch again. 2 o'clock in the morning. It would be the same time in Paris. He wondered for a moment whether Maxime Baudin had flown back into the French capital yet – and considered the idea of waiting until the next morning.

"No," Tremaine shook his head. Mankind couldn't wait.

He stabbed at the cell phone with his fingers and when he heard the ring tone, he began to pace with urgent purposeful steps. Blisters of anxious and exerted sweat squeezed out across his brow, and he wiped them away with the rumpled sleeve of his suit. The ring tone went on for a very long time – and then the call disconnected.

"Fuck!"

Tremaine stormed to the reception desk. A pale-faced woman stood behind the counter, her gaze fixed on the television screens in the foyer, her mouth open and her eyes dark pools of dread. She caught Tremaine standing impatiently before her from out of the corner of her eye but the automatic smile that crept onto her lips was tight and strained.

"Yes, sir?"

"I need you to dial a number for me," Tremaine said anxiously and it put a jagged edge to his voice. "Right away."

The receptionist arched her eyebrows, taken back by the grim-faced man's tone. She composed herself. "Who would you like to call?"

Tremaine thrust the phone at the young woman. "Him," he said. "The French Minister for Health, Maxime Baudin. That's his number displayed on the screen."

For a long moment the receptionist was taken aback. She dialed the number from the hotel phone and stood with the receiver pressed to her ear, staring politely out through the tall glass windows, her expression blank.

Tremaine drummed his fingers on the polished wooden counter. After a full minute the receptionist carefully replaced the phone in its cradle. "I'm sorry, sir. There was no answer at the number you gave me."

Tremaine snapped his hands into fists and clenched his jaw. He could feel a clock ticking down time in his mind, counting away precious seconds that could not be spared. He drew a deep breath, and then let it out. The tension remained etched deep into the lines of his face.

"Can you check the train timetables for me please?"

"Certainly, sir. Where would you like to travel to?"

"Avignon, in the south of France. As soon as possible."

The woman tapped at the keys of a computer monitor and Tremaine stood impatiently, growing aware that suddenly there were more people standing behind him, waiting in line. He turned slowly and saw as many as twenty people with their luggage, lining up to check out of the hotel. The receptionist lifted her eyes and pressed a buzzer on the counter to call for assistance.

Tremaine frowned. The faces behind him were ashen with fear and nervousness. He looked past them to the nearest television and saw a yellow flashing ticker-tape running across the bottom of the screen beneath a broadcast that showed iconic images of England. Tremaine went with slow dread towards the monitor, his eyes narrowed. When he could read the urgent announcement, his blood turned to ice in his veins:

*Breaking News: First cases of undead infection reported in London.*

Tremaine stood rooted to the floor for long seconds, unable to move. The contagion had reached Europe. The silent clock in Tremaine's became a rapid ticking… counting down to something explosive.

He pushed his way back through the unruly crowd to the reception desk. The woman behind the counter had a harried, panicked expression on her face. A man in a long dark coat hissed at her belligerently. He threw a wad of papers down on the counter. He was a big man, heavy in the gut and shoulder from too many expense account dinners, dressed in a dark suit. At his feet lay a single suitcase. He saw Tremaine and glared defiantly at him.

"Back of the fuckin' line!" the man growled. His accent sounded English, his breath foul with the stench of stale alcohol. Tremaine held the man's threatening gaze evenly for long seconds and then turned deliberately to the receptionist.

"Any luck with the train schedule?"

"Yes," the receptionist said.

"Hey! Didn't you hear me?" the businessman beside Tremaine jabbed him in the ribs with his elbow. "I said to get to the back of the fuckin' line."

Tremaine let out a sigh and turned to face the man. They were about the same height. The businessman's eyes were dark little specks in a fleshy florid face.

"I'm in the middle of something," Tremaine said reasonably. "And it's important."

"I don't give a shit!" the man snarled, his face swelling. "*I'm* important."

The man swung an awkward punch at Tremaine, but he was cramped against the counter and his arm slowed by the drag of his heavy coat. Tremaine took the blow on his shoulder and then lunged forward and seized the lapels of the man's coat with both his hands. He pushed the man hard and he went reeling backwards, tripped on the leg of a table and sprawled to the ground. Behind Tremaine's back, the crowd of people waiting to check out of the hotel made an ugly, restless sound and Tremaine sensed they were on the verge of panicked riot. He slammed his hand on the top of the counter and the receptionist flinched.

"Tell me!" Tremaine hissed.

"There is one train tomorrow," she said, scrawling the information onto a scrap of paper. It departs from Barcelona at 8:05 in the morning and arrives in Avignon at 12:30 in the afternoon."

"Direct train?"

"There is one stop in Nimes for thirteen minutes to change trains," the receptionist's face flushed red with agitation. In the background a security alarm sounded from somewhere in the hotel.

"There's nothing sooner or faster?"

"No," the receptionist said. "That's the only train."

Tremaine nodded grimly, then turned and glowered into the faces of the crowd. Their expressions were ugly, pressed in a pack close about him. Someone helped the English businessman unsteadily to his feet. The man dragged the back of his hand shakily across his mouth and glared with seething menace as Tremaine pushed his way through the wall of bodies and out once more into the warm Spanish night.

Tremaine stood at the street corner and redialed the number for the French Minister of Health. Cars were racing past the intersection, something frenetic about the way they were moving. A police siren wailed out of the darkness and went speeding by in a strobe of flashing lights and an ugly roar of engine noise. Cars honked and drivers shouted and gestured aggressively at each other. Tremaine pressed the phone to his ear as the ring tone went on and on.

Finally there was a click on the other end of the connection and Tremaine heard a tired, weary voice, the accent familiar. "Hello?"

\* \* \*

"Maxime!"

"Steven? Is that you?"

"Yes. Where are you, my friend?"

Boudin sounded exhausted. "I have just arrived back in Paris. The plane – there were delays. Are you still in Barcelona?"

"Yes, Maxime, I am."

"And am I to assume that you have seen the dreadful news?" Boudin asked confidentially with a thin edge of fear in his voice.

"I have."

There was a long silence. Tremaine could hear the French Minister talking to someone in hushed urgent tones, and then came the sound of a car's engine revving in the background.

"So…?" Boudin's voice became very quiet. "What can we do to save the world, Steven?"

Tremaine took a deep breath. "Maxime, the contagion has reached London. I just saw it on the news."

"Yes," Boudin said heavily. "I have learned this also."

"It's coming your way, Maxime. There's nothing you can do to stop this virus from spreading into France."

The sudden silence lasted for so long that Tremaine feared that the connection had been broken. "Maxime? Did you hear me?"

"Yes," Boudin said. He sounded very old and tired. "Then what can we do, Steven?"

"Evacuate Paris, Maxime. Get as many people as you can out of the major cities and into the countryside. You need to disperse the population in the hope that the contagion will burn itself out."

Tremaine tried to imagine Maxime Boudin's face, his expression crumbling under the crushing weight of his responsibility. He could picture the man out front of an airport, or maybe still on the tarmac, waiting to get into a government car. Tremaine lifted his own face and looked into the streaming banks of traffic speeding past the intersection where he stood. A taxi went past in a hurry — too fast for him to wave the driver down.

"Maxime? Are you still there?"

"Yes, Steven. I'm heading to the Ministry."

"No," Tremaine said with curt alarm. "Maxime don't go into Paris. If you do it's a death sentence."

"Monsieur," Boudin slipped into French for a moment and put sudden steel and pride in his voice. "Since the time of Bonaparte the French have been proud warriors. We have conquered most of Europe. Our bravery has never been questioned. I, for onc, will not flee in the face of my responsibility to my nation nor my people."

Tremaine shook his head in frustration. "Maxime, I'm not talking to the Health Minister. I'm talking to you as a friend."

"Then as a friend, you should understand," Maxime's tone softened just a little. "And as a colleague you should respect my decision."

Tremaine sighed. "I have another option…" he began, measuring his words carefully. "The alternative to dispersing the population is to gather them together in a place that is absolutely defendable. A place that is

41

fortified and provisioned, where people would be safe from the infected."

"And you know of such a place?" the fatigue in Boudin's voice suddenly fell away.

"Yes."

"Where?"

"Avignon, Maxime. It's the only city I know of in the world that has a chance of standing like a bastion against this contagion."

"Avignon…" Boudin repeated the name as if trying to find a reference in his memory. Then, suddenly he had it. "The ancient walled city," his voice came alive. "My God, Steven. Yes. It would be perfect."

"Then meet me there, Maxime."

"No," Boudin said, emphatic and final. "I must stay in Paris."

Tremaine hung his head in frustration. "Then at least help me to save as many people as I can," he pleaded.

There was another interminable pause before Boudin answered. "Yes," he said, decisive and emphatic. "I can do that. Tell me what you need."

Tremaine thought quickly. "I'm catching the morning train from Barcelona tomorrow. I'll be arriving in Avignon at 12:30 in the afternoon. Maxime, I need someone to meet me at the train station."

"Done. I will have a police escort organized and waiting."

"And I need you to call the mayor of Avignon on my behalf. I need you to talk to the man directly – tell him who I am."

"Steven, I don't have the influence to – "

"Then find someone who does, Maxime!" Tremaine's voice rose with irritation, and then dropped again immediately into something that sounded more patient.

42

He tried to keep his tone neutral, his reasoning logical. "All I need is for the mayor and his staff to listen to me. I need them to hear me out. And I need to use whatever authority you do have to get their attention. Do that for me, old friend, and I can save thousands of people."

Boudin grunted into the phone and then his voice became firm with renewed authority. "Okay, my friend. I will do it. But Steven, don't miss your train. At 2pm tomorrow, the President is going to announce that France will be immediately closing its borders. It's only the second time such an unprecedented measure has been taken since 1962."

"It won't help."

"Perhaps not," Boudin conceded grudgingly. "But the last time the borders were closed was after the Paris shootings. The government has also heightened its alert status to one that is similar to an imminent terrorist threat."

"Meaning?"

"Meaning that by tomorrow afternoon every crossing point into France will be a heavily guarded checkpoint. If you aren't on that train, you won't get into the country."

"Maxime," Tremaine said ominously, "If I'm not on that train, then you can assume I am already dead."

"I hope that is not the case, my friend," Boudin said seriously. In the background Tremaine heard car doors opening and closing, and the noise of the revving engine became louder, almost insistent.

Tremaine raised his voice. "Take care of yourself, Maxime."

The Frenchman almost smiled wryly into his cell phone. "If that was all I had to do, Steven, I would be on the next plane to Avignon," his voice became grave. "But I must do what I can to take care of my people, and for that reason, I must stay in Paris. It is you who should take care of yourself. The people of Avignon will need you. You might be the world's last best hope for survival."

\* \* \*

Tremaine spent the night sleeping in a seat at Barcelona train station, so that when the train arrived into Avignon station the following afternoon, he stepped onto the platform feeling utterly exhausted. The journey north from Spain into the south of France had been painstakingly slow, and not even the passing view of the lush green countryside could distract him from his nightmare thoughts.

The train was crowded, every available seat occupied by frightened people clutching their possessions close to them, and the air in the coach was thick with sweat and the coppery tang of fear. Tremaine stood very still on the platform while the other disembarking passengers swirled around him like rushing water around a rock.

Tremaine waited until the train drew away from the station and went to the high glass windows. At the bottom of a concrete slope he had a view of a parking lot, sprinkled with vehicles that were baking under the warm afternoon sun. At one end of the lot stood a taxi stand, and drawn up beside a long row of waiting drivers was a police motorcade; three motorbikes in an arrow formation around a police Renault hatchback with darkly tinted windows. The rear door of the police car hung open and one of the motorbikes was unmanned. Tremaine headed towards the station exit and was met at the doors by a policeman wearing leathers and holding a helmet in one of his hands. The man looked young, with an unshaven gun-metal blue stubble of new beard across his jaw. He snatched off his sunglasses and studied Tremaine speculatively.

"You are the Professor, yes?" his English was stilted.

Tremaine nodded. "I'm Steven Tremaine," he said.

The policeman narrowed his eyes. Tremaine still had on the same rumpled suit he had worn to the seminar the previous evening. His tie had been folded and stuffed into one of his pockets, and his shirt hung open-necked and stiff with his dried sweat.

"Your baggage?"

"No," Tremaine said simply. He was wearing everything he owned. He followed the policeman down a wide set of concrete steps and across the parking lot. The other two motorbike outriders saw him coming. They kick-started their machines, and the police car's engine whined into life.

Tremaine came to a halt in the parking lot and turned in a slow full circle. He could hear the distant hum of heavy traffic, but could see little. Trees, their leaves autumn brown and orange, fringed the entire area.

"How far is it to the ancient city?" he asked the motorbike cop.

The policeman shrugged. "Just five, maybe ten minutes," he said. "The train station is a little way out from Avignon. We have another domestic train station nearby the old city. This one is for trains that come from, er… country to country, yes?" the inflection of his voice rose into a question to be sure Tremaine understood his fractured English.

Tremaine nodded.

The passenger door of the police car opened and a thin, wiry framed man climbed out and stood stiffly beside the vehicle. He wore a police uniform, his cap

45

tucked under his arm. His hair was grey, cropped close to his skull and his face was tanned leathery brown, creased and wrinkled as an old pair of shoes. His eyes were brown, his mouth turned down at the corners as though he smiled rarely. He came towards Tremaine with crisp steps, his hand extended.

"Monsieur, I am Captain Benoit Devaux, of the Police Nationale. It is my pleasure to welcome you to Avignon."

Tremaine shook the man's hand. His grip was firm, his hand cool. "Thank you, Captain," Tremaine said. "And thank you for the escort. You will take me to the mayor?"

"Yes," Devaux said, snapping out the word. His English was good. "These men are from the local Police Municipale. We will escort you to the mayor's office. He is expecting you."

Tremaine looked bemused. He frowned and smiled curiously. "You have two different police departments operating within the same city?"

Captain Devaux shook his head. "In France we have three tiers of enforcement," he explained, very measured and precise with his words, speaking carefully to ensure his English pronunciation. "The Police Municipale are the local police. They deal with the mundane civil matters," he gave an elegant shrug of his shoulders. "Things such as parking tickets, yes?"

Tremaine nodded.

"And then the Police Nationale, of which I am the local captain in Avignon city, is for the solving of murders. Crime… robbery and such."

Tremaine began to understand. He nodded again.

"And then we have the Gendarmerie. They are the French military. They have a headquarters in Avignon."

Tremaine widened his eyes hopefully. "Where in Avignon, exactly, Captain? Is their headquarters in the old part of the city or the new city?"

"The old quarter," Devaux said. "As is the office for the Police Municipale. My own division's building is directly across the road from the old city. I can see the ancient walls from my office."

Tremaine felt a little lift of relief. Avignon had a population of around ninety thousand people, but only twelve thousand of them lived within the ancient great walls of the old quarter. The rest of the city sprawled for miles into the outlying country. To know that all three arms of the national law and enforcement were headquartered so close gave him a renewed surge of optimism.

Tremaine climbed into the back of the Renault alongside the police captain and the lead motorcycle drew away, weaving through the parking lot. The car followed with the two outriders keeping position on either side of the vehicle. The car's lights were flashing, siren wailing in the still afternoon air.

The interior of the car was cramped but air conditioned. Tremaine felt his eyes become heavy and the fatigue turned his arms to lead. The view through the tinted windows showed rows of tall autumnal trees lining a wide road. Through the filter of foliage he caught occasional glimpses of a river, shimmering under a clear blue sky. Then the road veered into a wide sweeping loop. The river disappeared as the car came down a gentle slope and, suddenly before him, stood the ancient fortified wall of Avignon; a twenty five foot high solid limestone rampart with battlements spaced every hundred yards or so for as far as he could see.

Tremaine gaped in awe.

47

"Stop the car!" he shouted from the back seat.

The policeman driving the vehicle shot a perplexed glance over his shoulder and slowed. Tremaine already had his hand on the door handle, pushing it open. The car came to a lurching stop across both eastward lanes of traffic. One of the motorbike outriders slewed to an ungainly halt.

Tremaine flung open the door, ignoring the traffic that was quickly snarling behind the police car, and lifted his eyes to the top of the wall with a kind of wonder. He had seen photos of Avignon's famous medieval walls and had referred to the city many years before in a paper he had prepared on disease quarantine. Now he was looking at the imposing height of the structure and it awed him.

The nearest battlement stood about forty feet high – well above the height of the intervening wall itself – and was surmounted with a crenellated parapet so that the top of the tower looked like a row of square stone teeth. Built into the bottom of the tower's battlement stood a high open breach, wide enough for two intersecting lanes of traffic. The stonework was sprinkled with green moss and streaked with rivulets of mud lines, and the vaulted arch of the gateway looked darkened with soot and exhaust smoke. In front of the tower stood a sign:

*Porte St. Roch.*

"I don't believe it…" Tremaine said incredulously. He turned and saw the police captain climbing out of the other side of the police car. Tremaine pointed to the wall.

"Captain Devaux, how long is the wall?"

"Over four kilometers," Devaux said.

"And it encircles the entire old city?"

"Oui, monsieur," he said. "Although part of the northern wall near the Pope's Palace is natural cliff-face."

Tremaine pointed to the sign next to the gate. "Porte Saint Roch? Where is that?" he asked, confused.

"It is not a place, monsieur. It is the name of this gate. They each have a name."

Tremaine stared back at the wall, shaking his head in slow disbelief. In the distance cars were honking their horns and several drivers had abandoned their vehicles and come forward to the police motorcycle riders, gesticulating angrily. Tremaine saw and heard none of it. He pointed to the tower. "How many other towers like this one are there?"

"Thirty five, complete with the battlements you see along the top of the tower, monsieur, and many more that are merely bulwarks."

"Gates?"

"Fourteen, I think," Devaux looked a little uncertain, "and there are also many small walking gates, especially along the western wall."

"Walking gates?"

"Oui," Devaux spread his hands, miming something the shape of a doorway. "Such as this," he gesticulated. "For people to walk through."

Tremaine nodded his understanding.

"And where are we now?"

"Monsieur?"

"Where are we in relation to the wall?" Tremaine asked more precisely. "We're at a corner, right?"

"Ah, yes," Devaux understood at last. "We are at the south-west corner of the wall," he said. The road we are on will take us to the main entrance into the ancient city. The corner tower marks the wall's western face. It runs parallel to the Rhône River."

Tremaine put his hands on his hips and walked to a grassed and tree-lined area that stretched between the

49

road and the wall. The ground was sprinkled with crinkled orange leaves. He looked directly up at the top of the wall.

"Twenty five feet?"

"Eight meters."

Tremaine frowned and tried to do the maths. Twenty five feet sounded about right. The wall had been built of huge limestone slabs, each cut and laid with incredible masonry skill. He walked slowly back to the police car and noticed several hotels on the opposite side of the road. He slumped into the back seat, his mind reeling but his hopes buoyed.

"If all the gates can somehow be blocked…" he thought furiously, "and if we can maintain food, water and order…"

The police car drew away from the intersection and cruised eastward. Tremaine kept his face pressed to the tinted glass window, following the unbroken line of the great wall until suddenly the car turned left at a set of traffic lights, and they drove through a breach in the wall, wide enough for two lanes of traffic in either direction. Standing like bastions on either side of the entrance were two more crenellated towers, but they were disconnected. Pedestrians scurried across the broad intersection and the police motorcade weaved their way through the crowd, the driver in the front seat pummeling his fist on the car's squeaking horn.

"This is Rue De La Republique," Captain Devaux explained. "It will take us directly to the mayor's office. And the gates we passed through are called Porte De La Republique. They are the main gates into the old city."

Tremaine felt overwhelmed. The police motorcade sped past huge government buildings on either side of the road with the French tricolor flying from every window,

50

and then into a long tree-lined retail strip, populated with restaurants, cafes and designer clothing stores. The sidewalks were crammed with people, and the gutters filled with leaves.

At the end of the boulevard the lead motorbike rider came to a standstill. The police car slowed and then braked. Ahead, Tremaine could see an open air plaza – a wide cobblestoned space in the shape of a rectangle with imposing stone buildings on the left behind more trees, and to the right, a long line of restaurants with outdoor table settings. The plaza was crowded with milling groups of pedestrians.

"Are we stopping?" Tremaine sounded confused.

"We have no choice," Benoit Devaux said and pushed open his door. "There are steel bollards across the road. We can go no further. This is Place de L'Horloge – it is a pedestrian square. No vehicles allowed."

Tremaine got out of the police car with a weary sigh and the sounds of the old city came to him in a wave; the hum and bustle of a thriving marketplace filled with the voices of locals and tourists. The cobblestones were covered in a confetti of stiff orange leaves. Tremaine looked around him. To his left snaked a narrow side street that meandered down a gentle slope, and to his right were the tables, chairs and umbrellas of the restaurants behind which he could see more narrow streets, leading off from the plaza like arteries.

"How far to the mayor's office?"

The police captain pointed to a grand stone building through the canopy of leafy trees. "A hundred yards on the left," he said. "Follow me."

"You're coming?"

"Oui," Devaux said. "As the senior policeman in the city I have been summoned to the meeting."

51

With the three motorbike cops still wearing their helmets and flanking them like bodyguards, Tremaine and Captain Devaux wound their way through the lunchtime crowds and stopped suddenly at the steps of a grand two story building with marble columns on either side of a high arched entrance and banks of long ornate windows. On the top floor, overlooking the plaza perched a balcony from which flew a trident of three flags. The middle one was the French flag but the two other flags Tremaine could not identify.

Devaux gestured courteously and Tremaine went up the stone steps and in through the ornate doorway.

"This is the Town Hall," Devaux's voice became hushed as if they had entered a museum. "It was built one hundred and seventy years ago."

The interior of the building was elegantly breathtaking – a mixture of grand design and French flair. The foyer was a vaulted open space and the staircases that wound around the outer walls were all decoratively balustraded. Tremaine's footsteps echoed harshly on the checkerboard marble floor as he looked around the walls.

He saw a reception cubicle to his right with a middle-aged woman behind the counter. Devaux approached the woman and spoke to her briefly. She nodded her head and reached for a phone. Devaux gently took Tremaine by the elbow and lead him to the back of the building where a wide stone staircase stretched up towards a mezzanine level. The steps were worn and rounded. Tremaine followed the French Captain of Police and they halted at a glass door to their right. Built into the wall beside the door was a security keypad. Beyond the glass outer doors, Tremaine saw a set of elaborate wooden doors and a sign; *'Mayor's Office'*.

Tremaine frowned. His eyes followed the staircase to where the steps ended at the upper level of the building. He had expected the mayor's office to have a sweeping view that overlooked the square – perhaps an office that led out onto the balcony he had seen from the entry steps. He looked quizzically at Devaux but before he could raise the question, he saw a young woman come out through the inner double doors, and then pull them carefully closed behind her. She crossed to the glass door, smiled politely at Devaux, and then used a security card on a strap around her neck to swipe through the lock. She pulled the glass door open and stood aside. Devaux stepped into the air conditioned space and Tremaine dutifully flowed him.

"Camille," Devaux's smile became charming. "What a pleasant surprise. I did not expect to see you here."

The woman shrugged her shoulders. She was in her mid-twenties with shoulder-length blonde hair and a slim figure. She wore a simple silk blouse and a knee-length skirt. She propped one hand on her narrow waist and stared at Tremaine with frank open appraisal for long seconds before flicking her green eyes back to the uniformed policeman.

"Hello, Captain," the woman smiled. "I have been asked to attend the meeting to represent the interests of the Avignon Chamber of Commerce," she explained. Her voice was husky, her English very good but still accented. She lifted her chin and brushed a loose tendril of hair away from her face in a distinctly feminine gesture as she turned back once more to Tremaine. She wore a couple of sterling silver bangles around her wrist. They tinkled together like delicate little bells.

"And you are the Professor, yes?"

"Yes," Tremaine said. The girl's eyes were bewitching – deep mesmerizing pools the color of a high mountain lake. "Steven Tremaine. Nice to meet you."

"I am Camille Pelletier," she held out her hand. Her grip felt firm, her fingers long and delicate. "I wish that we were meeting under happier circumstances."

"Yes," Tremaine said significantly. "So do I."

The girl held his hand for a second or two longer and then blinked her eyes. In that split second her demeanor changed and her body became stiffer, more formal. She turned on her heel and reached for the inner wooden doors. "Everyone else is assembled and ready," she said over her shoulder to Tremaine. "They're all waiting for you in the mayor's office."

\* \* \*

The mayor's office occupied a large area on the mezzanine level of the town hall building; curtained windows were built into the west wall and there was a closed door marked 'Private' on the far side of a vast board room table that dominated the space. The table was ornately decorated wood with vine leaves carved into the solid legs, the surface polished but chipped and marked with the signs of its antiquity.

The room had been lavishly appointed; a high ornamentally plastered ceiling from which hung a crystal chandelier, and there was plush grey carpet underfoot, slightly worn into pale tracks around the doorways.

Seated around the table were just four men.

One of them pushed back his chair and got to his feet, striding towards Tremaine with a forced smile on his lips. He was a small-framed figure, aged in his fifties or sixties. He was thin and narrow shouldered, so that the

54

expensive suit he wore seemed to hang from his frame. His face was round and fleshy, his hair thinning grey and swept carefully across the pink of his balding pate.

"Professor Tremaine," the man shook his hand, speaking in accented English. He smelled of coffee and garlic. He stood an inch or two shorter than Tremaine with brown eyes hidden in a web of wrinkles. "I am the Mayor of Avignon, Henri Pelletier." He looked askance at the American and wrinkled his nostrils to suggest that he found the man's rumpled appearance distressing.

Tremaine shook hands with the mayor and forced a thin smile. "Thank you for agreeing to meet with me, sir," he said. "You got the call from Minister Boudin?"

"Yes," the mayor nodded. "He phoned me personally at my home in the early hours of this morning. It is a grave business we are dealing with. Very grave indeed," the mayor shook his head sorrowfully and his eyes darkened. "The Minister told me you were one of the world's leading authorities on such matters. It is some comfort for us all for you to be here." As he spoke the mayor turned and made a gesture that embraced the other three men gathered around the table. He took Tremaine gently by the arm and steered him towards the far end of the big room.

"This is my Deputy Mayor, Jacques Lejeune," the mayor introduced Tremaine to a very tall, gaunt-faced man with sallow cheeks and a sickly, pallid complexion. The man was stooped, and bony angled within his suit. He had a shaggy cut of coarse black hair. Tremaine and Lejeune shook hands.

"And this is Colonel LeCat, of the Gendarmerie. He is the current commander of the men stationed within Avignon."

55

The Colonel shook Tremaine's hand. He was a tall, rangy man with close-cropped grey bristle and the heavily weathered, suntanned face, of someone accustomed to the vast outdoors. He had steely blue eyes and broad squared shoulders. "Temporary commander," LeCat clarified. He had a grip like a vice. Tremaine nodded, already confused. He had never been good with names, and the weary sense of fatigue that numbed his mind became overwhelming. He shook hands with another man, though could not remember his name or position.

Everyone in the room had turned towards him expectantly. Camille Pelletier had her arms folded across her chest, her weight thrown onto one leg so that the flare of her hip was accentuated. She watched him with level steady eyes, and an expression that might have been almost hostile. All the men in the room re-took their seats, and Captain Devaux of the Police Nationale, drew back a chair and sat heavily, dropping his cap onto the table and clasping his hands before him like a student in a classroom.

Tremaine planted both hands on the edge of the table and took a deep breath. His head hung lowered, as though in some great moment of contemplative thought. Then, slowly, he lifted his face and made eye contact with everyone in the room individually, fixing their attention with the force of his dreadful gaze.

"The world has collapsed over the edge of apocalypse," he said clearly. "America was the catalyst for the contagion and since then it has spread consistently to several other countries around the world. The mortality rate is one hundred percent," he paused for a moment to gauge the impact of his words. "No one who comes in contact with the virus survives. They

56

turn," he hesitated for another instant, seeking the correct word, "into some kind of predator. That's why the media is calling this virus Raptor. It's because the dead rise and become instinctive hunters. They kill in packs."

Tremaine swept his eyes around the table and saw heads nodding solemnly. "And last night the contagion arrived in London. I saw it on the news broadcasts. What began as America's disaster has now become a catastrophe for the entire world. *That includes France.* England is so close... the contagion reached the United Kingdom from America. There is no reason to think that it will just miraculously stop. If it isn't already sweeping across the northern reaches of France, then it will be – soon. Maybe by tonight, if not sooner."

Tremaine shrugged his shoulders and lowered his voice so that those gathered around him barely caught his words. "Death from this contagion is imminent," he said. "It's coming this way, and no one can stop it."

The silence around the room was morbid. At last the Deputy Mayor, Jacques Lejeune, shifted uncomfortably in his seat. He was shiny with nervous sweat. He wrung his hands plaintively. "But, monsieur, you believe that Avignon can be protected from this terrible disease, yes?"

Tremaine nodded his head. "Yes," he said, his voice flat and emphatic. "I believe that Avignon can be fortified and defended against the undead when they sweep down from the north of the country. I believe that with the urgent co-operation of the police and the gendarmerie that the twelve thousand people who live inside the walls of the ancient city can survive. But we must act urgently."

"And what becomes of everyone else?" the mayor asked. He had risen from his chair and come to his feet, the fleshy folds of his face paling.

"They will die," Tremaine said harshly. "Anyone who is not inside these walls when the gates are barricaded will ultimately become infected." He shrugged off his jacket and draped it over the back of an empty chair then thrust his fists deep into his pockets, his shoulders hunched as he studied the faces around the room. They were subdued and unsettled.

A pall of despair had descended on the room, hanging like a toxic cloud over the table. LeCat, the Colonel of the Gendarmerie, folded his muscled brawny arms across his chest and balled his fists. They were lumped with scar tissue across the knuckles, huge as hammers. "And just how would you hope to fortify the gates, monsieur?" he asked.

Tremaine shrugged. "I was thinking that we could use buses," Tremaine mentioned an idea that had come to him on the train ride north from Barcelona. "We could turn them onto their sides, and stack one bus on top of the other."

"Why would you turn them on their sides?" Jacques Lejeune looked mortified.

"Because the infected are hunters," Tremaine said with a patient sigh. "They'll climb under the wheels of the buses, or they'll find a way through the windows. The gates of the old city must be barricaded and there can be no gap, no chance for a breach. If even one of the infected gets inside the walls, we are all dead. All of us."

Henri Pelletier made a suppressing gesture with his hands like he was quieting a noisy crowd. "Monsieur," he said breathlessly, "as mayor of the city, I cannot sanction any measures such as you are mentioning," his voice rose an octave and consternation twisted his mouth so that he looked like he was in pain. "Yes, perhaps we could fortify the old city... but to leave so many people outside the walls... that is murder."

"No, it's not," Tremaine shook his head grimly. "It's a question of survival. We simply cannot house nor feed nor control a hundred thousand people or more within these walls. It's not practical, and it's counter-productive. Those people you would seek to save, you will kill through starvation or even other disease. We are talking about a siege, gentlemen... and madam," he nodded to the young woman inclusively. "And we have no idea how long the contagion will continue before it begins to burn itself out. It could be days – but it might be weeks or months."

Henri Pelletier sat back down heavily. His face seemed to have crumpled. He fidgeted with the watch on his wrist, gnawing at his bottom lip. Beside him, his Deputy sat staring blankly at one of the curtained windows. Tremaine clawed fingers through his hair and closed his eyes. He felt the first vertiginous sway of fatigue and had to clutch at the edge of the table to hold himself upright.

Colonel LeCat gazed around the room and saw fear and panic on the faces of the men he knew and lived amongst. He cleared his throat.

"Perhaps there is time, Professor, to begin at the beginning with your theories and your experiences? After all," he shrugged to avoid giving offense, "we have only your word that these events will unfold. Can you explain how you have come to your conclusions?"

"Yes." Henri Pelletier sharpened his eyes, thankful for a chance to stall making a decision. "That is an excellent idea. We should make a considered judgment based on the facts, gentlemen. Not merely on the word of the Professor alone."

He glanced sheepishly sideways at Tremaine but did not meet his eyes. "First we must truly understand what is at stake here. If we barricade the city and leave eighty or ninety thousand people hammering at the walls to get in… and the contagion does *not* reach Avignon…" the mayor cocked his thumb and drew it slowly across his own throat. "We would be hung in the plaza."

A murmur of sound rippled around the room. Captain Devaux shifted uncomfortably in his chair and his eyes became nervous.

Tremaine nodded. "Very well," he said, and took a deep breath.

He was about to launch into the prepared content of the seminar he used to address assembled world leaders when Camille Pelletier cleared her throat and held up her arm to show her wristwatch. "Forgive me, Professor Tremaine," she interrupted. "But it is 2pm. "The President is giving a speech about the contagion. Perhaps we should watch that first?"

The man Tremaine had been introduced to, whose name he could not remember, sprang from his chair and disappeared through the closed door. He came back into the board room wheeling a monitor on a steel frame. On the television flickered footage of a news anchorman speaking in French. Everyone drew their chairs around the television just as the image cut to an empty podium in front of the French flag. The President appeared from the left of screen holding a thin sheaf of papers in his hand. He stood wearing a severe black suit and grey tie. A scrolling tickertape across the bottom of the screen flashed the message:

*'Live broadcast by the President of the French Republic from the Élysée Place'.*

The President positioned himself behind the podium and stared directly into the television camera. Tremaine stood behind the seated men gathered around the board room table with the young woman close beside him. She looked sideways at him and their eyes met. Her gaze was enigmatic and her perfume smelled of sandalwood and lavender... subtle enough so that through its scent he could still sense the palpable fear of the gathered men. Their worry seeped from the pores of their skin, and clung thick to their clothes like cigarette smoke. Tremaine crinkled his nose.

"He is going to announce the immediate closure of all French national borders," Tremaine said from the back of the room. "He'll declare a national state of emergency – which will be only the second time that has happened since the 1960's. All border crossings will be protected by heavily armed troops. No one will be allowed into, or out of France."

Henri Pelletier glanced, irritated and dismissive, over his shoulder, but Colonel LeCat's head turned, more considered. He appraised Tremaine thoughtfully, looking him up and down the way he might inspect a soldier on the parade ground. He turned back to the television just as the French President began his address.

His voice grave and his face solemn, the French President started speaking in English. Tremaine raised an eyebrow in surprise. Clearly the address was being broadcast to an international audience.

"Effective immediately, I have ordered the closure of all borders into France and declared a state of emergency," the President said without glancing at his notes. "Furthermore, all flights into Paris are being grounded indefinitely and all train services into the capital are being cancelled. On the advice of my Minister for Health, only outbound flights and trains from the capital will be permitted to proceed."

The President pauscd at the podium and took a long deep breath. "We take these measures in response to the Raptor virus that is sweeping the world. Citizens in populated areas are advised to disperse. Evacuate the cities, return to your ancestral homes. The contagion spreads quickly in densely populated areas. Your best hope to survive the spread of this terrible plague is to be in low population or rural areas. Leave the cities."

There was another pause while the President shuffled the papers before him, even though he did not refer to them as he spoke. To Tremaine it showed a measure of the man's nervousness. He narrowed his eyes and watched the President's face closely. Under the bright studio lighting a sheen of perspiration showed across his brow.

"Armed soldiers will be on the streets of Paris and every other major city within the hour. Armed troops will be blocking every crossing point into the country. Anyone attempting to enter France by any means will be dealt with in the same manner as a suspected terrorist – they will be shot."

That last word rang out like the doom-laden tolling of a bell. The President looked unapologetic. "This is only the second time since the Algerian crisis in 1962 that a state of emergency has been declared," the President went on. At this stage, it will remain in effect until the infection is contained."

He cleared his throat, scooped up the pages into his hands, and had begun to exit the room when a chorus of journalist's voices called out from somewhere beyond the view of the camera. The loudest voice was that of an American journalist, the accent instantly recognizable.

"What can you tell us about the virus, Mr. President? Are there any developments?"

The French President stopped in mid-stride and came back to the podium. He took a moment to settle himself and the silence was crushing.

"This is a plague upon mankind," The President said hollowly. "Already we have estimates of almost seventy million dead around the world, mainly across America at this stage, but the death toll is rising in every country affected. So far the Raptor virus has been found in twenty-three countries, including confirmed cases in the United Kingdom. There seems no cure. Those bitten or otherwise infected die a gruesome painful death, and then are re-animated within just one or two minutes. They can only be killed with a shot to the head – and they seem mindless and impervious to pain of any kind. Fire does not stop them. Nothing stops them."

"Are there any reported cases in France at the moment?"

"No," the President shook his head emphatically. And then went on. "And that is why we must take the draconian measures I have just announced – to preserve France and its people against infection for as long as possible."

"Is there a cure?" this time the accent was less obvious. Tremaine guessed the journalist as British, or maybe South African.

"No," the French President said again, shaking his head as he answered. "There is no known antivirus, nothing at all that can protect anyone from the spread of this infection. The advice from my Minister and those experts in the field of disease ecology has been that the only hope remaining is to thin out major population areas in the hope that this infection will extinguish itself. It has been barely four days. We don't yet know how long the contagion remains virulent within those infected." The President shrugged his shoulders. "Perhaps in a week the undead will simply expire. Perhaps the contagion has a short infection life and those who have been re-animated will simply become dead once more. We just don't know…"

"And if they don't? If the infection remains virulent for a month or maybe a year… what happens then?"

The President stared at the journalist who has asked the question for long silent seconds, staring slightly off-center of the camera while he formed an answer to the question. Finally he sighed. "Then, it is the end of the world," he said softly. "No one will be left alive. Mankind as a species will entirely cease to exist."

There was a blinding strobe of camera flashlights and the President's gaunt face became lit brightly in a long flare of white light. The assembled journalists turned into a clamoring rabble. The President seemed unaffected – almost detached. He turned away and walked slowly off camera. For a moment the shot stayed on the empty podium with the French flag in the background, and then cut back to the news anchor in the studio. The reporter seated behind the desk seemed visibly shaken.

Slowly the men around the table in Avignon sat back in their chairs as though awakened from the nightmare of a hypnotist's trance. They turned their eyes towards Tremaine. Henri Pelletier's face had turned as pale as wax.

\* \* \*

The television stayed on in the mayor's office through the afternoon, the sound turned down so that it became background noise to the panicked debate that roiled around the table.

"We must be sure!" Jacques Lejeune said. He had a desiccated voice, dry as parchment, and the manner of someone who had spent his entire dour life in a musty office. His fingers scampered across the tabletop and he snatched at a glass of water. He took a long gulp, then loosened the noose of his tie. His face was shiny with his sweat, his eyes shifting nervously.

"How much more certain do you need to be?" there was a harsh frustrated edge to Tremaine's voice. He was no longer able to stay still. He began to pace restlessly about the room; it suddenly felt too small for him, cramped and suffocating. He went to one of the windows and twitched aside the heavy curtains. The afternoon had turned to dusk. They had been in the mayor's office for over four hours, discussing the President's announcement, and the implications of barricading the ancient city of Avignon against an undead swarm... and still the mayor and his deputy were vacillating.

Tremaine turned back to face the room and the men seated around the table. His hands became fists, the knuckles whitening with frustration and tension, yet his face remained a neutral mask. "Eighty-five percent of the world's population lives in cities," he said. "And the population is so vast now that we've overcrowded the planet. Seventy percent of all pandemic diseases are passed from animals to man, so by encroaching into the areas once left to nature we have seen a huge rise in new viruses – something like three hundred in the last sixty years or so." He shook his head. "I'm not saying this Raptor virus originated through animal infection – it

65

probably didn't – but the fact remains that the virus now sweeping the world was inevitable. It *had* to happen eventually. Previously governments have been able to limit the spread of contagions. The Chinese did it with SARS back in 2002. Once the virus found its way into the travel network it spread like wildfire around the world, ultimately infecting over eight thousand in a matter of weeks and killing ten percent of those people. The Chinese finally controlled the epidemic by quarantining everyone infected and limiting all unnecessary travel. But the contagion almost crippled the Chinese economy in the process. It cost billions of dollars through stifled international travel, and impacted business across a dozen different sectors. Compared to the Raptor virus, SARS was nothing. How could we hope to quarantine the infected of this new contagion? We couldn't. And how can we quarantine half the world's population? Where would we put them? How would we arrange the quarantine without the huge danger of further infection? Jesus!" Tremaine's temper finally reached its simmering boiling point. Every second wasted in this room was another moment the population of Avignon was put at risk. "This thing is out of control. It's not a question of *'if'*, it's a simple question of *'when'*. And I'm telling you," he thrust an angry threatening finger at Henri Pelletier and Jacques Lejeune, "that it's just a matter of hours… maybe a day or two. Then death is going to be at your doorstep and you'll either be prepared, or infected."

Henri Pelletier stared querulously at Tremaine, his face darkening with color. He drew himself to his feet and tinkered with the knot of his tie for a moment. "Monsieur Tremaine," he said indignantly. "The government has closed the borders right across the country. The President himself said there is no sign of the infection yet within France. Therefore, perhaps your threats are unfounded at this stage, yes?" he spoke deliberately to provoke and saw Tremaine's eyebrows narrow into dark pointed lines.

"No," Tremaine snarled. "The President said the state of emergency would only protect France *'for as long as possible'*. He didn't say it was a complete measure that would ensure safety. Because he knows the infection must come. Nothing can stop it. It's inevitable."

"And how would he know such a thing?"

"Because I told your President's Minister for Health exactly that. It's how I knew what the President was going to announce. Everyone is operating in a vacuum of panic, terror and dread. But if you separate the emotion you can see the reality, and *this* is the reality!" Tremaine slammed his fist against the board room table. The sound was like the crack of a whip. "You are wasting time," he glared around the room. "Twelve thousand – maybe fifteen thousand people can be saved. Avignon has the unique opportunity to provide the last stand of mankind. Please," the tone of his voice became anguished and imploring, "Please don't waste this one remaining chance to save lives."

Tremaine could see in Henri Pelletier's eyes that he still had not made his case – the mayor remained clinging to the hope that somehow the contagion that had swept through over twenty countries would miraculously sidestep France. The mayor glanced over his shoulder and made eye contact with his Deputy, Jacques Lejeune. A silent message passed between the men. The mayor turned back to Tremaine and the tension in his features softened and became sympathetic for a moment.

"You are tired, Professor," he said with silky condescension. He took Tremaine's arm and began slowly guiding him towards the doors of the boardroom. "Your trip has been exhausting and this meeting has gone for too long." When they reached the doors, Pelletier stopped and stared Tremaine in the eyes. "My colleagues would like some time tonight to consider your views in privacy. We have heard your arguments. Now you must give us the time we require to reach our decision about what action should be taken. In the meantime, we have a hotel room reserved for you within the walls of the old city, and my daughter here," he gestured to the young woman, "will take you on a tour of the old fortifications and then to a local restaurant for dinner."

"No," Tremaine shook his head, his eyes furious. He shrugged off the mayor's grip on his arm. Somewhere in the back of his mind he had the startling realization that the pretty young woman was the mayor's daughter, but at that very moment he was too aggravated, too incensed, to recognize the fact. "This cannot wait for you to waste more time talking. You must decide now."

Pelletier shook his head. "No, Professor. That is what you want, of course, but that is not what we are obliged to do. We will instead, continue with our private discussions and re-convene here at 7am tomorrow morning."

"It will be too late!" Tremaine snarled.

Pelletier looked stoic. "I hardly think so, Mr. Tremaine. We are many hundreds of miles away from Paris and the coast of England. Even if the infection is as virulent as you say, it cannot reach Avignon before tomorrow morning. There will still be time to act… if indeed a course of action is the decision we arrive at."

\* \* \*

Tremaine followed the young woman down the staircase and out through the front doors of the Town Hall. At the rear of the imposing building they climbed into a Peugeot hatchback. The young woman hitched her skirt above her knees and threw the car into gear.

"My name is Camille," she said brusquely. Her eyes were slanted and narrowed.

"You're the mayor's daughter," Tremaine nodded wryly. "I didn't realize."

"Does it make a difference to you?" her tone became defensive. She had been watching his face, but the instant Tremaine turned to answer, she lifted her chin in a gesture of disdain.

"Nope," Tremaine sighed. He tried to sit back in the passenger seat, his legs cramped under the dashboard of the compact little car. Camille Pelletier reversed, spun the wheel hard and slipped the car into first gear, her movements smooth and precise. She stomped her foot on the accelerator and wound down her driver's side window at the same time, flicking a glance into the rear view mirror as a kind of apologetic afterthought to anyone else who might be using the road.

She drove with her brow furrowed, her soft pink lips pursed. Tremaine watched her from the corner of his eye. Clearly, she was unhappy with the task of escorting him on a tour of the old city. Well it went both ways, he decided. He didn't want to be run around town. He wanted to start drawing up plans for the fortification of the walls. He let out a long weary sigh and folded his arms across his chest.

"Why were you at the meeting?" Tremaine asked.

69

Camille flicked him a glance as she turned left, and then took a sharp right onto a narrow cobblestoned road that ran parallel to the open air plaza. "To represent the business community," she said.

"Why you?" Tremaine persisted.

"Because I am the night manager of a local hotel," Camille said, narrowing her eyes and then lifting her chin arrogantly. Her mouth was a hard line and her eyes darkened and gleamed dangerously. "I wasn't at the meeting because I am the mayor's daughter, if that is what you are implying, Professor Tremaine," the stiffness came into her voice. "I have studied hospitality for six years, and the hotel I run is the most successful in Avignon."

Tremaine tried to look apologetic, but didn't try too hard. "Well good for you," he said dryly. She was pretty he decided, but typically French – there was something grating and prickly about her attitude. "How do you feel about what I presented to your father and the others in that meeting? Do you believe me… or are you your father's daughter?"

"I am both," Camille's eyes glittered like the sharp point of a knife. "I am a believer in what you said, and I am my father's daughter. You are American, Professor Tremaine. You do not understand Avignon, or her people. We are a small place in the south of France. This is not Manhattan or Los Angeles. We are different people. We approach things differently."

"I understand that," Tremaine said with frayed patience, "but if your father doesn't pull his thumb out of his ass, he is going to be responsible for the unnecessary deaths of up to fifteen thousand people." Despite the almost pleasant tone of his voice, there was real tension and strain in his words. "So if you can do anything…

70

anything at all. If you can say something that will make your father act – please, do it."

Camille arched her eyebrows and huffed. "So you think I am at the meeting merely because I am the mayor's daughter, and for that reason you are cynical of me. Now, you would wish me to influence the mayor on your behalf because I am his daughter," she slowed at a pedestrian crossing and stared coldly at Tremaine. Her knuckles were white on the steering wheel and there was an angry splash of color on her cheeks. "In France we would call you a hypocrite," Camille said bluntly. "Is it the same word in America?"

Tremaine said nothing.

Camille threw the little Peugeot into a right-angled turn and suddenly they were racing along a narrow street with flower stalls on one side and another open air plaza on the opposite side. The square was filled with crowds of people dining at outdoor cafes. A flock of pigeons took to startled flight and the faces of the diners turned to watch the car flash past.

"Place Pie," Camille said, pronouncing the word *'pee'*. "It is a popular place for the University students to come to eat."

Tremaine nodded. Then Camille turned again and Tremaine felt his heart leap into his throat as a crowd of pedestrians flashed past the windshield in a panicked scatter. Camille pointed ahead.

"The university is at the end of this street," she said casually. "It is the first place you should see. Just a few more moments."

The road became choked. Parked cars lined the sidewalk. They sped past an orange-vested crew of workmen who were digging up part of the blacktop. Camille put the car to the narrow gap without slowing

71

and Tremaine felt himself instinctively stiffen and brace for collision.

"The University security guard should be expecting us," Camille glanced at Tremaine, her voice almost conversational. "The gates, they should be open."

She swung the wheel over and then came back on the clutch and accelerator, her feet dancing as the Peugeot gathered speed. Ahead, Tremaine could see the narrow road hook into a sharp left turn. He held his breath.

Camille eased her foot off the accelerator and a wide iron gate swung open directly ahead of the Peugeot. Camille put the little car into the gap and then stomped hard on the brake. The surface was gravel and the back tires juddered and skidded for traction. Trees flashed past and then the car came to a halt in a billowing cloud of dust. A dozen young people came slowly, unconcerned, towards the vehicle. Camille killed the engine and kicked her door open.

"We're here," she glanced across at Tremaine.

They were parked inside the gates of the University between two huge buildings. One was a massive two story edifice built in the grand tradition of French architecture with rows of windows and columns either side of vast doors. The other building was a more modern structure, featuring lots of grey tinted glass. Between them – where the car sat parked – ran a slash of concrete paths and grass. At the far end of the open space Tremaine could see the continuation of the ancient wall and a wide archway. He went towards it with Camille at his side.

"Is that one of the traffic gates into the old city?" Tremaine pointed ahead, his voice confused.

"No," Camille swept hair away from her forehead. "It is only used to gain entrance to the University by

72

students who live outside the walls. No cars are allowed."

"There are iron bars across the gates."

"Yes," Camille said. They brushed past a cluster of students sitting in a circle on the grass, their heads bowed over their textbooks. Tremaine quickened his stride.

The vaulted stone entrance had been built into a gatehouse, the same as the Porte Saint Roch gate he had seen from the police car, except this entrance had a motorized set of steel barred gates that opened and closed. Tremaine ran his hand over the cold metal and shook it. He turned back to Camille.

"Are any of the other gateways like this one – do they have the same steel gate system?"

"No," Camille shook her head. "Only this one."

Tremaine grunted. These gates could be chained. There would be no need for barricades. He stood back from the vast limestone wall and stared up to the top, studying the crenellations. It was the first time he had seen the wall from the inside and he marveled at the good condition of the stonework and the sheer monumental size of the structure. The wall had a platform built along the inside for firing down at attackers with narrow stone steps leading up into the heart of the tower. The steps were covered in moss and weeds and the walls were streaked with dirt, the masonry chipped and rounded in places by antiquity. But there seemed no way to quickly access the upper level of the wall.

They would need ladders.

Tremaine stood and turned a full circle. The great bulwark muted the hum of traffic beyond the University. To the west he could see the sun setting behind the glass-faced building. He stared at the milling University students for a long moment, watching them as they went from class to class or just lazed on the wooden benches without a care in their worlds.

"If only they understood what was happening," he grunted.

Beside him Camille remained silent. She had grown up in Avignon. The great walls had been part of her life since childhood. She saw no particular fascination with them. Instead, she watched Tremaine's face, studying his features as he frowned in calculating thought.

"Do you know anything about Avignon's history?" she asked at last. Some of the surly edge had gone from her voice, the tranquility of the location seeming to soften her attitude.

Tremaine shook his head. "Just a little," he said vaguely. "I wrote a research paper about Avignon, but it was a long time ago, and it didn't relate to the city's history as much as its suitability as a stronghold against pandemic infection," he admitted. "But I think these walls were built in the 14th century, right?"

Camille nodded conditional agreement. "Avignon's history reaches back into antiquity," she said. Some of the natural huskiness had come back into her voice. "Its foundations can be traced back to the time of Roman Emperor Augustus when this part of the world was known as Gaul. It's always been of strategic importance – and armies and rulers have always fought for its control. During the 8th century it was controlled by the Arabs. They invaded the Provence region and turned the city into a stronghold. It took two sieges for them to be ousted, but the city's history is drenched in blood, right up until the 14th century – as you suggested – when Avignon experienced almost two hundred years of prosperity."

"Because of the Popes, right?"

"Right," Camille nodded and the faintest hint of friendliness crept back into her smile. "The installation of the papacy within the walls of Avignon turned our little town into the capital of Christendom. Quickly life changed. There were maybe five thousand people in the city, and the walls that had been built over the previous centuries were crumbling. But when the Popes turned Avignon into the papal city, a great palace was built called the *Palais des Papes* – the Palace of the Popes – and the walls that you see now were constructed."

Tremaine watched the way the young Frenchwoman gestured with her hands to emphasize a point as she spoke. They were pale mobile hands with gracefully tapered fingers. The nails were short and painted pale pink. She wore no rings.

Tell me about the palace," Tremaine became suddenly interested.

Camille shrugged her shoulders. "When the Popes came to Avignon, the population of the city grew to maybe thirty thousand. There was a crumbling old Roman wall around the city at the time, but there was no room to house the new businesses and the courtesans who were needed to support the papacy. In the middle of the 14th century the Pope Innocent VI became worried about the vicious gangs of marauding bandits that roamed the countryside. A new wall was begun in 1355, which included all the new businesses and homes. That's the same wall you are looking at right now."

"And the Papal Palace still stands?"

"Yes," Camille said. "Of course. Now it is a tourist attraction on the other side of the city. The stone walls of the palace are seventeen feet thick."

Tremaine arched his brows in surprise. "I would like to see it."

Camille nodded. "My father told me to take you wherever you would like to go. I am at your beck and call, monsieur," her mood changed again. Now her eyes were sparkling with a hint of provocative amusement, and an impish dimple appeared in her cheeks.

Tremaine said nothing. He turned and stared back up at the top of the walls and when he spoke, his voice sounded distant and detached, as though he was talking to the sky. "They're going to come," he said gravely. "Thousands of them – maybe hundreds of thousands of infected. They're going to come, and these walls are the only chance the people of Avignon have to survive. If we don't barricade them and find a way to defend the city against a siege of the undead…"

He turned round at last, the dreadful sense of foreboding still upon him and seemed startled that Camille was still standing close by, watching him curiously. Tremaine shook himself and smiled, but it was a poor effort, his expression shadowed by a profound fear that hung draped about him like a black shroud.

Death was coming to Avignon.

Tremaine knew it with utter certainty.

\* \* \*

They drove around the city's walls, eventually abandoning the car when they reached the western wall to inspect several small breaches which were like doorways cut into the thick stone. By the time Tremaine had seen most of the gates that entered the city night had fallen. He stood watching the traffic swarm past under the yellow street lights. On the far side of the road was the Rhône River, shimmering like a silver thread under a rising moon.

"The Palace will be closed," Camille said. "You will not be able to see it tonight."

Tremaine grunted. "What's that?" he pointed suddenly to a high rise of ground far across the river, hazed by distance and smog, where some vast slab of solid stone reflected the last of the day's dying light like a mirror.

Camille turned. "That is Fort Saint-Andre," she said. "Phillippe le Bel, who was the king of France, commissioned it in 1292. The fort commands the entire valley."

"Is it still intact?"

"Oui," Camille said. "The watchtowers and fortifications still stand, and the gateway to the fort was restored several years ago by local historians."

"How far away is the fort?"

Camille shrugged and pouted her lips in a moment of thought. "Maybe three kilometers," she guessed. "A bus route exists between here and the fort. It takes about ten minutes."

Tremaine nodded, distracted, and his thoughts came back to barricading the ancient city. Defending the western wall worried him. There were four wide traffic gates here and just as many pedestrian entrances, serving the snarl of heavy traffic that bypassed the city. Two of the traffic gates were carved into the base of battlements, but two others were wide breaches that even an overturned bus would not span. He frowned into the darkness until he felt a gentle tug at his elbow and turned around, distracted.

"I asked if you are hungry?" Camille repeated herself, with a little frown on her brow.

"Sorry," Tremaine apologized. "I was just thinking…"

"Thinking or worrying?"

"Panicking, actually," Tremaine admitted. "Barricading the breaches in this western wall – I just don't know how we would do it."

Camille shrugged. "The pedestrian entrances are easy," she said in a matter-of-fact voice. "The wall was not only built to defend against marauding bands of criminals. It was also built to protect Avignon from the River Rhône flooding. We have boards and doors to barricade the narrow entrances."

"Really?"

"Of course."

"And the wide traffic entrances? What about them?"

"The two entrances built through the gatehouses also have boards that can be used," she said. "This one…?" she looked about where they were standing on a traffic island with cars flowing past and others diverting into and out of the city, "is less easy."

"That's an understatement," Tremaine muttered.

Camille seemed not to have heard him. She turned on her heel like a ballerina and started to walk back along the narrow cobblestoned roadway towards where the car was parked. Tall dark buildings crowded the sidewalk so they were cast in dark shadow. Tremaine followed.

On the next street corner something moved and then groaned in the night. Camille stopped mid-stride and went stiff with alarm. Tremaine caught up to her and they stood silent for a second. Camille pointed into the shadows.

"Who's there?" Tremaine gruffed his voice.

There was another groan. Tremaine looked a question at Camille and then a shaky voice called out of the shadows, speaking in French.

Camille's tense poise loosened. She let out a little sigh

of relief.

"It is only a beggar," she said to Tremaine. "For a moment I thought we would be mugged."

"A beggar?"

"Of course," Camille said. "There are many in the city." She plucked at Tremaine's elbow to steer him onto the opposite side of the narrow path but he shook her off. He went into the darkness and crouched down before a middle-aged man with a grey scruffy beard. He sat slumped on a piece of cardboard with a white Styrofoam cup at his feet. His back was propped against a wall and he was dressed in tattered soiled rags. Beside him lay a plastic shopping bag, crammed with all his worldly possessions.

Tremaine reached into his pocket and felt for loose change.

"What are you doing?" Camille's voice became edged with impatience. "Please, do not give him money. It encourages them."

Tremaine looked over his shoulder and frowned. "Camille, this man has no food, no water and nowhere to sleep except on the street. We have to be charitable to those less fortunate than ourselves."

Camille folded her arms across her chest. The little spark of temper came back, glinting in her eyes. "He is homeless. It is a fact of life."

"It's not a fact of life," Tremaine's own voice turned stony. "And remember this," he thrust a finger at her. "In just a couple of days we are all going to become homeless. We're all going to struggle for food and water and shelter. We're going to be no better than this man. Homelessness and hunger and thirst won't be a fact of life. It will be a way of life for everyone who remains inside these walls."

79

* * *

At the end of the street, crouched under the south-west corner of the high wall, was a pizza restaurant. Camille led Tremaine up the steps and they found a table for two near a high serving counter that separated the dining area from the kitchen. There were French posters and small works of art on the walls. Clarinet music played in the background. Bustling behind the countertop, Tremaine saw two young chefs hard at work. One of the men gave Camille a familiar smile and friendly wink. The restaurant was filled with the aromas of pizza and wood smoke.

"Do you come here often?" Tremaine asked. Set out on the table before him were brown paper placemats.

Camille nodded. "I am a regular," she said lightly. "The pizza here is the best in all of Avignon." She glanced over her shoulder. The tables and chairs were an eclectic gathering of mismatched pieces. "Normally it is very busy," she said with a shrug of her shoulders. "But it is still early."

Tremaine had the peculiar sense that the ceiling in the restaurant had been lowered; the atmosphere felt intimate and close. The lighting was soft, and lit candles flickered on each table. He picked up a menu and glanced at it. "What do you recommend?"

"Are you hungry?"

"Starving."

Camille nodded. She caught the eye of one of the chefs and he came through an open side door to the edge of the table. They spoke quickly in French and the chef nodded. He scribbled notes onto his pad with an elegant flourish and disappeared again.

80

Camille turned back to Tremaine. She clasped her hands together and set them down on the table. "So…" her expression turned solemn. "Do you think Avignon can be barricaded?"

"Yes," Tremaine said with more conviction than he actually held. "If we act quickly enough."

Camille smiled wanly. Her eyes swept the walls like she was looking for inspiration. She seemed unaware that he still watched her. He wondered what she was thinking about – what secret thoughts and fears were lurking below the outwardly calm exterior. At last Tremaine filled the awkward silence with a question of his own.

"Where is the hotel that you manage?"

Camille looked around at him quickly. For a few seconds they stared into each other's eyes. Color blushed on her skin and a tendril of hair fell forward against her cheek. She swept it away with the back of her hand, and then she pointed airily. "Just on the other side of this wall," she said. "I am the night manager at the Grande Hotel. It is one of the biggest in Avignon. One hundred and twenty rooms."

Tremaine was impressed. "And you are the manager?"

"The night manager," she corrected him.

"What does that mean?"

"It means I start work at 10 pm each evening and run the reception desk and all the service staff until the morning when the day managers arrive. It's a great responsibility."

Tremaine listened attentively, but his expression turned grave. He reached across the table impulsively and snatched at Camille's hands. "Don't go into work tonight," he urged her. "Call in sick. Make any excuse you want. Just don't go outside the city walls this evening."

"What?" Camille blanched as if she had been slapped.

"I mean it," Tremaine's eyes became fierce. "Camille, you have no idea – no concept – of how imminent the spread of this contagion is. If your father gives his approval, then tomorrow morning the gates into the old city will be barricaded, if it's not already too late. Anyone trapped outside the walls isn't going to get in again... and that means they will die."

"But I must go to work," Camille's sense of duty and pride was bruised. "People are relying on me."

"To hell with them," Tremaine snapped. A blaze of fanatical desperation filled his eyes. Camille leaned back in her chair, putting space between them. Tremaine hunched over the table, his voice hushed but intense. "They will be dead in twenty-four hours," he said brutally. "And unless you listen to me – unless you do as I tell you to – you will be dead also. This contagion doesn't care who you are, or how much money you have... or if you're a nice person or not. It's not called the Raptor virus for no reason. By this time tomorrow, France will be overwhelmed by the infected. No one will be left alive, Camille. No one."

There was another long silence, charged with electric tension and antagonism. Camille's face was stony, her eyes like flint. She glared at Tremaine, searching his face for some sign of deceit but could find none. The tension went from her shoulders slowly, and her eyes widened just a little. She inclined her head in a gesture of grudging capitulation.

"You truly believe this, don't you?"

"I know it," Tremaine said earnestly. "I am certain."

Camille's eyes shifted and settled on the empty space beyond Tremaine's shoulder for a long moment as if she were suddenly daydreaming. "Very well," she sighed without meeting his gaze. "I will not go to work tonight," she told the lie to appease him and saw instantly the relief in his face. "I will phone and tell them I am too ill."

"Good," Tremaine let out a breath of air he had been holding and visibly relaxed. The fire went from his gaze like cooling lava, and the touch of a relieved smile tugged at the corner of his mouth. "Thank you," he said.

The pizza arrived, carried high overhead by the chef on a serving platter. He set it down in the middle of the table and stood back satisfied. Tremaine inhaled the aromas and felt his mouth water. He knew he was hungry, but he hadn't realized just how famished he was until this instant.

"Enjoy!" the chef smiled like the pizza was a personal triumph. Camille flashed the young man a dazzling smile of appreciation. The chef gave a curt little bow and scuttled back behind the serving counter. Camille picked up her knife and fork. "We share," she said. "It is the house specialty. I hope you will enjoy. And after we have finished eating, I will take you to your hotel."

Tremaine attacked the food with single-minded determination.

Outside it began to rain.

\* \* \*

Henri Pelletier shrugged off his rain coat and trudged up the narrow stairs to his home, located above a shop that sold hand-made chocolates. He could hear his wife in the kitchen and smell the aroma of cooking, but Henri was not hungry. He hung his coat on the back of the bathroom door and slumped down in the sofa that faced the television. His wife heard him. She came bustling into the room, wiping her hands on a dishcloth. She was a large woman with huge shapeless breasts beneath her blouse. Her dark hair, woven through with grey strands, had been pulled back in a bun, and her face flushed red and perspiring. The loving maternal smile on her lips faltered and froze when she saw Henri's expression.

"What is wrong, Henri?" the mayor's wife asked in a whisper. Her hand clutched at her throat instinctively.

He shook his head and forced his face into a dismissive grin. "Nothing, chéri," he said. "Everything is fine."

She came cautiously towards him. They had been married for thirty years. She knew when her husband was lying. His face seemed to have collapsed, the flesh hanging in unexpected pouches and folds. She put her hand on his shoulder. "Are you hungry?"

He looked up into his wife's eyes and tried to keep the smile going just a little longer. "Not at the moment," he said softly. "I wish to watch the news first."

He switched the television set on and his wife left him alone in the darkened living room. On the wall, a clock chimed 9 pm. Henri switched to a news channel, and the bright flickering lights from the screen lit his face into a death-like mask of hollows and deep haunting shadows.

The spread of the Raptor virus was a continuous news feed; linking outdoor live footage back to a pair of female news anchors back in a studio. Henri watched with the cold slithering fear of dread coiling tighter in the pit of his guts. The contagion had breached France's borders. The broadcast showed footage of armed troops at crossing points and then cutting to a live feed from the streets of Paris. Henri leaned forward in his chair, pressing his horrified face closer to the screen.

He could see police cars in the foreground parked at

crazy angles across a shadow struck street. The blue flashing lights were like a strobe. Darkened by their uniforms and riot gear, French troops were filing through the gap between the cars and jogging in two lines down the middle of the road. They were carrying shields on their arms and wore dark paramilitary helmets. At the far end of the street was an intersection. The camera zoomed in, but for a moment nothing happened. The troops reached a traffic sign and spread out across the road in a line, linking their shields like a wall. Henri Pelletier held his breath and felt a trickle of ice-cold sweat run down the back of his shirt. Over the images a reporter was broadcasting, but Henri narrowed his gaze and blocked out the sound. He concentrated on the intersection, the road lit up by the neon lights of nearby shops. The armed soldiers started to move forward in a straight line, stretching from one side of the road to the other. The camera tried to follow their progress by zooming further, but the image became shaky. Henri swallowed hard.

Then, suddenly, there came a blood-curdling scream from somewhere off camera and the line of soldiers froze. Someone barked an order, and the men braced themselves.

A wall of snarling, blood-drenched figures came around the corner and spilled out across the intersection like a wave of bodies; a heaving seething mass of snarling growling faces. They were clawing and biting at the air, surging forward towards the thin line of soldiers. Henri felt his breath jam in the back of his throat. A spotlight cut through the darkened gloom like a knife, falling on the faces of the crowd. They were inhuman, their features distorted, their faces ravaged and greyed. They hissed at the soldiers and then charged.

85

Henri Pelletier sat back in his chair and watched numb with horror and fear as the tide of infected undead crashed into the line of soldiers, and then overwhelmed it. The center buckled first. One of the soldiers fell screaming to the ground with three of the infected thrashing at his body. In an instant the entire line collapsed into a terrified rabble as men tried to escape back towards the police cars. The camera picture shook madly and then suddenly tilted side on and froze.

Quickly the image switched back to the studio. One of the women behind the news desk wept softly.

"We repeat," the other broadcaster announced. "The Raptor virus has reached Paris. Three thousand people are already believed to be infected, with that number rising dramatically by the minute. Police and Army are unable to contain the spread of the contagion at this time. The government has declared a state of martial law in Paris, Nantes, Strasbourg and Lille. All other major towns in the northern region of the country are on high alert…"

Henri Pelletier's skin crawled and prickled with a thousand insects of terror. He had delayed fortifying the city, and now he felt filled with cringing fear. He sat very still for a long time, staring blankly at the television screen. His only movement was the fluttering tick of a nerve at the corner of his eye. His face was white as marble, shiny with a sheen of perspiration.

Quietly, as if in slow motion, he leaned over the side of the sofa chair and vomited across the living room carpet.

\* \* \*

Jacques Lejeune pulled up the collar of his overcoat

and turned the corner, walking slowly with his head bowed, deep in thought. The night was a pearlescent mist; an Impressionist painting of soft hazy edges and blurred halos around the streetlights. The mist drifted like smoke, turning the figures that passed him on the street into vague ethereal shapes.

"If the American is right, then it is the end of the world," Jacques heard the echo of his footsteps on the ancient cobblestones, walking without purpose or direction. "And if that is the case, then what have I done with my life?"

He was a sixty-year-old man and still a virgin. As the Deputy Mayor he had some prestige in the community, *but as a man?*

He had lived in his mother's home with her until she had passed away just the year before, and had never dated, never married. Now he was staring into the precipice of his own mortality and the view from where he stood was not a pleasant one.

Without realizing it his feet carried him towards the old city's imposing walls, and as he stepped beneath the vast arch of the Porte Saint Roch gate, a young woman with lewdly painted lips appeared from out of the darkened gloom.

She wore a short skirt, a handbag dangling by her side. She sauntered towards Jacques with a polite invitation in her eyes and in the way she smiled. Jacques hesitated. His feet shuffled on the wet ground. The young woman was very beautiful.

"Twenty-five euros –" the prostitute came closer to him, confident in the way she moved her body. She began slowly unfastening the top buttons of her blouse. At every sway of her hips the fabric of her shirt gaped open, and Jacques had to tear his eyes back to her face.

"I'm… I'm not interested," he said stiffly, without conviction. Her lips were soft, painted red.

"Twenty then," the prostitute lowered her price. "And for that I promise you the time of your life."

Jacques shook his head but his resolve began crumbling. The woman's top gaped wide open and her breasts were soft in the moonlight. A car drove past, slowing as it passed through the gatehouse but Jacques did not notice. He took a step backwards into deeper shadow. The woman came close enough that he could smell the scent of her cheap perfume. "Come on," her voice purred. Possessively she ran a delicate hand across his chest, smiling up into his face with sparkling eyes. "You know you want to…"

A wave of unaccountable despair washed over Jacques, hopeless longing and the emptiness of his fear. He hung his head for a moment and felt the oily taste of his shame in the back of his throat. The woman heard him sob.

When he lifted his eyes again, the movement shook loose a tear; it spilled down his sallow cheek.

"My mother died…" he made a helpless gesture with his hands like a plea for understanding. "And I'm very lonely. I've never been with…"

The young woman reached for Jacques hand. "Come with me," her voice firmed and became husky. "My name is Paulette. I will look after you."

"Come with you? To where?"

"My apartment," she said softly. "It is just around the next corner."

Jacques cuffed at the tears in his eyes and nodded passively. Paulette led him down a shadowed laneway.

\* \* \*

"I was starting to worry about you," the woman behind the reception counter at the Grande Hotel smiled her relief at Camille Pelletier. "Half the night shift staff have already called in sick this evening."

Camille groaned. She flung her handbag behind the counter and pulled off her sweater. "Why? Is there something going round? A flu?"

"Fear," the woman behind the counter said with scornful condescension, pouting her lips. "They're all worried about the Raptor contagion that has been on the news."

"They said that?" Camille sounded shocked. She thought for a moment about Steven Tremaine and the lie she had told him at dinner.

"No," the woman shook her head. "They all made the usual excuses, of course. But you can tell. It's in their voices."

Camille said nothing more. She swept through a doorway to an inner office and dropped into a chair behind a computer monitor. She glanced at her watch while she waited for the latest data on hotel occupancy and reservations to spill down the screen. It was a few minutes before 10 pm.

"Glad you could make it," a matronly woman's voice called out from over her shoulder. Camille spun round on her chair. It was the day manager – a bitter woman in her forties with a dry withered face and a surly expression. She eyed Camille with open resentment. "I was expecting to have to cover your shift as well. Most of your staff have already called in absent. I thought you would be one of them."

Camille widened her eyes into an artless challenge and stared defiantly at the woman with her jaw set and determined. "Then you were wrong, Marguerite. *Again.*"

The day manager sucked air through her clenched teeth so the sound was like the soft hiss of a snake. Her eyes flashed venomously. In her hand she held a thick folder stuffed with dog-eared sheaths of paper. She threw it onto the desk beside Camille.

"These reports need to be completed and sent to head office before midday tomorrow," the woman declared. "I've done most of it. You will have to do the rest. It's a full inventory of all… and I mean *all*… of the hotel's current cleaning and maintenance supplies. Everything needs to be counted and signed off. That's your responsibility."

"Mine?" Camille was about to protest. Her tasks were not administrative. She oversaw the reception counter and customer check-ins. "Why me?"

"Because I put your name on the bottom of the forms," the older woman smiled vindictively, flashing crooked, discolored teeth. She turned and left without another word, her footsteps echoing hollowly on the parquetry floor.

Camille flipped open the cover of the folder and sighed. Ahead of her waited twelve hours of work in dark cramped storerooms in the bowels of the building. She closed her eyes, sighed as her shoulders slumped. "I should have called in ill," Camille muttered darkly.

\* \* \*

They came for Tremaine at 6 am — a frantic pounding on his hotel room door drove him from the bed and he stumbled to his feet, bleary-eyed, his head still stuffed with the cotton wool of fatigue. The television was still on. He saw the face of a man dripping blood

90

flash upon the screen, the stranger's mouth wide open in a silent shriek of agony. He drew the door open suspiciously and saw Henri Pelletier and Captain Devaux of the Police Nationale standing in the hotel corridor. The mayor wrung his hands with anxiety, shuffling impatiently from foot to foot while the Captain of Police stood stoic and stiff to one side.

"Monsieur, you must come immediately," Henri Pelletier insisted. There was naked unholy fear in his eyes. "The meeting at the Town Hall has been brought forward."

Tremaine swayed on his feet. He scraped his hand across the unshaven stubble of his jaw and blinked myopically. He had not slept long enough. "What's happened?" his voice croaked.

"The contagion," Pelletier lowered his voice to a coarse whisper. "It reached Paris last night. France is infected and the virus is spreading down from the north. The capital is under martial law, and we have had no contact from those government authorities in Paris, or any of the other major cities since the early hours of this morning."

Tremaine listened in silence, the fury and outrage growing like a fire in his eyes as the French mayor explained. He glowered at Henri Pelletier and his voice snapped with scorn.

"I told you this would happen," Tremaine came fully awake in an instant, grappling with the ominous implications of the mayor's update. "Now you're in a panic because everything I warned you about is coming crashing down around you."

Pelletier lowered his eyes with regret and shame, and his face reddened. He nodded his head and when he looked up again his expression was twisting on his lips as though he were in great pain. Tremaine saw weakness in the man's eyes. Henri Pelletier lacked the instinct for ruthlessness. Most men were reasonable; they sought to avoid confrontation. But there would be no room for the luxury of compromise in the dark days ahead.

"Yes," he conceded. "You were right, Professor Tremaine. The contagion has reached France, and it is spreading south towards us. I have cost us twelve hours of preparation. I can only hope that there still remains enough time for us to save as many people as we can. But right now we need your help – not recrimination. There will be time for that later, I assure you, and I will go to my God to be judged. But now – *right now* – we need you to come to the Town Hall. The others have been summoned and are assembling there, waiting for us."

\* \* \*

There was just four of them in the conference room: Tremaine, the mayor, Captain Devaux and Colonel LeCat from the Gendarmerie.

"Deputy Mayor Lejeune is not answering his phone," Henri Pelletier apologized.

"And your daughter, Camille?"

Pelletier shook his head dismissively. "She was not notified," he said. "This matter is beyond the involvement of the local business community."

Tremaine grunted. The building was eerily quiet. He glanced out through the curtained window. The new day was dawning.

"Very well," Tremaine turned back to face the room, his voice filled with determination and authority. "What do we know for a fact that we didn't know when I left here last evening?"

Pelletier shrugged his shoulders. "I have told you," he said, frowning. "Paris is being overrun by the infected. It was on the news last night – the first cases in the capital began appearing late in the evening."

"And you cannot reach anyone in Paris?"

Henri Pelletier shook his head. Tremaine glanced at LeCat. "Colonel?"

The burly French commander unfolded his arms and straightened his shoulders. "Communication with headquarter elements has been disjointed," he chose the word carefully.

"Meaning?" Tremaine fixed the man with a stare.

"Meaning that we have no direct link to an active command," LeCat was forced to admit. "The contact we have had has been with broken elements of the Army in various regions surrounding Paris."

"What about other headquarter elements here in the south?"

"There are none," LeCat sighed expressively. "We cannot make contact."

"Meaning the majority of the French Army has deserted?"

"Or been infected," LeCat said.

Tremaine and LeCat stared at each other through the tense crackling silence. Tremaine nodded his head slowly. "How many men do you have based here in Avignon?"

"Two hundred and thirty six," LeCat answered automatically.

"Any tanks… things like that?"

"A dozen APC's," LeCat said. "No tanks."

"Are there other elements of the Gendarmerie in towns nearby?"

"They're not responding," LeCat said abruptly.

Tremaine clawed his fingers through his hair and turned to Captain Devaux. "Your men, Captain? How many members of the Police Nationale are there in your headquarters outside the city walls?"

"One hundred… maybe a few more," Benoit Devaux said, his voice a somber rumble.

"How many on duty right now?"

"Less than half that amount."

"Thirty?"

"Perhaps."

Tremaine looked grim. He turned back to Henri Pelletier and planted his knuckles on the polished tabletop. "Mr. Mayor, you need to step aside and give full authority to the Army and the Police to impose martial law here in Avignon, effective immediately."

Pelletier leaped to his feet, an outraged protest on his lips.

"Never!"

Tremaine cut the mayor off with a curt slash of his hand, his features hard as granite, his voice blunt and brutal. "You cost us twelve hours of preparation time because you're a politician, sir. By considering your own position first, and the people last, you have jeopardized everyone's lives. It is impossible to prepare Avignon for defense if these two men," he thrust a finger at LeCat and Devaux, "constantly need to come to you to decide if a measure is politically savory. They don't have the time to consider whether their actions will be popular. They're not looking to get themselves re-elected. They're practical men. You are not."

"I will not stand aside," the mayor persisted, but his voice had lost much of its outrage.

Henri Pelletier had seemed to wither under the searing heat of Tremaine's simmering temper. The shape and poise went out of his body and his shoulders sagged. The tight lines around his jaw softened, blurring his features so that he looked suddenly aged. He shuffled his feet, looking uncertain for one more moment, and then silently capitulated. He nodded his head. "Very well," he muttered. "It will be so."

"Immediately," Tremaine insisted.

"Yes," Henri Pelletier said, suddenly just a sad middle-aged man in a rumpled suit. He steeled himself, formally handed control of the city's defenses to the Police Captain and the Colonel of the Gendarmerie, and then sagged into his chair, his gaze far away, his eyes empty.

Tremaine felt himself relax just a little. He took no pleasure from wresting control of the city's defenses from the mayor. But the time for sensitivity had long passed. Now urgent action was required and if the consequences of saving thousands of lives were this one man's bruised ego, then it would be an infinitely small price to pay. He turned to LeCat and Devaux.

"Captain, call in your men. Order every police officer inside the city's walls. Don't tell them why. It will only cause unrest. They need to be assembled before 8 am. I suggest you get started."

Benoit Devaux nodded his head and snatched his cell phone from his pocket. He bounced out of his chair, went to a corner of the room, and began talking urgently and earnestly.

"Colonel, LeCat, your men will need to fortify the town's gates and will be responsible for the armed defense of the city against the undead infected. The police, under Captain Devaux, will maintain civil control. Does that make sense to you?"

"It does," LeCat came to his feet. "But two hundred

95

men...?"

"We will need the help of the civilian population, of course," Tremaine conceded. "Once the gates have been sealed and the threat is real, I'm sure we will have no problem. But closing the city off from the rest of the world is the first, and most pressing challenge. We need to block each gateway completely with buses, APC's... anything and everything you can think of. Can you do that?"

"We have some engineering equipment," LeCat said vaguely. "A couple of cranes that can be used. What about the buses?"

"We'll commandeer them," Tremaine said bluntly. "That will be the police Captain's responsibility. No bus arriving inside the walls will be allowed to leave again."

"This is going to cause great unrest," Henri Pelletier mumbled a dire warning from his chair.

"Yes," Tremaine agreed. "But that can't be avoided. "We need every gate – large and small – blocked off completely by 9 am. And we need supplies. How do we handle that?"

"Food and water, you mean?" Pelletier asked.

"Yes."

The mayor shrugged. "There are supermarkets within the city..."

Tremaine shook his head irritably. "That won't be enough for us to sustain ourselves when this turns into a siege."

"There are several large food markets beyond the old city," LeCat said. "They could be raided."

"Good," Tremaine nodded. "Get all the men together you can divert from sealing off the gates and send them out in trucks, Colonel. Under the regulations of martial law, take all measures necessary."

"But…" Pelletier looked aghast. "That will encourage looting across the entire city, monsieur."

Tremaine shrugged. "If looting hasn't already started, it was about to anyhow," he said flatly. "The world has tipped over the edge. Civilization as we knew it no longer exists. It's anarchy, Mr. Mayor. Only the strongest and those who are prepared will survive. You can't think of this in any other way. We're at war."

\* \* \*

They came out through the conference room doors, Henri Pelletier ashen and visibly shaken, Colonel LeCat and Captain Devaux grim faced, their jaws set and steel in their eyes. Tremaine felt exhausted, his tightly strung nerves beginning to fray as fatigue and tension took their toll.

Deputy Mayor, Jacques Lejeune was coming up the stairs, still fastening the buttons of his suit jacket. His tie hung awry around his neck and his face looked rumpled and unshaven. He appeared to have slept in his clothes, and his hair hung disheveled, falling lank into his puffy red-rimmed eyes. He started up at the phalanx of men above him on the mezzanine foyer and paused.

"I am sorry," he said hastily. "My cell phone… I only just got the message." A slow throbbing pain beat inside his skull.

Henri Pelletier's eyes narrowed with disapproval. Lejeune smelled of cheap perfume and stale sweat. He glared at his deputy and drew him aside into a quiet corner of the hallway.

"Jacques, you are too late," he said stiffly, examining his deputy closely. He saw that Lejeune was a physical mess. His eyes had a gaunt, hunted look. "I have handed over authority for the defense of Avignon to the Colonel and the Captain. Lejeune's long drawn face reflected his shock, but secretly he felt relieved. The decisions that would have been necessary for him to make were simply beyond his ability and fortitude. He let out a long sigh of breath and then nodded. "Perhaps it is for the best," he conceded weakly. "We are not fighting men, Henri. This is something extraordinary that is beyond our levels of understanding, yes?"

Pelletier studied Lejeune's expression suspiciously for long minutes, noting the shift in the taller man's eyes, and the little tightening of nerves along his jawline. Lejeune's long nicotine-stained fingers were fidgeting. Finally the tall man looked away, self-conscious under the intense scrutiny.

"Yes…" Henri Pelletier said slowly, mistrust in his tone. "But I for one will do whatever I can to assist the Captain to maintain civil order. That is our responsibility, Jacques. *And we do understand the fears of our people.* It will be our task – yours and mine – to aid the Captain, and to sooth the people when calamity and death comes to our city's door. Do you agree?"

"Yes," Lejeune nodded his head. "That is the least we can do."

\* \* \*

Tremaine came down the steps of the Town Hall and stood for a moment on the cobblestones of the outdoor plaza. Early morning sunlight was rising above the rooftops and filtering tranquilly through the trees. The city was silent, still asleep. Beside him, the police Captain and the Colonel of the French gendarmerie were talking urgently to each other, their faces earnest.

And suddenly Tremaine didn't know what to do with himself.

He reached for his cell phone and dialed Maxime Boudin in Paris. The phone rang out, unanswered.

"Come on, Max," he muttered. If Paris had been overrun by the infected he wondered whether the Health Minister and the other members of the French government had escaped to safety or if they had died at their desks. He dialed again and stood clutching the phone to his ear for long anxious seconds, tapping his foot impatiently, until Colonel LeCat came and stood abruptly before him.

Tremaine shut down his phone and looked up into the soldier's harsh face. "Yes?"

"You must come with me," LeCat said simply. "I will need you at the main gates to supervise."

Tremaine held up his hands and shook his head. "Colonel, I'm not an engineer, and I can't drive a crane. I wouldn't be any help to you."

The Colonel's expression did not change. "It's your plan," he said simply. "You must see that it is carried through."

"What about the western wall? I was told that the city had boards of some kind and doors that were used to block the gatehouses during flooding. Do you know anything about them?"

LeCat nodded. "Captain Devaux has men enough to complete that task," he said dismissively. "It has already been decided. It is the other gates we must worry about, monsieur. They will need to be barricaded, and the longer we stand here in useless discussion, the less time we have to complete the task."

\* \* \*

There were eight buses parked at the Avignon bus terminal by the time Tremaine and LeCat pulled up in a jeep-like Peugeot P4 four-wheel-drive. Tremaine got out of the unarmored, camouflaged vehicle and looked around him, taking in everything in a matter of seconds.

Behind them stood the imposing grand edifice of the Avignon Post Office, and ahead were the wide open gates he remembered being driven through under police escort when he had arrived in the city. The buses were parked at awkward angles and the drivers were protesting in loud agitated voices with police officers. On the sidewalk a crowd of disquieted and confused bystanders had gathered. LeCat glanced around quickly and checked his wristwatch. "This is the largest, most used gate on the south side of the city," he said. "It will also be the most difficult to obstruct. We need to block the entire expanse of four lanes. We have these buses to do it."

Tremaine frowned, deep in thought. It was just after 7 am in the morning. Traffic off the road network beyond the walls was still light. He flicked a sideways glance at LeCat. "When will the crane arrive?"

"We have one at our barracks on Boulevard Raspail," he said. "It is on its way here."

"Where is that?"

LeCat pointed northwest. "Just a few minutes away," he assured Tremaine. "And we have a civilian crane being brought in from a nearby construction site."

"Will it come through these gates?"

"Yes. It should be here within the half-hour."

Tremaine strode towards the gates, crossing the wide expanse of the bus depot and walking towards the nearest battlement. There were stone steps inside the structure and another set of narrow steps connecting to the firing platform that ran the length of adjoining wall. He turned back to LeCat and pointed. "We'll need ladders," he said. "Lots of them. Once we get men up onto the upper level of the wall, we're fine. But there's no other way to access the firing platform."

LeCat arched his eyebrows, and his mouth pressed into a thin pale line, aggravated by his own oversight. "Yes," he said grimly. "This was unforeseen. I will attend to it." He turned on his heel and reached inside the driver's seat of the P4 jeep. Tremaine heard the Colonel in the background barking orders over a two-way and shut the sound out of his mind. Instead he went and watched the passing traffic with a rising sense of unease.

There was something in the air; something intangible that was just an instinct – a sense of foreboding that seemed to vibrate. It was as if the world were trembling, the ground softly rumbling under his feet. It was in the harsh sounds of the passing traffic, and it was on the faces of the drivers.

It was unholy fear – not expressed; not given voice… but lurking like a sinister shadow in the depths of men's souls.

Tremaine shivered and something cold and creeping slithered along his spine.

Behind him he heard a snarling rumble of heavy engine noise and Tremaine turned to watch the Army's crane come trundling along the main street of the old city. Following it were three truck loads of French soldiers and two police cars, their lights flashing. The sound jarred the eerie hush of early morning. Two of the Army trucks did not stop. Instead they drove out through the gates in a surging cloud of black diesel exhaust. Tremaine propped his hands on his hips and watched

101

the camouflaged trucks join the traffic streaming past the open gates. In the distance, moving against the grain of vehicles heading east, approached the high hanging arm of the other crane LeCat had promised. Tremaine grunted and glanced fretfully at his watch.

\* \* \*

With the police parked across the main highway outside the gates and all traffic halted from entering the old city, LeCat ordered the first bus to be driven between the two battlements and then overturned. The huge vehicle went crashing onto its side, with the roof of the bus facing out at the world and the ugly black chassis facing into Avignon. Glass windows crashed, upended tires spun on their axles. The two cranes worked like prehistoric monsters picking over the carcass of dead prey until the bus could be dragged into place. Then the second bus was overturned and the gateway made impassable to traffic. Tremaine stood back, looking on critically. He went to each battlement to be sure the buses overlapped the old stonework and then windmilled his arm at LeCat. The next two buses were overturned and then hoisted precariously into the air. The first bus swung like a pendulum while the cranes inched it into position. Then it was dropped onto the broken shell of the bus below it. When the second bus was finally in place, the barricade stood two buses high; a wall of crumpled broken metal that reached twenty feet above the road.

"It looks good," Tremaine admitted. He dragged the sleeve of his shirt across his brow. Even in the cool early morning air he was sweating.

"There is one way to find out," LeCat grunted. He

sent a man at a run along the inside of the wall until he reached the next gate and then ordered him to try to escalade the barricade of buses. The soldier came back fifteen minutes later, red faced and dripping sweat through his fatigues. He shook his head in defeat. LeCat allowed himself the faintest mirthless smile.

"Very well," he agreed with Tremaine. "Now we will move on to the next gate."

* * *

"Preacher, you must come and see. Satan is at work!" a man came into the abandoned warehouse gasping and out of breath. He stood in the darkened doorway, staring through flickering candlelight and swirling incense smoke to where an imposing man dressed in a flowing black robe stood on a raised platform.

The tall man on the stage stared venomously for a moment, outraged at the interruption to his sunrise sermon, and then his face lapsed quickly into a benevolent mask. He combed his fingers through the silver pelt of his beard, and then his gaze shifted to the crowd that had assembled, kneeling on the cold concrete floor, to listen to him speak.

For months his dire doomsday predictions had drawn just a dozen faithful lost souls. Now his flock counted into the hundreds, each of them driven to find God and salvation since the Raptor virus had spread around the globe.

The man on the stage closed the bible he had been reading from.

"Speak," his voice rumbled like thunder across a storm-filled sky. "Why do you interrupt God's word?"

"The Army and police are on the streets," the man's

voice became querulous and intimidated. "They're sealing off the city's gates."

* * *

Two buses were driven to the Porte Saint Roch gate with one of the cranes trundling awkwardly along the narrow road that ran inside the wall, following close behind. Several civilian cars had to be moved from the roadside and the whole operation took a frustrating hour before the crane could overturn the first bus and wedge it into place across the open gatehouse. Tremaine drove in the P4 with LeCat, while a police car raced ahead of the procession to block off traffic. LeCat was furious – precious minutes ticking away. He barked threats at his men and threw his arms about, red-faced and seething with impatience. The first bus crashed onto its side in a rending screech of broken glass and crumpled metal, but beneath the clamor came suddenly another sound – a noise like waves crashing on a beach.

Tremaine turned, frowning and puzzled. The sound became a muted roar. Tremaine felt a slow leaden weight of fear fill his legs. His mouth turned dry. He turned and saw LeCat narrowing his eyes warily, his soldier's instincts prickling the fine hairs on the back of his arms. LeCat had just six armed men with him, the rest of the troops sent to seal another gate with the civilian crane. Suddenly he wished he had not been so blasé. He reached slowly for the sidearm holstered to his waist and drew the weapon, just as a crowd of angry people came spilling across the intersection of a narrow road, surging with their fists clenched towards the soldiers. They came as a solid phalanx of people, swarming past the houses that lined the street like a river

104

in flash flood. They were chanting, their faces distorted and swollen. There were men and women and children, all of them incensed and outraged.

"Get back," LetCat told Tremaine levelly. "Get the men into a line and keep them calm. No one is to open fire without my orders."

LeCat kept his weapon lowered by his waist and strode out to meet the line of protesters. Behind him, the soldier in the crane and half-a-dozen troopers shuffled themselves urgently into positions. There were two policemen standing by their vehicle. They drew their weapons and took cover behind the car, guns raised and pointed into the mass of protesters.

LeCat held up one hand, palm facing out, like a traffic cop halting vehicles. The crowd filled the roadway from one side to the other, and still they came on, pouring out of a narrow side road like a rushing wave. Ten feet short of the gendarme Colonel, they suddenly paused, strangely hushed to silence by the stern imposing figure that had strode forward to confront them.

"What do you people want?" LeCat's voice cracked like a whip.

For a long moment there came no answer. The front ranks had been cowered by the Colonel's stone-like defiance. Then, from within the milling mass, a man's voice called out strongly.

"We want to be free to leave the city!" the voice cried out. "You're barricading us in. We have rights!"

LeCat smiled but there was no humor in his eyes. "You do not!" he told the crowd. "Avignon has been placed under martial law, effective immediately. Gatherings like this are unlawful. You will disperse back to your homes, or you will be fired upon by my men."

A little ripple of uncertain movement washed through

the gathered crowd. They swayed back from the intersection, and LeCat felt himself steal a small breath of relief. But then the voice from amongst them called out again, and the moment turned suddenly dangerous.

"God is the only one who can judge us!" the voice shouted. It was a man's voice, strong and clear.

"I am not judging you," LeCat snarled. He narrowed his eyes, trying to pick out the trouble maker but in a sea of faces it proved impossible. "We are taking these measures to barricade the city and seal it from the contagion sweeping the earth. We must fortify the city. No one will be allowed to leave. No one will be allowed to enter. It is for your own protection."

"The contagion is God's will!" the voice cried out. "This is the Lord's way of cleansing unbelievers from the face of the earth and creating a new Eden for those who follow His divine teachings! You have no hold over us, for we are all God's children. We will walk amongst the infected and our righteousness will be our shield, our love and devotion our sword."

The sound of the crowd swelled in support and turned into a snarl. LeCat turned and glanced over his shoulder. His men were raising their weapons. They were drawn into a line in front of the overturned bus. Tremaine stood beside them. He came forward to join LeCat.

Tremaine held up his hands in an appeal for silence, but the crowd's angry noise jeered and swirled around him.

"Listen to me!" he cried out. The rumble amongst the protestors became a roar. Then, suddenly, the mass of bodies seemed to peel apart and Tremaine saw a man pushing purposefully towards the front of the rioters. He was tall, dressed in a long black robe that hung baggy about his waist but was stretched tight across the broad of his shoulders. He had a great silver beard, a thick long grey mane of hair, and the burning blazing gaze of a zealot. His features were biblical – broad and gaunt faced with a large beaked nose and penetrating eyes; fanatical dark eyes that burned with fierce conviction.

The man came out of the crowd and strode towards LeCat and Tremaine. He had a battered leather-covered bible clutched in one huge hand. His face was grim, his mouth a harsh slash. He turned back to the crowd and raised his arms high.

"Do we trust our God to deliver us?" the man's voice boomed.

"Yes!" a hundred voices called back with devotion.

"Do we demand the right to leave the city?"

"Yes!"

"Will anyone stop us from doing the work that is God's will?"

"No!" the crowd roared, gaining voice and determination.

The black robed man lowered his arms and turned to stare implacably at Colonel LeCat. "This plague is God's work," he said, his voice low and quivering with restrained passion. "It cannot touch us for we are God's children."

LeCat raised a cynical eyebrow and raised his pistol until it pointed into the stranger's face. "What is your name?"

"My followers call me Kane," the dark man said.

"Well, Kane," LeCat spoke slowly and deliberately, "I don't care whether you are your God's chosen children or not," he said. "This city is not under his law. It's under martial law. No one enters. No one leaves."

"You're making a mistake…" Kane's voice became edged with dire warning.

107

LeCat ignored the threat. "Tell them to disperse," he ordered through clenched teeth. "Right now, or my men will open fire."

Kane turned back to face his followers, and his shoulders slumped. "They will not let us leave," he said heavily. "Just as the Israelites were kept slaves in Egypt – "

He got no further, for suddenly, from somewhere deep inside the pressing mass of bodies a piece of brick was thrown. It sailed in a high arc above the heads of the crowd and struck the soldier standing beside Tremaine on the arm. The man spun around, dropping his weapon, his face wrenched into a mask of agony.

It was the spark that ignited the combustible temper of the crowd. In an instant they turned into a wild mob and came rushing forward.

"Kill!" they cried.

LeCat swung his pistol and aimed instinctively at a charging man in the front row who had a long wooden post in his hands, raised high above his head like a club. His mouth hung wide open in a hateful howl. LeCat fired, striking the man in the face. The bullet snapped the man's head back, and flung him to the ground, dead in a spreading pool of his own blood.

The crowd froze, the sound of the bullet's retort loud as a giant bell, echoing off the city's old walls and reverberating along the narrow alleyway. The silence was stunned; shocked. The rioters drew back from the body on the ground aghast with astonishment and seething fury. Then a wail of outrage went up, and the crowd rushed forward once more, lashed into a frenzy by Kane's voice as he urged them on towards the guns. The air became thick with dust and the cloying stench of blood and sweat and terror.

108

LeCat fired again, hitting a middle-aged man in the arm, the impact spinning him around in a tottering circle. The bullet struck with the sound of a solid meaty thump. The man's arm was flung wide. He staggered and fell, and was instantly trampled by those who pressed close behind him. The mob overwhelmed the soldiers until suddenly a ripping roar of automatic gunfire tore the air apart.

One of the gendarmes had dropped to his knees, white-faced with horror and blood gushing from his forehead. A young woman with wild crazy tangles of dark hair stood over him, her skirts clutched in one hand and an iron bar in the other. She wielded the cold steel like a sword, bludgeoning the soldier's head and shoulders. She was screaming with fanatical madness, hissing spittle at the young trooper. The soldier threw up his weapon and fired instinctively. The range was so close that the muzzle flash seemed to join the barrel to the woman's stomach, and the impact so fierce that she was flung back in the air, her body broken almost in half before she hit the cobblestoned ground. Two other men crammed close to the woman also went down, clutching at wounds to their chests. They reeled away from the melee, staggering in pain.

LeCat clawed a hand for the tall dark-robed leader, but the man was lithe and elusive. He slipped out of the Colonel's grasp and melted back into the mass of swarming rioters, still screaming at his followers, urging them to violence. LeCat snarled, and kicked out at a teenage boy who came running at him with his fist bunched. His boot caught the young man in the midriff, and he folded over in red-faced pain. LeCat spun around, the teenager already forgotten, and drove the stiffened palm of his hand into another man's face. The man was dark-skinned with a scruffy moustache and black beady eyes. The blow snapped off two of the man's teeth and he flopped to the ground like a landed fish, kicking and flailing his legs while blood gushed from his cawing mouth.

For an instant there was a space around him and LeCat stole a quick fearful glance over his shoulder. His men were backing away, pressed up against the chassis of the bus that been overturned across the Porte Saint Roch gateway, with the rioters seething and heaving all around them, throwing punches and lashing out with their feet. The two policemen were firing wildly into the edges of the crowd, their faces white shaken blobs behind their weapons. LeCat bellowed an order, his voice honed and hardened by years on the parade ground.

"Open fire!" he shouted.

The small wavering line of soldiers began shooting in short jarring bursts of semi-automatic fire that buzzed in the air like chainsaws. In just a few seconds more than a dozen rioters were laying dead or injured on the bloody ground, clasping at wounds and groaning in shocking pain. A woman and a young child lay on their backs beside each other. Their arms were flung out, the child's eyes open and staring, unseeing, at the wide blue sky. The woman's heels drummed a macabre tattoo on the cold stone ground.

Tremaine saw a running man struck by two bullets as he charged towards the barricade. He was jerked back as though he had reached the end of a tethered chain. He tottered for a few staggering steps and Tremaine saw one of the bullets come out through the man's shoulder blades. A vaporous puff of cloud erupted through his shirt. The man sagged to his knees, his eyes wide with shock and his gaping mouth wrenched in dreadful pain.

At last the crowd broke, fleeing back down the narrow laneway, yelling and sobbing and gasping with fear. They turned on their heels and ran like hunted rats, disappearing into the shadows, through doorways and around corners, melting away from the intersection like mist. LeCat stood, shaking with anger and rage, the barrel of his sidearm still hot in his hand. His face was streaked with sweat and dust. He was standing in a puddle of sticky congealing blood. He didn't seem to notice.

A deathly shroud of silence draped itself over the intersection. The police officers came from behind their car, wandering through the carnage of bodies, dazed and dismayed, their weapons hanging limp in their hands. One of the soldiers, disheveled and still shaking, knelt over the body of the dead child. He saw the dreadful wound, the torn frail body punched open by the impact of semi-automatic fire, and he sobbed silently.

Tremaine stood aghast amidst the bloody killing ground, numbed with his own horror. His eyes were huge and unblinking, cold sweat trickling down his spine. He stared down at his hands. They were trembling. His ears still thumped with the echo of gunfire. He turned in a slow bewildered circle, and all around him the cobblestones were drenched in blood, the dead and dying slumped like ghastly broken dolls upon the street.

He saw LeCat standing in the center of the chaos, stiff shouldered and gaunt. The French Colonel's face looked ashen, the sharp edges of his features blurred by the tragedy.

"What do we do?" Tremaine asked, his voice made small by shock.

"We finish barricading the gate," LeCat said with grim resolve. "And we call for an ambulance and support troops – in case they come back."

\* \* \*

Camille Pelletier stood up, stretched her back, and stared dejectedly at the shelves of serviettes, blankets and stationery items on the walls around her that still needed to be counted. Her hands were grimy with dust, her bottom numb from sitting too long on the hard wooden chair. She went to the doorway of the hotel's basement storage room and drew a breath of cool air.

The sound of the elevator descending made her pause with curiosity. She switched off the light to the storage room, thankful for any excuse to break the monotony of the stock take, and went towards the end of the hall. Behind the stainless steel doors she heard the elevator yo-yo to a stop. The doors glided open and the woman who had greeted her when she had arrived at work was standing, trembling and wide eyed.

Camille went to the woman. "Eve, what is wrong?" The woman was sobbing, the makeup around her eyes smudged. Under the touch of Camille's hand the young woman's arm trembled.

"The city…" the young woman named Eve gasped in disbelief. "Camille, they are closing off the city!"

Camille blanched, recoiled. Slowly a sense of fear stirred at the base of her spine, tingling up across her back. She stepped into the elevator and stabbed her finger at the 'Ground Floor' button. The elevator doors closed very slowly. Camille felt the first creep of her own alarm prickle the flesh at the nape of her neck.

She took the young woman by the shoulders and shook her like a rag doll. "Tell me!" she insisted. "Tell me what is happening."

Eve sobbed. Tears rolled down her cheeks, dripping off her chin. "They have blocked off the gates into the old city," Eve blubbered. "The police and the Army. They have sealed the gatehouses with overturned buses. No one can get in, Camille."

Dread filled the pit of Camille's stomach, a weight like heavy lead. The elevators doors finally glided open on the ground floor and she went striding through the hotel's front doors. Eve scurried behind her, the sound of her shoes echoing loudly across the high-ceilinged lobby.

"See!" she flung her arm out, pointing across the four lanes of traffic that were snarled to a standstill. "The undead must be close by. We're all going to be killed."

A hundred yards east from the hotel stood the blocked and barricaded Porte Saint Roch gates. Camille stared in shock. She could see the crumpled yellow carcasses of two buses wedged across the gateway, cast in shadow by the vault of the high arch. She shook her head in slow dread and disbelief.

"And there was shooting," Eve gasped beside her. "I heard it, Camille. Machine guns were firing."

"When? Camille turned on Eve. Her eyes filled with her own fear. She felt a lurch of despair clutch her stomach and wring the tenacity from her. Suddenly her legs turned weak under her.

"Maybe ten minutes ago," Eve said. "It went on for several minutes."

Camille ran onto the street, weaving her way through the stalled cars, squeezing between bumper bars until she reached the intersection of roadway that lead through the gatehouse into the old city. She stood trembling with her hands on her hips, her head thrown back in disbelief. The gateway had been completely blocked. There were two buses, each of them overturned onto their sides, stacked and crumpled on top of each other. She could not see daylight through the barricade. It was a solid wall of yellow rumpled metal.

Camille cupped her hands to her mouth and cried out as loudly as she could. It was no use. The wall and the battlement were deserted, and the sounds of her shouts were drowned out by the irritated clamor of car horns on the road right behind her. Her cell phone was in her handbag down in the basement storage room. She ran back across the street and into the hotel. She snatched up one of the front desk phones and crushed her finger at the numbers. She held the phone to her ear, listening to it ring out unanswered, while Eve stood fretfully beside her, weeping with fear, her shoulders heaving, her body beginning to shake.

"What will we do?" Eve's voice sounded small and filled with terror.

Camille slammed down the phone and picked it up again. She dialed another number. Her lips were pressed together, her heart racing. She could feel fear tremble in her fingers.

"Pick up the other phone," she snapped at Eve. "Dial anyone you can think of who lives inside the old city. We must get a message to my father."

\* \* \*

The rioters scattered into the narrow alleys of Avignon's old city, dragging their wounded with them as they retreated from the bark of the guns. Kane fled back to the abandoned warehouse that was his church, and with him ran a dozen of his followers, sobbing with shock and fear, their faces masks of stunned horror.

Candles still burned in the dark cavernous warehouse.

The lingering perfume of incense still hung in the air. Kane threw himself down in a corner of the building, his chest heaving, and the fire of his fanaticism fanned into a seething blaze.

"The unbelievers!" he raged. "They have cast themselves into the pits of Hell with their defiance of God's children."

It was a critical moment. The chaotic bloodshed at the city's gates would shatter the resolve of the timid amongst them unless he could galvanize their allegiance. He snatched up his battered Bible and forced himself to his feet, holding the book high over his head like a rally flag on a battlefield.

Two years ago he had been Father Pierre Gullette; a lowly Catholic priest serving in the suburbs of Bordeaux. Driven from the church and excommunicated in the face of an adulterous sex scandal, he had fled south to Avignon and built a new flock of adoring followers who had been drawn to Preacher Kane's hellfire sermons that foretold the imminent end of the world.

"We won a great victory today," Kane filled his voice with fervent passion and glared into the frightened faces around him, daring them to defy him. "We forced the unbelievers to declare and condemn themselves. We have won God's favor, and this is only the beginning. As word spreads, more and more of the faithful will flock to us until, like a mighty battering ram, our will to do God's work will force the city's gates open!"

A shaft of sunlight filled with moving dust motes spilled through a nearby window, illuminating the preacher as if he stood beneath a spotlight.

Someone in the shadows gave a reedy half-hearted cheer. The sound was strained in the ominous silence. Then a second voice joined the first. It was just enough to drown out the sobbing and the muted painful groans of the wounded that lay bleeding in the shadows.

Kane went amongst the survivors, talking to them all individually, putting booming confidence into his voice as he clapped a man on the shoulder and then hugged a woman who was still trembling. Gradually, more frightened followers returned sheepishly to the warehouse, seeking the comfort of other supporters, drawing strength from their zealous leader.

"And who are you?" Kane came to a young girl in a white dress that was spattered with blood. She was sitting alone in a corner beside a cluster of candles. The flickering light painted the perfect features of her face golden. The girl lifted her eyes to his. She had been crying. Kane guessed the girl was eighteen or nineteen years old. She had long black hair and the serene beauty of a Madonna.

"My name is Josephine, Preacher Kane," the girl sniffed, awed to be so close to the man she revered. Her face looked pale as bone china, and there were bruise-colored smears beneath her haunted eyes. Her tears had dried, cutting streaky runnels down her cheeks. Her dress was torn.

"Where is your mother, your father?" Kane looked down on the girl.

"My father was shot," the girl's voice choked and fresh tears spilled down her face. "One of the gendarmes killed him."

Kane dropped to his haunches, so he was face-to-face with the young girl. She shivered with cold and shock. He caressed her arm from the elbow to her shoulder with his strong fingers, and then reached to grip her hand. The girl shuddered and squeezed her eyes closed.

"Where is your mother?" his big booming voice

116

turned obscenely soft and slimy with kindness.

"She died when I was a baby," the girl gnawed at her lip. The enormity of being left alone in the world was beginning to crash through the trauma of her father's savage death.

"You have no other family?" Kane surreptitiously ran glittering snake-like eyes over the girl's body, lingering on her breasts. She was slim, and on the brink of blooming into womanhood. The tattered dirty hem of her dress had bunched around the tops of her slender thighs, so he could see the tantalizingly smooth skin of her legs. He felt a sharp bright rush of lust.

"No," the girl said, and then convulsed into a fresh outburst of heart-broken tears.

Kane reached for the girl and pulled her into his arms, engulfing her with a bear-like embrace. He could smell the sweetness of her young flesh and the scent of apples in her hair. The girl pressed her innocent face into the long silver pelt of his beard.

Through the coarse material of his black robe Kane could feel the girl's tender body clinging hard against him. He closed his eyes as if in silent prayer, and felt a peverse brew of wild emotion bubble up inside him. His body engorged and stiffened almost painfully, but at the same time the reckless temptation shook him into trembles.

"You are no longer Josephine," when Kane spoke again his voice was suddenly thick and husky. "From this moment on, you will take the name Mary… and you will serve God through me, child, for you are the divine vessel I have been searching for," Kane's voice rumbled as he formulated the lie and told it effortlessly. "And it is God's will that you have been delivered to me."

The girl went very still in his arms. He could feel the

rhythm of her heart through the thin stuff of her dress.

"I would be honored," the girl whispered, her voice small and strained.

"But you must give yourself to me completely," Kane said, and made the warning sound like a dire threat. He felt a giddy thrill of arousal. "You must give to me your mind, your soul and your body so that through you, I can serve God's will and lead our people to Him. To defy me in any way is to defy God Almighty."

"I will," the girl promised fervently. Her face was up-turned to his and her expression solemn. She felt overwhelmed by her chance at salvation and completely trusting. Kane was God's messenger on earth. That she had been chosen as his divine vessel was a profound miracle. She heard a roar of blood in her own ears and felt her heart hammering.

Kane tightened his embrace and drew Mary away from the light of the candles. The girl went willing and pliant in his arms. He touched her breasts through the thin fabric of her clothing, and she did not pull away.

"Good girl," he crooned and licked his lips.

Deep in the shadows, and far from the eyes of the others, one of Kane's hands slipped beneath the hem of the girl's dress.

It was God's will at work.

* * *

Ten o'clock.

Right on time the radio on Colonel LeCat's hip squawked.

"Oui?" He turned from Tremaine and strode a few steps away with the radio pressed to his ear. The two men were standing in the old city's leafy open plaza,

118

surrounded by growing crowds of frightened people. Across the front steps of the town hall, a blue French VAB 4x4 armored personnel carrier had been parked, painted in the livery of the French Gendarmerie. The vehicle was a steel monster mounted on four huge tires. A nervous corporal stood hunched behind the machine gun mounted directly above the vehicle's cockpit.

"That call was from one of the teams charged with securing the city," LeCat came striding back to where Tremaine waited. The French Colonel was grim-faced. "The last of the gates have at last been blockaded."

Tremaine nodded. "So that's it then," he allowed himself to relax. "There is no way for the infected to breach the walls."

"Oui," LeCat confirmed. "But that does not mean the challenges facing us are any less insignificant," he gestured with a wide sweep of his hand. The crowd was building in the plaza and voices became shouts that demanded answers. Tremaine cast an anxious glance along the Rue De La Republique. It was the main artery into the heart of the ancient city, lined on both sides by expensive boutiques, restaurants and curbside eateries. The pavements were swarming with people, all heading towards the plaza. Some of them were marching and waving hastily painted banners. Patrolling the road was a second VAB 4x4 and two police cars, their blue lights flashing.

"The people are scared and confused," LeCat said. "They are fearful… and fear leads to violence and rioting unless they are made to understand."

When the phalanx of people marching along the Rue De La Republique reached the plaza, the mood of the crowd turned ugly. There were shouts and pushing; violent scuffles broke out and the crowd turned on the patrolling troops to vent their frustration. They were like a surly horde of football fans. People got crushed as the crowd surged like an angry tide towards the steps of the town hall. The plaza became choked with a struggling mass of humanity. A glass was thrown and a woman fell to the ground with blood streaming from cuts to her face.

LeCat waved his arm urgently and one of the police cars patrolling the route to the plaza braked to a halt nearby. The officers got out of their Renault with their handguns drawn. The second police car came racing towards the plaza as back-up. LeCat went to the closest vehicle and snatched up a megaphone from the back seat.

Over his shoulder he heard a shop front window smash and then a wild roar of triumph as a looters broke in to a clothing store. LeCat turned and sensed the rumbling volcanic mood of the crowd was teetering on the verge of eruption.

Tremaine broke from the swarming tide of bodies, gasping. He had almost been swept up in the crush. He was white-faced and panting. LeCat drew his sidearm from its holster and fired twice into the air. The shots were great deafening thunderclaps of sound that startled the crowd and caused them to back away in fear.

The looters who pushed and shoved their way through the broken plate glass window of the clothing shop froze in sudden alarm. On the sidewalk a young man crouched on his knees in a puddle of blood, crumpled over and clutching at a jagged blade of glass buried in his stomach. The crowd in the plaza stopped surging towards the town hall. A woman gave a shrill, terrified scream and then fainted. Voices that had been raised in violent fist-pumping shouts suddenly fell mute.

LeCat's voice boomed in the fraught silence.

120

"Attention citizens of Avignon. In one hour an announcement will be made from the steps of the Place of the Popes. You are to assemble and congregate in an orderly fashion. Police and armed gendarmes have orders to arrest anyone inciting violence against people or property. All your questions will be answered during the announcement. You must disperse from this plaza immediately."

From somewhere amidst the press of bodies a lone man's voice cried out abusive defiance. LeCat snarled and sent the two armed policemen scything into the crowd. They came back frog-marching a handcuffed overweight man who wore a torn shirt spotted with blood. One of the policemen had lost his cap, and buttons had been torn from his uniform. He was disheveled and heaving for breath. The policemen threw the man into the back of the nearest patrol car. The handcuffed man's face swelled with anger. He had a cut above one eye.

"Rebellion will not be tolerated!" LeCat's voice crackled with menace as he turned on the crowd, trying to cower them into obedience, and yet aware of how tenuous the thread of his authority was. If the mob turned violent, there would be nothing at all he could do to stop the rioting; the police and troops inside the walls would be overrun.

"You will disperse the plaza now and move in an orderly fashion to the square outside the Popes Palace."

As if to reinforce the Colonel's command the APC that had been patrolling the Rue De La Republique arrived and began to nudge its way forward at slow speed, forcing the milling crowds to separate. The engine of the second APC parked across the town hall steps roared into life. Like sheepdogs, the two thirteen-tonne

121

steel monsters with *'Gendarmerie Francaise'* painted on their sides went wading into the press of bodies until the crowd broke. They dispersed through the narrow streets towards the ancient papal palace that dominated the rising ground of the old city's northern quarter.

LeCat set down the megaphone and called urgently on the radio for reinforcements. Then he turned to Tremaine.

"A near-run thing, Colonel," Tremaine croaked. His voice sounded strained and hoarse.

Colonel LeCat said nothing.

\* \* \*

Hotel staff had gone from room to room, knocking on every door and herding all the guests downstairs to the lobby for an urgent announcement. Camille waited impatiently for everyone to assemble. She stood grim-faced, gnawing on her lip and fretting. She paced the lobby floor, wrestling with her own anxiety, but aware also that everyone watched her. She needed to remain composed. With a deliberate effort she forced a confident smile onto her face and smoothed away the edge of tension from her voice.

"Quickly!" she waved her arm at a crowd of startled guests that had arrived in the elevator. "Don't worry about your baggage. Leave it where it is."

The lobby was densely packed with people. Most of them were middle-aged tourists, huddled in couples or small groups. They were haggard and ashen faced. The stench of unwashed bodies mixed with cigarette smoke and the sweaty taint of raw fear to cloud the air a haze of blue. The news of the undead infection was being broadcast on every television and radio station. Under the murmur of rattled voices and the scuff of shuffling feet, Camille could hear someone sobbing softly.

It was Mrs. Chantilier. Camille went into the crowd and put a comforting arm around the old lady's shoulder. The woman had been staying alone in the hotel for the past two weeks, visiting grandchildren before a return trip to Lyon. Camille had grown fond of her.

"Don't cry, Mrs. Chantilier," Camille smiled into the old lady's face. Mrs. Chantilier wrung a damp handkerchief between arthritic fingers. Her eyes were shiny with welling tears. "Everything will be fine."

"I… I'm so afraid."

"We all are," Camille admitted. "But you are a woman of France. You must show these foreign visitors that you are brave."

The elderly woman gave a last shuddering sob and then wrenched her mouth into a quivering smile. "I lived through the Second World War…"

"I know," Camille said. "And you will live through this too. You just have to be courageous."

When the last of the hotel's staff had returned from the upper floors and all of the guests were crowded into the lobby, Camille blew out a deep breath to compose herself and raised her hands above her head to attract everyone's attention.

"Ladies and gentlemen, please listen to me," she stepped up onto a low coffee table. Every face turned towards her. She saw expectation and confusion in their expressions. She saw fear and uncertainty. They were scared.

"We have no choice but to evacuate the hotel," Camille began to speak, lifting her voice to be heard above the ripple of moans that rolled around the room. "As you have all seen and heard on the news, the infection has reached Paris and is quickly spreading south. This hotel will not be secure."

People began to protest and complain. Camille appealed for silence but the voices became panicked and bickering, drowning her out. One of the other hotel staff took off her shoe and hammered it against the reception counter like a judge's gavel.

"We have to take shelter behind the walls of Avignon," Camille went on in a rush. "There is an American Professor inside the old city. He has been making preparations for such an eventuality. If we can get into Avignon we will be safe."

She saw heads turn and stare. Through the hotel's high glass windows, the vast walls of the old city were visible beyond the lines of stalled traffic. People began suddenly to move, pushing others aside and using the suitcases they clutched in their hands as battering rams. A woman screamed in pain and a tall grey-haired man snarled as he shoved his way towards the hotel doors.

"Wait!" Camille shouted. "The main entrances into Avignon have already been barricaded with buses. No one is being allowed in or out."

She saw the panic seize them. Just minutes before they had been startled and fearful. Now they were on the brink of becoming a savage horde.

"What will we do? Where can we go?" a middle-aged woman near the elevators wailed. She was standing beside a portly man in a suit. The woman had an English accent. Other voices rose above hers, howling accusations and threats. The room erupted in uproar, and then two men in the crowd threw a flurry of punches at each other. Someone screamed and one of the men went tumbling backwards, knocking two elderly women over like bowling pins.

"Stop it!" Camille cried out. "Stop it!" Hotel staff rushed into the group of guests, separating antagonists and helping the injured. One of the women who had been felled in the fracas had blood streaming from a cut to her leg.

Camille glared at the crowd, a flush of hot temper rising up from beneath the collar of her blouse. She bunched her fists and propped them on her hips, seething with contempt.

"You men behave like pigs!" she scolded. "This is the time we need heroes. But instead of being brave, you think only of your selfish selves. Shame on you," she flung her arms at them and her words were clipped by her accent and bitterness. She was thirty years younger than them, but they hung their heads, embarrassed by the lash of Camille's words. For a moment she had control again, and she went on quickly with blazing anger still in her eyes, daring anyone in the lobby to defy or interrupt her.

"There are several small pedestrian gates along the west wall, facing the Rhône River. These gates were built to allow people to move in and out of the city at night in ancient times when the main gates had already been closed. These gates will be our way into Avignon. Soldiers or police will probably guard each of them. We can call out to them to let us in."

The crowd around her had settled into uneasy silence. She sensed the panic still upon them all, but now – with hope and a plan – they were calmer. But they remained anxious. Every few seconds heads would turn, or people would jerk and stifle a cry of fright at the sudden blare of a car horn. At any moment they expected an infected horde to come through the hotel doors like a crashing wave of death. They began to sway and shuffle restlessly, as if desperate to flee. Camille saw people hastily reach for luggage while others flung their suitcases open and began discarding anything unnecessary.

Camille spoke over the top of the rustle of noise.

"We will separate into groups of twenty," she had to shout at the top of her voice to be heard. "I will lead the first group. Eve…" Camille turned and Eve came forward to stand on the low table at her side. The girl had been crying. Her face was grey, her mouth wrenched and twisted as though she fought back more tears. "… Eve will lead the second group, and Maria the third," Camille pointed to another member of the hotel's staff.

"You will not take any luggage with you. It will slow you down and put your life at risk. Carry only the items you can fit into your pockets."

Maria had a clipboard clutched to her chest. She was nineteen years old and training for a future management position at the hotel. In a quavering, faltering voice she read out the names of each hotel guest and the leader they were assigned to.

The lobby fell into sudden stony silence as each guest listened for their name to be called. Camille drew Eve into the hotel's back office.

"Try your phone one last time, Eve," Camille kept a brave reassuring smile on her face.

"I did, out in the lobby. I can't get your father or anyone from the town hall. No one is answering my calls."

"Then we must get all these people to safety in the way we have planned," Camille said. "I will take the first group out through the doors and across the street. Have your people ready to follow, but let me get my people to the grass outside the walls before you leave the hotel. Tell Maria the same thing. If anything goes wrong, you must

126

stay in the hotel and do your best to barricade the doors. Do you understand?"

Eve's eyes began to well and glisten with tears. She nodded and choked down a sob of terror.

"I understand. Let's hope it does not come to that."

"Oui," Camille's brave smile slipped. Her voice dropped to a hollow whisper. "Let us pray the soldiers at the gates hear us and let us in before the infected arrive."

\* \* \*

The Palace of the Popes was one of the largest and most significant remaining medieval buildings in the world; a towering, sprawling palace and fortress that had been the seat of western Christianity during the 14th century. It was the spiritual heart of the old city, built to face a vast open square and adjoined by ornate gardens that connected the promontory rock of Doms to the palace's outer walls.

Now the square was choked with a mass of humanity, milling, standing; waiting impatiently in the warm mid-morning sun. The sound coming from the square was the noise of a million buzzing bees.

Standing in the shade behind the vast old palace's walls, Henri Pelletier shivered. He was flanked by Captain Devaux of the Police Nationale, and Colonel LeCat. Both men stood over the mayor like tall bodyguards, their faces grim and expressions set. Henri Pelletier felt like his tie was a noose around his neck. His palms were sweaty. He licked his lips nervously.

"It is time?"

LeCat nodded. He handed the mayor the megaphone he had seized from the back of the police car an hour earlier.

**127**

Pelletier stepped through the high arched entrance to the palace, known as the Porte des Champeaux, and into the sunlight. LeCat and the Captain of Police stayed a pace behind on either side of the mayor.

The entrance opened onto a raised platform, accessed on one side by a long stone ramp, and from the other side by steps. In years gone by, it had been here that Church officials would greet visiting dignitaries who arrived for an audience with the Pope.

The platform stood like a high stage. Pelletier could see clear across the space of the square to the buildings that faced the palace. There were people watching him from every window.

Directly below the stone ramp were parked the two blue VAB armored personnel carriers. A line of armed soldiers defended the approach to the ramp and a dozen policemen were blocking access to the steps. There was another VAB parked in the middle of the square, standing like a steel island in a sea of sun browned faces.

"Citizens of Avignon," Henri Pelletier's voice squeaked nervously. He had addressed large crowds before, but those masses of people had never teetered on the brink of rioting. He cleared his throat and began again.

"Citizens and Avignon, we face a terrible moment in the history of the world." Speaking into the megaphone distorted his voice and filled his ears with a numbing crackle like electronic feedback. He winced and turned to LeCat for reassurance. The Colonel of the gendarmerie urged the mayor of the city to continue.

"Much of Europe, including France, has been overcome by the so-called Raptor virus. Millions upon millions have been infected, and much of society has collapsed. Our government and our military cannot be

128

contacted. We have tried. Paris has been overwhelmed by the infected. Soon all communication and power networks will fail."

It was ominous, shocking news. The crowd in the square seemed to sway like a field of corn in the breeze, and a sound like a strangled wail of fear washed through them. It was news they had been hearing on their televisions and radios for days, yet somehow it seemed more shocking to hear it in person, the message delivered by their mayor surrounded by armed police and soldiers. The surly impatience that had bubbled through the crowd just an hour before evaporated. They listened with growing horror.

"Avignon stands a chance of surviving this apocalyptic plague," Henri Pelletier went on, gaining confidence. "Provided we all work together. We must ration our food and water. We must be patient behind these high walls that protect us. Rescue, I fear, may not come, and so instead we must wait until the infection burns itself out – until there are none left to infect, or until the virus runs its course."

The crowd had fallen eerily silent, hanging on his every word. Henri Pelletier was their mayor. He wanted to say something more; something Churchillian that would galvanize his people in this moment of unprecedented crisis.

"We are proud Frenchmen," he puffed out his chest and put fire into his voice. "And we stand defiant and united against this undead plague because here at Avignon we must survive. We represent the last stand of man. We cannot fail. There can be no surrender. We must be stubborn in the face of danger and brave in the face of death."

They cheered him. It started as a ragged cry by just a

few men and women standing closest to the platform, but it spread quickly, the salute taken up by ten thousand voices until they were hoarse. Pelletier felt tears of pride sting his eyes and a lump of emotion choke in his throat. When he handed the megaphone over to Colonel LeCat, he was weeping.

LeCat let the cheering subside. He stood with his feet braced, his shoulders squared and his back straight. He stared out into the sea of faces and when they fell silent at last, he explained their new reality.

"Martial Law has been declared across the entire old city for the duration of this emergency. Everyone within these walls is compelled to abide by instructions issued by my soldiers or the police. Mayor Pelletier has handed over control of all normal civilian functions to the Gendarmerie."

The Colonel paused, letting the news and its implications sink in. He saw heads turning, but there were no defiant cries of objection. Satisfied, he put the megaphone back to his lips.

"All retail and service businesses within the old city will be closed and remain closed. This afternoon, troops and police will go to each food store and commandeer all non-perishable items. The university will be closed and the buildings used for the secure storage of all food and water supplies. Rationing will commence in two days time. The town hall will become the headquarters of all civilian operations, and staff will be on hand day and night to deal with any issues that arise."

The crowd murmured and LeCat could sense the first rustle of their rising resentment. He went on remorselessly. "Looting and civil unrest will not be tolerated. Armed patrols will operate around the clock patrolling the streets, and my men will have orders to shoot."

He had laid down the law. Now at last he could rally them.

"Within hours, the undead infected will be swarming around the walls of Avignon. They will try to breach our defenses. If just one of the infected gets inside the city, it will be the death of us all. Everyone must remain vigilant. Everyone must perform their duty. We need men to defend the walls. If you have a weapon of any kind, you will present yourself to my officers at the Post Office within the hour. They will allocate you a position and provide you with ammunition. If you are an able-bodied man and you do not have a firearm, you will present yourself to the Gendarmerie barracks on Boulevard Raspail where you will be provided with a weapon and rudimentary training. Any woman with military or law-enforcement training must also report to the barracks. The walls will be manned in shifts until the crisis is averted."

LeCat set the megaphone aside but stayed in the foreground, watching the crowd with narrowed eyes, gauging the sentiment of the masses. He had told them brutal reality of their situation. The time before the undead attacked the city would be dangerous, the Colonel knew. Until the people were confronted with the desperate reality of survival, there would continue be elements of skepticism and bitter resistance.

Once they were fighting for their life, they would conform and obey.

LeCat handed the megaphone to Benoit Devaux, and the Captain of police explained to the crowd how his officers would maintain order and work with civilian authorities until the crisis had passed. The radio on the LeCat's webbing belt squawked and he snatched at it, turning his back on the vast crowd and disappearing from the platform, into the shadows of the Papal Palace.

"Oui?"

"Colonel LeCat, this is Captain Gireau at the university. The convoy of supply trucks we dispatched this morning has just returned from the city's supermarkets. Every vehicle is fully loaded with food and water."

"Good. Store everything in the university buildings and post guards," LeCat said gruffly. He was relieved. The steel-gated entrance that connected Avignon University with the outside communities was the last link to a secure perimeter.

"I have ordered the Port Saint-Lazare gates closed and padlocked."

"Good," LeCat said again. "Did your troops meet any resistance or see any signs of the infected?"

"There was an incident," the Captain's voice remained clinical and detached. "Two of my men were confronted by a woman. She demonstrated and shouted at the soldiers. She was covered in blood, sir. She refused instructions to move away… and was subsequently shot and killed."

LeCat said nothing. A chill of foreboding ran down his spine. If the infected had reached the outer suburbs, it would not be long before they were attacking the old city's walls. He was about to end the call when a sudden sickening lurch of alarm struck him.

"Captain? The trees outside the Port Saint-Lazare gates…" he gasped.

"Sainte merde!" Captain Gireau swore.

A dozen tall leafy trees with spreading branches grew dangerously close to the university entrance. In the panic and chaos, their perilous threat had been completely overlooked.

"Get men with chainsaws at work immediately!" LeCat barked the order. "Cut every tree down and clear a field of fire."

"Sir!" Gireau snapped.

LeCat cut the call and swore bitterly. He cursed his oversight, and as he did, fear came creeping upon him. He prayed that Gireau would have the time to rectify his mistake.

# Part 2:

Outside gendarme headquarters on Boulevard Raspail, lines of men and women were already forming by the time Tremaine arrived at the barracks and was shown into Colonel LeCat's office.

It was a sparsely furnished, functional room with a large window behind the Colonel's desk. The French flag was displayed in one corner and there were oil paintings depicting famous battles hanging on the walls. Prominent was a painting of France's greatest soldier, Napoleon Bonaparte. The image showed Napoleon on a rearing white horse, pointing the way ahead with a golden robe draped over his uniform.

"It is, alas, a copy," LeCat rose from behind his desk and smiled a vain apology. He gave a Gaelic shrug of his shoulders. "Napoleon was always my inspiration."

Tremaine nodded. "Napoleon Crossing the Alps, right?"

"Correct," LeCat seemed impressed with the American professor's knowledge. "It's one of several versions of the same work painted by Jacques-Louis David. This happens to be my favorite."

It was just after midday and Tremaine already felt himself fading with fatigue. He noticed on the Colonel's desk a detailed map of the city, weighted down at one end by a platter of cheese. Benoit Devaux arrived.

"The crowds have dispersed from the papal square," the Captain of police announced with a sigh. He snatched off his cap and clawed his fingers through his hair. There were two empty chairs in front of the Colonel's desk. Devaux slumped down into the closest with the weary groan of an old exhausted man.

134

LeCat went to his own side of the desk and stabbed at the map with his finger. "The university," he said. "It is the last gate that remains vulnerable. At the moment men are taking chainsaws to the nearby trees that encroach on the battlements. Once that work has been done the gate will be padlocked. Then, maybe we can relax a little, yes?"

"Any word on the infected?" Captain Devaux asked.

Tremaine shook his head. He had spent the past hour trying to contact Paris. "I can't reach anyone on the phone, and the television coverage has become intermittent," he said. "Parts of the world are simply shutting down, or being overrun. We're blacked out. French television went off the air an hour ago. The only broadcast I could pick up was from Berlin. The plague is sweeping through Germany, just as it has here, America and the United Kingdom."

"The soldiers who brought supplies back from the suburban supermarkets encountered a person they believe was infected," LeCat spoke into the dark ominous silence. He gave the two men across the desk a brief outline of the incident.

"Then they must be nearby," Tremaine flicked his glance out through the big window as though he might see a tide of undead somewhere in the distance. All he could see was a haze of smoke. France seemed to be ablaze.

Neither of the Frenchmen took up the thread of speculation. Instead, LeCat drew Tremaine's attention back to the map on his desk. "We have a little more than two hundred gendarmes and about forty police," the Colonel said grimly. "Twenty of my best men will be kept in the plaza near the town hall with two of the APC's. They will be our reserve, able to respond and

135

mobilize immediately should the undead find a breach in our defenses, or if they somehow threaten to overwhelm a gateway. The rest of the troops and Captain Devaux's police will be spread along the battlements to supervise and set an example to the volunteers beside them."

"Do we have enough people to man the walls?" Tremaine asked.

LeCat shrugged. "We are processing the volunteers as we speak," he said, referring to the long columns of men and women beyond the barracks gatehouse. "And my men at the post office have had sixty three people bearing weapons present themselves for duty. They should already be on the ramparts." It wasn't an answer. The French Colonel shrugged and picked up a biro and lowered his voice like he was confessing. "We could always do with more," he said obliquely. "With so much wall to defend, even four thousand might not be enough if the ramparts were lower and the enemy intelligent," he scribbled the number on the map. "But they are mindless, professor. Savage, yes. We have seen ample situations on the television news that show us the vicious brutality of their attacks. But our best defense is the height and thickness of the walls we defend. They cannot be breeched. They cannot be climbed. The only danger is that the blockaded gates might fail in some way."

Captain Devaux sat back in his chair and Tremaine fell silent. Each of them were imagining the dreadful carnage if the undead were able to breach the city's defenses. No one would survive, and there was nowhere to escape. The entire world would soon be infected. Mankind teetered on the very brink of being rendered extinct.

The door to the Colonel's office suddenly flung open, jarring Tremaine and the French Captain of Police from their dark fears. A woman wearing the gendarme uniform of a lieutenant came from the outer office. Her face looked pale, her eyes wide with urgency and agitation.

"Forgive me, Colonel," the lieutenant blurted. "But I have an urgent message. Guards at the Porte De La Republique gates report that large masses of people are gathering outside the walls. We have also received frantic reports from men at Porte Saint Roch gates and Porte Magnanen."

"The undead?" asked Tremaine.

The lieutenant looked devastated. "No, monsieur. They are the soon to be dead. They are refugees, and they are begging for our protection."

LeCat's eyes turned dark and flinty. "Have there been any reports from the troops guarding the western wall?" All the gates reporting in were on the southern side of the old city.

"No, Colonel," the lieutenant said.

LeCat grunted. He glared at the two men on the opposite side of the desk and made his decision. "Captain Devaux, please return to the town hall and continue with your preparations to seize all available supplies. You must send your men to every shop, every restaurant and every retail store before goods can be horded or sold on the black market. Professor Tremaine; you will come with me to the city gates."

\* \* \*

"We will disperse, and meet again tonight," Preacher Kane announced. He could hear police sirens criss-crossing nearby streets, and through the dusty cracked windows of the old building he saw crowds of people

137

moving about the old city with urgent, panicked strides. It was unsafe to stay here. He imagined police patrols searching the narrow alleyways for the ringleaders of the morning riot. He was a hunted man.

"Return to your homes. Go about your business," Kane urged them, waving his hands as if to shoo them away. "Come back here after nightfall, for there is much we must discuss. I must speak with God, and listen for His answer."

They shuffled timidly from the warehouse in small groups, merging into the passing crowds and blinking owlishly in the sudden bright light of the day.

When they were all gone, Kane hastily discarded his black robe and changed into a fresh shirt and trousers. He took the girl by the hand and led her through the narrow streets towards his apartment. "Follow me, Mary," Kane's voice cracked treacherously, edged with the thrill of anticipation, and fueled by the memory of the girl's slender squirming body in the dark shadows. His heart raced in his chest, and the sweat that beaded his brow was not from exertion. He was sick with lust, and trembling with wicked desire.

* * *

It was a short drive from the gendarme barracks to the Porte De La Republique gates. Driving one of the jeep-like Peugeot P4's, LeCat took the corners like a grand prix driver, stomping his foot hard on the gas pedal and scattering pedestrians that blocked the way. They raced past the post office that was the staging point for the men defending the southern perimeter, and Tremaine saw armed civilians sprinting across the road towards steps that lead to the top of the walls.

Other entrances around the city were vast towers with arched gateways built into the sandstone, but the main entrance was a wide thoroughfare. The 14th century remains were solid towers erected on either side of the roadway, each with crenelated battlements. Between the two stone sentinels were the overturned carcasses of four buses.

LeCat braked to a halt at the bottom of the closest tower and snatched the megaphone off the backseat of the P4. Beyond the barricade and thick stone walls he could hear a roar of screaming, pleading voices undulating like the sound of a storm-tossed ocean.

"Come with me," LeCat took the weather-worn stone steps up to the top of the tower two-at-a-time, and Tremaine struggled to keep up with the French Colonel. Other parts of the wall no longer had steps leading to the ramparts and soldiers had erected ladders in their place. Here the old stone slabs were moss-covered and treacherous. When Tremaine reached the battlements, he was wheezing for breath and sweating from the exertion.

What he saw made him gasp.

Crowded outside the main gates were over a thousand people, pressed together in swarming knots of terror and desperation. Some were trying to clamber over the stacked bus carcasses. Others were hammering on the solid stone walls with their fists.

"Please!" women wailed, their faces wrenched in the agony of their fear. "Let us in! We have children."

People thrust clutches of money into the air, trying to buy their safety. Fights broke out as terror turned the crowd savage. Women threw rings and heavy gold bracelets. One middle-aged woman held her infant child over her head. The baby was pink and wriggling in the

139

sunlight, squealing wretchedly.

"Take my baby!" the woman pleaded. "Save my son!"

The crowd surged and people closest to the walls got crushed. One woman stumbled to her knees and the press of terrified bodies drove her underfoot in the stampede. The air filled with the infectious greasy tang of fear.

LeCat stood at the ramparts overlooking the chaos and held the megaphone to his lips.

"You must disperse!" his voice blared. "Return to your homes. It is your best chance to survive the approaching infection. No one will be allowed inside the walls."

A wail of despair went up from the crowd. They surged again, as if their weight could somehow shift the crushed buses that barricaded the road between the two high towers. Someone threw a rock. It smacked off the wall near LeCat. A beer bottle followed, shattering on the stone and showering the crowd with glass.

"Return to your homes," LeCat repeated the order. "If you do not disperse in an orderly fashion, my men will be forced to shoot."

LeCat signaled across to the opposite tower where three armed soldiers stood watching the crowd nervously. The soldiers raised their weapons and aimed between the crenellations. They were uneasy. There was a feeling of dread on them all. They moved with mechanical restraint into firing positions, and they did not meet their Colonel's eyes.

Centuries before these same jagged gaps atop the walls had allowed archers to defend the city against raiders, firing a hail of arrows into an advancing army. Now the battlements bristled with the barrels of automatic weapons.

"Disperse!" LeCat demanded.

The woman holding her squirming baby aloft suddenly cried out and fell. The child in her arms slipped from her embrace. The woman howled her horror, but the sound was drowned out by a thousand other wailing voices. The baby was crushed to death under trampling feet.

Tremaine watched the unfolding drama, helpless and heart-sick. His mouth felt dry, and the skin along his forearms crawled with prickling insects of horror. He turned away, tears stinging his eyes, and did not see another pack of people running across the wide road that ringed the old city. A dozen figures drenched in blood and baying like wild beasts charged into the crowd outside the gates.

Their faces were ravaged by disease, their eyes huge and crazed by madness, their lips and cheeks swollen with ulcers, and their bodies slashed with wounds and running sores. Their ruined blood-streaked faces leered and contorted as they attacked, flailing arms that were gnarled and knotted as tree branches.

LeCat saw them, and understood immediately.

The undead had reached Avignon. The fight for survival had begun.

The infected tore into the crowd, mauling and savaging the people that were crammed against the walls. Some people turned, screaming, and fled for their lives. Others were torn to shreds where they stood, their hands pressed to their faces, cowering. A middle-aged man heard a howl close behind him and when he spun around, he came face-to-face with a snarling rabid ghoul awash in fresh blood and staring with wild-eyed madness. The man's bladder voided, and he died in a puddle of his own piss.

"Open fire!" LeCat gave the order.

The three soldiers atop the opposite tower began firing into the crowd. LeCat drew his sidearm and shot one of the snarling infected in the chest. The figure was hurled back by the savage punch of the bullet, but stayed on its feet. It growled and hissed – then mauled a teenage boy who had been trying to flee the chaos. The boy went down in the milling madness and did not get back up. LeCat fired again and again.

"More men!" the Colonel waved his arms urgently. Along the wall overlooking the mayhem, stutters of automatic fire punched the air.

LeCat threw aside the megaphone and snatched at the radio on his hip. His hands were shaking. He prayed there would still be time.

"Gireau! Captain Gireau!" LeCat stared eastward in the direction of the university. Somewhere beyond the walls, buildings were ablaze. A thick pyre of black smoke roiled into the blue afternoon sky.

"Gireau!"

The radio crackled.

"Sir." Captain Gireau's voice sounded strained and breathless.

"Get your men back behind the walls and seal the gates immediately, Captain. There is no more time to remove any more trees. The undead are upon us! You must seal the Porte Saint-Lazare gate now!"

\* \* \*

Captain Arnaud Gireau was a seasoned soldier who had once served in Iraq. Two years earlier he had worked as part of the Republican Guard that protected the French President's offices in Paris and the Elysee

142

Palace.

He was a veteran… and he was terrified.

He had eight men stripped to their waists and working manfully with chainsaws outside the gates to cut down the trees that grew close to the high stone wall, while up on the parapets ten more soldiers stood anxious guard. Half-a-dozen trees had already been felled; there were three more targeted for cutting. Gireau paced the roadway outside the steel barred gate impatiently, his eyes searching the nearby buildings for signs of danger. The surrounding suburban streets beyond the old city were eerily quiet, but he could hear a rise of noise coming from further to the west, gradually becoming louder, and seeming to come closer.

When the radio on his webbing belt hissed with sudden static, he snatched for it, just as a two-story office complex across the street suddenly exploded in flames and smoke.

"Mon dieu!" Gireau gaped, then flinched and ducked as a second explosion tore through the building sending bricks and rubble and glass in a deadly hail across the pavement. The ground beneath his feet shook. A few stunned seconds later, the intersection directly across the street became choked with a running horde of screaming people, rampaging towards the old city's gate, as if fleeing for their lives.

Hunting within the crowd were the bobbing snarling heads of blood-drenched ghouls, slashing and tearing at the press of living flesh all around them. The infected undead attacked like wild animals, throwing themselves onto the back of a running figure and lunging for the neck with gaping, gnashing jaws. When the person collapsed under the jarring shock, three, four or even five undead would swarm over the body, tearing it to shreds

143

and howling their crazed triumph.

It was a scene of savage brutality and horror unlike anything Captain Gireau had ever witnessed.

The radio in his hand crackled a second time. Gireau held it to his ear. He heard Colonel LeCat barking urgent instructions.

Gireau had just time to acknowledge the order before the crowd of terrified people and the infected undead amongst them came rioting and screaming towards him. He threw down the radio and shouted the order for the men on the parapets to open fire.

"Shoot!" Gireau snatched up an assault rifle and fired at the edges of the crowd where the undead had brought down a young woman. The girl had been thrown onto her back. She thrashed her legs and flailed her arms wildly. She lay in a spreading pool of blood. Her dress had rucked up around her waist, spattered with gore. Two of the undead hunched on their knees, leaning over the woman and clawing at her. Gireau shot one of the infected in the shoulder. The ghoul spun, flung backwards by the impact. It had once been a woman, Gireau saw. The ghoul had long black hair disheveled and matted with blood. It rolled away from the struggling girl and then pounced back to its feet. Gireau stared aghast. He could feel his heart crashing wildly against the cage of his chest. He fired again and felt the assault rifle buck hard against the muscles of his shoulder. He shot the infected ghoul in the head and its skull collapsed in a thick grey cloud of custard-like gore that splattered across the blacktop.

The woman's second attacker shrieked and snarled. It clawed its fingers into the soft flesh of the girl's neck and ripped out her throat. The girl's legs began to spasm uncontrollably and then her heels drummed against the

144

road. The ghoul thrust a handful of warm wet flesh into its mouth.

"Retreat to the gateway!" Gireau's voice cracked, hoarse with horror. The gendarmes with chainsaws had already fled, discarding their uniform coats and running for their lives. The sliding steel-barred gate began slowly closing, powered by an electric motor. Soldiers posted at the university had come running the wall. They were pushing at the gate, trying to force the barrier shut before the undead reached them.

Gireau backed away from the crowd, swinging the barrel of the assault rifle in an arc and firing at the nearest threat. The sound of the riot came like a crashing turmoil of shouts and terrified screams. Two panicked men threw themselves at the gendarme captain, wailing with their fear. They clung to him, screeching for his help. Gireau had to club them down with the hard stock of his weapon, catching one man full in the face and smashing in all of his upper teeth. The man bellowed and reeled away, howling in pain and spitting gouts of bright red blood. The second man staggered backwards, his arms pin wheeling, until he crashed against a street sign and fell. The undead pounced upon the victim and tore his chest open while he flailed and whimpered beneath them. Blood sprayed in a fountain and Gireau saw the gaping mush of the moaning man's guts. The undead were like wild dogs. One of them buried its gnashing face inside the open body cavity. When it lifted its head, the ghoul was gnawing on a tangle of the dead man's thick ropy entrails.

"Run!" Gireau heard his men on the parapets urging him to break for the gates. "Run for your life!"

Another the undead broke from the horde and charged at the gendarme captain. Gireau spun towards the threat and fired instinctively from the hip. The muzzle was almost pressed against the belly of the disfigured undead wretch when the assault rifle bucked in Gireau's hands. The clattering roar drummed against his ears and the blood-covered beast flew backwards. Its arms flailed and it fell.

"Run!"

The troops along the top of the wall fired into the melee indiscriminately, trying desperately to clear a path for their Captain to retreat to the closing gate. A dozen more soldiers inside the walls knelt in the entrance, firing through the gate's bars. Bodies littered the pavement, twisted in the gruesome agonies of their deaths. Blood washed across the sidewalk in rivers and ran dripping into the gutter.

Gireau felt someone lash a fist at him, and the strike of the blow to his shoulder was so violent that he staggered off balance. He teetered on the sidewalk, just twenty short paces from safety, and then tumbled backwards over the gnarled branch of a felled tree. Gireau hit the ground hard on his back and stared up, dazed and stunned, into a blue sky slowly filling with smoke. He heard the assault rifle go clattering across the concrete path and then his vision filled with a demented, terrifying face that dripped blood and smelled of putrid corruption.

He kicked out and drove his boot at the figure. It spun away but came back snarling. Gireau cried out in pure fear as the undead threw itself at him. He tried to roll away but there were bodies and kicking legs in every direction. The crushing impact as the undead ghoul fell upon him drove the air from the gendarme captain's lungs and cracked the back of his head hard against the pavement.

Gireau heard a flurry of far-away gunshots. He heard the terrified cries of the dying all around him. He saw the steel bars of the gate close at last through a tangle of legs, before black fluttering shadows wheeled through his vision. The pain came then; the terrible torture of being mauled to pieces. He lay on the concrete pavement and felt down across his chest, sensing there was something dreadfully wrong. He groped towards his stomach and felt the hard jutting fragment of a broken rib – and then nothing. His hand fluttered like a dying bird. His guts had been torn from his torso, leaving wet flaps of flesh and a gaping hole of warm stinking mush. Blood spurted hotly over his fingers. Gireau's mouth fell open in a silent groan, and the shadows at the edges of his vision grew dark. He blinked and gasped with shock. He felt suddenly cold. Another of the undead came to crouch over him, its eyes wild with infected madness.

Soft treacherous lethargy spread through Gireau's mauled body, and then a serene sense of calm washed over the gendarme. He felt no fear, and his pain turned into chilling numbness. He felt suddenly overwhelmed with a vast sense of sorrow. He thought about his young wife, staying with her parents in Toulouse, and he wondered whether she had fled the infection, and if she was safe. His mouth moved in a quick, whispered prayer for her survival, and then looked up into the hideous ravaged face of the ghoul. Its eyes were wild, its cheeks blistered with running sores. The virus had withered the figure's lips, exposing bleeding gums and blackened stumps of teeth. The ghoul's bottom jaw hung open and the tongue lolled lecherously from the side of its rotting mouth. He could smell it; the stench of carrion long dead and festering with corruption.

Captain Gireau smiled. It was a benign expression of

147

forgiveness and melancholy and resignation.

"Finish it," he said.

For a few moments more Gireau suffered through fresh savage waves of unholy agony before the dark relief of death.

* * *

Camille pressed her face close to the glass doors of the hotel's front entrance and stared in wild eyed shock and confusion at the scene unfolding before her.

The road outside the hotel teemed with crowds of people. Some had abandoned their cars. Others had appeared in rampaging hordes from nearby streets. They were massing around the Porte Saint Roch gates a hundred yards to the east. The noise became deafening; people screaming and shouting, wailing in fear. It came through the glass in waves. Then, the muted echo of an explosion had rattled the windows. It sounded far away but the tremor made her flinch. A thick pall of smoke grew in the sky, rising like a black cloud beyond the nearby buildings.

Camille drew a deep breath and turned, forcing a tight smile.

Twenty terrified ashen faces were pressed close about her, their eyes filled with alarm, their expressions fearful. They were all elderly. Some were propped up with walking sticks.

"Be ready," she told them. "When I give the word, we go out through the doors and straight across the road."

The angry horde around the Porte Saint Roch gates had turned violent. Camille saw men on the fringes of the mob hurling rocks and abuse at the soldiers standing guard on the battlements.

Eve pushed her way through the elderly group. Her face was pale. "You can't wait any longer. You must go now or it will be too late."

"Let's go!" sang out Camille, and she flung the hotel doors wide open and stood aside as the group of elderly tourists came awkwardly down the steps. They milled there for long moments, seemingly dazed and overwhelmed by the violent protests around the nearby gatehouse. Rocks flew like hail and the voices of the horde were rabid and snarling.

Camille ran to the sidewalk and took an elderly man by the arm. "Follow me, gang!" she beckoned them. The man was a Jewish gentleman in his eighties, wearing a voluminous heavy black coat and a hat. His face had withered with age; the flesh hanging in freckled and spotted little pouches, and his Van Dyke beard and moustache were pelts of silver. "Stay with me, Mr. Goldstein,"

The man tottered unsteadily into the road with the aid of his walking stick and with Camille clutching his other thin arm. His body was gaunt and stooped, riddled with arthritis.

"Leave me," the old man protested. "Help the ladies." His voice strained, rusty with pain.

The rest of the hotel guests in the group followed, clinging to each other for support, their faces stricken with grief and fear.

The road was choked with abandoned cars, some still with their engines running. In places they were jammed bumper-to-bumper and Camille had to navigate a ragged winding course across all four lanes. She called to the rest of the group as they wound their way closer to the great wall. Over her shoulder she could hear heavy sobs of panic and exertion.

149

"Just a little further, gang!" she hoisted Mr. Goldstein onto the grassy verge of the opposite sidewalk and turned back to the others. There was a bus shelter on this side of the road. Camille sat the elderly man down and went back into the middle of the traffic jam to herd the rest of the group to safety.

The rioters at the Porte Saint Roch gates had banded together out of fear and desperation and were trying to batter their way into the old city by heaving against the side of the blockading buses. Troops on the top of the gate's tower were leaning over the battlements with their weapons raised. Shots rang out – fired into the sky as a warning.

Somewhere in the distance there came another noise. No, it was not an actual sound, but rather a sensation like a vibration in the air. Camille frowned and turned her head, bewildered and puzzled. She stood like that for three precious seconds before the tremor turned into the growling rumble of a heavy engine straining. It came louder on the breeze and then seemed to fade. Camille had an ominous, instinctive sense of foreboding. She looked about wildly, searching for the source of the sound. It came again; the howl of an engine being revved beyond its limits, growing louder but still lost from her view by the buildings that surrounded the hotel complex.

She took the arm of a middle-aged woman in a floral dress and dragged her across the street.

"Quickly!" Camille steered the woman towards the bus shelter. Three more old ladies from her group were clutching each other for support as they ran. They were weeping. Camille took the closest woman by the arm and pointed at a gap between two abandoned cars. "Go that way!"

Suddenly, from behind a nearby office building, a

huge eight-wheeled truck appeared, spewing black diesel smoke as it raced towards the intersection jammed with abandoned cars and the rioting crowd around the ancient gate. It looked like some kind of dump truck, Camille thought. The engine roared as it changed through gears, building dangerous speed. Behind the wheel she could see a man, hunched and shouting. In the back of the truck's steel tip-tray, a dozen people clung on for their lives.

"Run!" Camille cried out in helpless despair.

The stragglers in her group were still staggering their way across the road. They heard the bellowing engine of the truck and saw it careering towards the crowded intersection like a vast avalanche of steel. They froze in sheer horror.

A hail of spitting gunfire roared from the battlements atop the Avignon wall. The windscreen of the truck starred and shattered.

Camille started to run back towards the stranded elderly still in the middle of the road, but knew it was too late. The truck raced through the intersection without slowing, crashing into the litter of vehicles in its way and hurling them aside. A silver Fiat went under the truck's giant wheels. The huge vehicle rocked drunkenly on its suspension, then righted itself. A Volvo was struck on the front right fender and hurled high into the air. Steel and glass flew like missiles. Two of Camille's elderly group were killed under the overturned carcass of a red Renault. Four more were scythed down by flying debris. Their frail bodies lay broken on the road in pools of spreading blood while the huge truck jounced on, surging straight for the mass of rioters around the gate.

* * *

There were four gendarmes standing at the battlements of the Porte Saint Roch tower, and a dozen more men posted to positions along the high wall on both flanks.

Below them, the scene around the intersection turned chaotic. Wild-faced protestors were pummeling their fists on the overturned busses that barricaded the entrance. The sound of the drumming mixed with the hysteria of their frenzied shouts became the clamor of nightmares.

The gendarmes were rattled. Rioters started hurling rocks and one struck a young soldier in the head. He fell to the ground with a groan and threw his hands to his face, blood spurting from between his fingers.

A gendarme sergeant standing at a nearby section of wall slung his assault rifle over his shoulder and came marching along the parapet. He stared down at the fallen soldier and snarled irritably at him, then leaned through the battlements with his sidearm drawn.

"Get away from the gate!" the sergeant bellowed at the crowd. He had a deep voice that sounded like rolling thunder but the chaotic shouting of the rioters drowned it out. The sergeant aimed his pistol into the air and fired two warning shots. Instinctively the crowd pushing at the overturned buses that blockaded the entrance cringed and cowered away. They washed back from the gateway like surf receding from a beach.

"Get away from the gate or I will order my men to open fire," the sergeant repeated the command into the shocked silence. "Return to your homes."

The scene beyond the walls looked apocalyptic. The wide boulevard that ringed the old city had been choked with four lanes of abandoned cars, and the sky had darkened with smoke from a dozen nearby fires. People were pouring into the streets, running towards the old city walls with their arms full of belongings. He saw women pushing shopping trolleys packed with possessions, and others wandering, dazed and confused. Car alarms blared in the background, while from inside the city's walls he could hear police sirens. And then another sound added itself to the swirling cacophony of bedlam. It was the unmistakable bellow of a truck's engine straining. The gendarme sergeant narrowed his eyes and searched the skyline.

For long seconds he saw nothing, but still the sound of the truck engine seemed to be coming closer. He looked right, towards a corner. All he could see were local hotels and a ragged line of people spilling into the stream of choked traffic. He looked left. On the opposite corner stood the abandoned local police station – a sprawling collection of low-rise buildings with full-glass windows that glinted the afternoon sun. Then he heard the truck's engine noise alter, revving hard through a change of gear. The sergeant saw a gout of black exhaust smoke stain the sky, and a moment later a dump-truck appeared on the far side of the intersection, still a kilometer away, shadowed by an overpass.

The Avenue Eisenhower was a wide service road that joined an outer ring route to the old city; a four-lane thoroughfare through an area of greater Avignon undergoing re-development that had been blocked to all civilian traffic for several months.

The dump truck turned onto the avenue and surged towards the Porte Saint Roch gates like a charging bull shown a red matador's cape.

"Fuck!" the gendarme sergeant swore in English. He was a twenty-year veteran who had served alongside British Special Forces troops during operations in Yemen and Somalia. He snarled at the men around him and ordered them to take aim.

The truck crested a low rise in the road, still gaining speed. The gendarme sergeant saw a big burly man at the wheel of the vehicle. The truck slewed from one side of the road to the other and smeared the sky with its belching exhaust.

"Fire!" the gendarme sergeant snatched his assault rifle off his shoulder and took aim at the truck's windscreen. The glass starred and then shattered but the truck reached the jammed intersection and ploughed on like a battering ram. Abandoned cars in the destructive path were crushed or flung aside. One vehicle was clipped on the fender and flung high into the air. Rioters at the gates who sensed the new danger began to flee the destruction, but they were trapped by the sheer weight of bodies pressed so close together beneath the arch of the tower. Women began to scream. Fists flew as men fought to break free of the claustrophobic trap. People went down under the crushing panic, dropping to their knees to be stampeded to death under the frenzied throng.

"Fire!"

One of the gendarmes stationed on the nearby wall took aim at a tight knot of rioters on the sidewalk. They had picked up pieces of metal from the strewn wreckage and began charging into the crowd, swinging the crude weapons. Some shots kicked up spurts of dirt. One caught a rioter in the back as he turned to swing a jagged length of iron. The man was thrown a staggering step forward and then he arched his back like a drawn bow and threw his face to the sky. His mouth fell open in a silent cry of pain, and then a second bullet knocked him to the ground. The rioters around him scattered.

The truck reared up on one side as it crumpled over

154

the top of a Fiat and then slewed sideways for a perilous moment before righting itself. The gendarme sergeant saw the driver heaving at the wheel. He fired into the truck's cabin and saw the driver flinch then clasp at his shoulder.

The truck swerved again, lining itself up with the arched opening of the gatehouse. There were people in the back of the truck, clinging to the lip of the tip-tray.

"Fire!" the sergeant repeated the order and the air hissed with bullets.

One of the figures crouched in the steel tray at the back of the truck got shot in the face as the truck bucked wildly over crushed wreckage. It was a young man who had been staring wide-eyed with fright over the rim of the tray and bracing himself for the approaching impact and collision. The bullet took off the top of his head and flung him backwards.

"Fire!"

The truck bucked over the sidewalk, rearing up like a wounded beast and then crashing down on its front tires, flattening a steel sign post and careering into the stranded rioters pinned by the press of bodies around them and unable to escape. The truck smashed into the rioters and the sound of crushing bones and breaking bodies was appalling.

The truck was too wide and high to clear the stone arch of the gateway. It ploughed into the ancient sandstone tower at almost fifty kilometers per hour, crashing into the huge stone blocks before momentum carried the twisted mangled remains into the overturned buses barricading the gate.

The vast stone tower shuddered and shook. One of the gendarmes was thrown off his feet. Dust and smoke roiled into the air and in the stunned silence immediately afterwards came the first agonizing cries of the dying.

Bodies had been pinned between the front of the truck and the overturned sides of the buses. Others had been mangled under the eight rumbling wheels. The dead and dying lay in their dozens, flung like broken toys onto the pavement. The gendarme sergeant stared over the edge of the battlement and gaped in horror. He had seen two decades of death and warfare, but nothing like this. Everywhere he looked he saw bodies and blood.

Then, with a deafening *'crump!'* the wrecked truck exploded into flames.

"Get the Colonel here!" the sergeant turned and barked orders to his pale and shaken men. From the top of the tower he could see bodies in the back of the truck's twisted tipper-tray. Some of them were children. One small figure was on fire, its head burning like a torch. The sergeant heard himself gasp and choke. His gorge rose in a hot flood of nausea that scalded the back of his throat. He gagged it down and scraped the back of his shaking hand across his mouth.

The burning child began beating at the fire with its bare hands, shrieking in dreadful agony as the blazing flames burned off its ears, nose and flesh on its cheeks. The child collapsed into a pathetic bundle when the flames caught on clothing. The feeble wretched cries of agony were cut mercifully short.

The sergeant blinked back stinging tears and tore his eyes away from the gruesome skin-crawling horror. But the stuff of screaming nightmares was everywhere he looked.

Crushed beneath the tires of the vehicle were mounds of twisted limbs and mutilated bodies caught in the tangle of wreckage. Black greasy smoke billowed from the burning truck's remains, and a wall of heat rose to singe the sergeant's eyebrows. He swayed away, gasping and choking, hunched double and coughed smoke from his lungs. He heard more screams – tiny, tortured, child-like screams – but he did not look again. He did not watch them die.

The truck burned furiously and the stench of burning rubber and human flesh became overpowering. Fire from the blazing vehicle scorched the façade of the gatehouse black, and a column of dirty smoke rose a hundred feet into the air before the breeze smeared it across the sky. The gendarme sergeant ordered his men back to the battlements and gave the nearest man orders to shoot.

He thrust his craggy face close. "Anyone who tries to approach the gatehouse must be stopped. Do you understand?"

The gendarme flinched, intimidated and shaken. "I… I can't," the young man whispered, appalled by the carnage.

"Damn you!" the sergeant struck the man a stinging blow on the side of his face. "Until we know if the barricaded buses are still firmly in place, we are vulnerable. If we don't kill anyone who approaches, we could be overwhelmed!"

Some of the dead were incinerated as the truck burned, their bodies blackening to charred pulp as the corpses writhed and twisted in the furnace of leaping flames. Some of the survivors crawled, or staggered into the gutters to die, choking on ghastly rattling groans. People milled about in the dusty debris, wandering dazed and aimless.

Minutes later LeCat and Tremaine arrived at the gatehouse.

As he climbed out of the French jeep, Tremaine felt

his legs shaking beneath him. A hard lump of foreboding knotted in his chest, making his breath saw. He went towards the steps to the tower slowly. He could smell burning oil and rubber, and there were thick wisps of smoke hanging in the air. The buses that were the barricade had been scorched with soot, but they remained firmly wedged across the gateway. His relief was tempered by a perilous fear of what he would see on the other side of the wall.

The sergeant met the two men at the top of the tower. Colonel LeCat stared over the edge of the battlement and gaped down at the fire-blackened carnage for long moments.

Within the killing ground below the gatehouse he could still see movement. A man lay on his back in a pool of his own blood, waving his arm weakly for help. Both his legs were missing, while close beside the man laid a woman tucked into a ball of agony with her knees drawn up to her chest and her arms clutching at a gaping hole in her stomach. She made a soft keening sound as agony overwhelmed her. Others sobbed and staggered amidst the dreadful carnage, clutching at broken limbs, or with hands clasped over jagged wounds to stem the flow of blood. It was a charnel house of destruction and death.

Already flocks of squabbling birds had gathered amongst the cadavers. Hopping and flapping raucously from body to body, they bickered and croaked, pecking at eyes and soft flesh, tugging at lifeless hands so that they twitched as though the corpse looked still alive.

When the Colonel turned back to the waiting sergeant his face was tight and fixed.

"Should we help the injured, sir?" the sergeant asked LeCat stiffly.

"How?" the Colonel's voice rasped, rough with his

horror. "The barricades must stay in place."

"We could…" the sergeant searched delicately for the right words, "… put the dying out of their misery as an act of compassion…"

"No," LeCat said. "We cannot spare the ammunition."

The sergeant stiffened. The gendarmes nearby overheard the exchange and their faces betrayed their shock. LeCat lifted his voice so his words would reach the men stationed along the nearby walls.

"Well done," LeCat said thickly, struggling to contain his emotions. The bleeding bodies strewn across the road reminded him of the devastating car-bomb blasts he had witnessed in Iraq. "You all did your duty. And you must continue to do what survival requires. The undead are here. The infection has reached our walls. Thousands are already attacking the main gates and any moment the infected will appear here too. Do not lament the dead or the dying. There is no time for anything now but to fight for our survival."

* * *

Camille drew the remnants of her little group into a knot around the bus shelter. Just a dozen frail and weeping faces stared back at her. The rest of their number had been killed during the terror of the truck's suicidal collision into the nearby gatehouse. The elderly survivors were weeping, aghast at the horror they had witnessed, stunned into mute helplessness. They stood, trembling and shaken and gulping for breath.

Camille slumped against the wall of the shelter and a shudder of reaction overwhelmed her. She began to shake uncontrollably. Despair washed through her in waves, and she began to weep thick, slow tears.

Smoke from the burning truck drifted over the group in thick black clouds, and a half-human figure came staggering towards them, emerging through the choking haze. The man had been stripped of clothing and his skin hung in lacerated shreds of smoldering flesh; a disfigured gruesome thing with a ragged hole the size of a coffee cup in his chest and one arm dangling from its shoulder socket on a thin ropy sliver of gristle. He moaned in agony, his mouth gaping, his eyes blank and dazed. He stumbled blindly past the bus shelter and then collapsed, kicking feebly, in the middle of the road.

Camille cuffed brusquely at her tears with the back of her hand and drew a short, sharp breath, turning away from the carnage surrounding the gatehouse and focusing all her attention on the faces pressed around her.

The elderly tourists were almost child-like in their helpless appeal. Even old Mr. Goldstein sobbed, his rheumy eyes haunted with fear. His lips quivered, and the hand holding his walking stick fluttered with a fierce palsy. The old man seemed to have shrunk in the last few terrible minutes. The flesh seemed to have withered on his bones.

"Come on, gang," Camille sniffed back more tears and tried to put fire and promise in her voice. Her face had drained of all color so that her lips seemed rimmed with frost, and her skin had a waxen pallor. "We're going to run to the wall, and then we will follow it alongside the river. The small entry gates into the city are on the western side. Stay close to me!"

She went at a purposeful walk, and the elderly followed like a gaggle of baby geese. The grass underfoot grew lush and green with recent rain, littered with a carpet of autumn leaves.

When she reached the shelter of the vast wall at last, Camille turned.

Everyone was still with her. Mr. Goldstein lagged at the back of the line, struggling painfully to keep moving. Camille called encouragement out to the old man, and then her eyes were diverted back to the doors of the hotel by a sudden flurry of activity and noise. Eve's group of tourists were emerging into the smoke-filled horror of the day. Over the sporadic crack of gunfire and the wailing of the dying, Camille could hear the woman's high shrieking voice, edged with panic, as she implored her group to run towards the road.

"Come on, Mr. Goldstein," Camille's focus shifted back to the elderly Jewish gentleman. "You can do it. Just a little further."

She shifted impatiently from foot to foot, waiting for the old man to catch up, torn by the urgent need to press on. One of the women began plucking at the sleeve of her blouse for attention. Camille scraped her fingers through her hair and turned, her brow puckered with annoyance and her voice edged.

"What is it, Mrs. Doolan?"

"I... I'm sorry, dear. I don't think I can go on," the woman wheezed. Her eyes were wide with a look of astonishment. She was an Irish lady in her sixties, hunched by her age and by the weight of a heavy pink coat she wore. The garment was unbuttoned, and between the flapping lapels Camille saw a sudden red stain of blood bloom like a rose from between the woman's breasts. Camille choked a gasp of alarm and gaped open-mouthed in horror.

"I've been shot..." the elderly woman grimaced. Her expression became almost apologetic. She fell forward

161

into Camille's arms. Camille couldn't hold her weight. The woman was dead before she hit the soft green grass.

Along the high wall, Camille saw nervous pale-faced soldiers gesticulating down at the group and aiming their weapons. She shook her head in slow numb horror.

"We're from the hotel!" Camille cupped her hands to her mouth and shouted. "We need to get into the city."

The elderly around her were cowering in a huddle close to the body of the dead Irishwoman. They wailed in fear and panic.

"Help us. Please!"

There was a pause in the sporadic firing and for a moment the world seemed eerily silent. Then another shot rang out and Eve – standing in the middle of the road and waving furiously to the group of tourists she was shepherding – fell down, dead. The bullet caught her full in the chest. Its impact flung her off her feet and hurled her against the side of an abandoned car. Eve slumped there, her mouth gaping open, but her scream of pain trapped in her throat. She slid down the side of the vehicle, leaving a garish red smear on the door panel.

"Eve!" Camille cried out. Her instinct was to run back into the road to help, but one of the women in her group snatched at her arm, holding her back.

"Don't leave us!" the cry was filled with raw plaintive fear. The woman's face had blotched and stained with tears, and her voice rasped as though she were being strangled.

Camille doubled over with a cramping pain of despair, and then suddenly the last vestiges of her brave façade collapsed. She began to weep openly, sobbing with fear, with sadness and with frustration at the cruelty of their situation. She was inconsolable as she stood helpless and directionless in the lee of the high stone wall.

* * *

Standing atop the tower of the Porte Saint Roch gatehouse, Tremaine swept his eyes across the skyline. Smoke scarred the horizon. It hung in the air from a hundred far-away fires like the great pall of a battlefield. He went slowly to the battlements, mindful of the carnage around the foot of the tower and moving with dread for what he might see. His legs felt rubbery under him. LeCat's face was still ashen with shock, and Tremaine had to steel himself before looking down.

The breath jammed in his throat. The intersection resembled a slaughterhouse. Around the stone gateway lay piles of bodies and dark smears on the ground where people had dragged themselves to die. The skeleton of the truck was a black mangle of twisted metal. Tremaine reeled away, struck numb by the ghastly trauma – and from the corner of his eye glimpsed a huddle of people standing about a hundred yards to the west in the shadows of the wall.

Tremaine felt his heart trip, and then he was consumed by a moment of swirling outrage and fury.

"Christ!" he gasped. He spun on his heel and spotted a gendarme with a pair of binoculars slung around his neck. He lunged for the man and snatched for them.

"What do you see?" Colonel LeCat frowned. He stared west, scanning the line of the Rhône River through the trees and seeing nothing but dark, vague movement.

"Down there!" Tremaine thrust a finger urgently. He stared unblinking until his eyes stung with smoke. "Look!" His hand became a white-knuckled fist, and a sickening sensation lurched in the pit of his stomach.

"Against the wall near the bus shelter. It's Camille Pelletier."

Colonel LeCat snatched the binoculars from the American and pressed them to his eyes. The mayor's daughter was dressed in her work uniform, surrounded by a huddle of cowering elderly people. Then he traversed the binoculars until they were focused on that section of the high wall. Two uniformed gendarmes and one civilian man were defending the parapets west of the gatehouse. The gendarmes were aiming their weapons at a cluster of people running across the wide street. The civilian hefted an old double-barrel shotgun, and leaned out between the stone crenellations to fire on the milling elderly people directly beneath where they stood guard. LeCat threw down the binoculars and started to run. With dreadful certainty he knew what was about to happen.

"Don't shoot!" the Colonel roared. He had a barking voice that had been honed and trained on a thousand windswept parade grounds. As he ran he reached for his sidearm and fired a shot into the air. His face twisted with effort and rage. Droplets of spittle flew from his lips as he shouted.

"Don't shoot!"

The section of wall between the Porte Saint Roch gates and the southwest corner of the ancient city was about two hundred yards of uninterrupted parapet, but centuries of wear had made the narrow battlements precarious. LeCat leaped a small gap in the crumbling stonework, still shouting.

One of the gendarmes saw their Colonel charging towards them and blanched in shock. The civilian was a burly, unshaven man, with a dark curly mop of tousled hair. He was heavy in the chest and bulgingly obese in

164

the gut. He had the shotgun wedged tight against his shoulder.

LeCat was still fifty yards away when the civilian fired down into the knot of people standing beneath the wall.

* * *

Camille sagged at the knees, distraught and defeated. Her group was pinned against the wall, while Eve's clutch of tourists stood stranded and leaderless, cringing in the middle of the roadway.

Around them the madness seemed to reach a new level of chaos. Shots still spat from the wall high above them, and black roiling smoke swept along the street from the burning truck. There was other smoke too from nearby burning buildings and the blare of security alarms and sirens. Overlaying it all were the sobbing cries of fear and pain.

Then old Mr. Goldstein suddenly flung up his cane and pointed towards the corner of the street with a shaking, trembling hand.

"My God!" the old man croaked. His face seemed shriveled, collapsing in upon itself. Raw fear swirled in his eyes.

Standing on the far side of the nearby river, a horde of grotesque running shapes emerged, streaming towards a bridge that carried traffic from the far bank to the old city. Even at a distance their voices could be heard; lustful wild ululations like baying dogs as they take the scent.

Camille gaped in dismay.

"It's them," Mr. Goldstein took a few tottering steps as if to see the undead more clearly. "The infected have reached us!" his cry croaked alarm in his throat. He started to say more when the heavy charge of a double-barrel shotgun blast caught the old man in the back and ripped through his spine. It tore out through the front of his pelvis, throwing him forward in the grass as if a hammer blow had struck him from above. The dead man's cane went skittering across the ground and his hat was flung from his head.

Camille saw the gentle old man's body seem to break in half as a puffing pink feather of blood and tissue misted in the air and splattered gore across her skirt. She stood, rooted with shock for long stunned seconds, until a woman beside her began to cry mournfully.

Slowly Camille's expression altered. Her face became smooth and pale as a corpse. The last glimmer of hope faded from her eyes. She made her decision.

"Follow me," she seized the weeping woman and dragged her along. The rest of the survivors followed meekly. "We're going back."

From the bus shelter she could not see the nearby bridge; it was blocked from her view by other hotels – but she instinctively sensed that they had only minutes to find refuge.

There was no way forward. Their last hope was to barricade themselves inside the hotel.

And pray.

* * *

Chuck Gudinski drove the hire car with inspired abandon, anticipating the bends in the road before they leaped out at him, and slaloming the little Fiat from one side of the blacktop to the other to avoid abandoned vehicles that littered the highway in both directions.

He felt tired. His eyes were red and puffy. His eyelids

166

itched – but unholy fear kept him alert. The journey had been a nightmare of tension and strained nerves.

He had been driving for almost eight hours, and now the needle on the fuel gauge had dipped into empty.

He flicked another sideways glance at his fiancé but didn't smile.

Sherry Wilson sat curled up in the passenger seat, her face pale, gnawing at her bottom lip. Her eyes were huge and haunted, her features drained with exhaustion. Chuck felt his heart squeezed with concern as he saw the deep lines of worry at the corners of Sherry's mouth and the sickly waxen patina of despair on her skin.

"It will be okay," Chuck reassured her for the thousandth time. They had fled the city of Bourges in the small hours of the morning just moments before the infected had swarmed through the suburb where they were vacationing. "We'll make it."

Sherry said nothing. She had cried through the night, weeping softly and pitifully, until she felt she had no more tears left to shed. Now she felt like a hollow shell, slipping deeper into a morass of despondency as the endless miles sped by until she became so numb and immune to the nightmare landscape that the horrors no longer registered.

Chuck was the exact opposite. He was pumped full of adrenalin. He realized the lack of rest and relentless tension were corroding his physical and mental reserves, but fear drove him on. He caught a glimpse of himself in the rearview mirror and saw a reflection of dry skin and bloodshot eyes, gummed with yellow mucus and underscored by smudges of fatigue.

That they had driven so far before dawn had been a blessing. Most of the ungodly horror they passed had been blanketed by darkness. They had seen small rural villages on fire and dark shapes laying beside abandoned cars, but the ghastly details had been blessedly masked by night.

Now morning had come, and the road south stretched before them like a winding python.

A green signpost flashed past and Chuck grimaced.

"Twenty kilometers to Avignon," he spoke quietly out of the side of his mouth to Sherry. "It's going to be touch and go. If the gas runs out we might have to walk a couple of miles."

Sherry said nothing. She sat, staring fixedly ahead.

"There might be a boat we can board, or steal," Chuck went on optimistically. "I remember reading the brochures about this place before we left Washington. The city is built right on the banks of a river. They do a lot of luxury cruises and stuff from here. There's bound to be a boat. There's bound to be."

They had arrived in France two weeks before the world had slid into apocalypse, and Chuck had proposed marriage under the Eiffel Tower. Their holiday in France had been planned as the vacation of a lifetime...

Abandoned cars and trucks were strewn along the road as they drove further south, some of the vehicles simply left in the middle of the blacktop, while others had careered off the tarmac into ditches and trees. Under the bright morning sun, bodies had become distinguishable, and Chuck had seen the corpses of small children in the back seat of a Nissan wagon, the vehicle's windshield smashed and spattered with blood.

Five kilometers from Avignon the little Fiat surged and spluttered for the first time. Chuck eased his foot off the accelerator and slowed, trying to nurse the hire car the rest of the way. They passed another huge roadside sign indicating bridges ahead.

Suddenly the road network west of the ancient city became choked afresh by a new chaos of abandoned vehicles. Some were crumpled and mangled from collisions. There were others that were smoldering black shells. A truck had overturned onto its side, spilling its cargo of boxed electrical goods across three lanes. Great flocks of squawking birds wheeled and hung in the sky, screeching raucously as the Fiat rolled past. The air became tainted with the smells of oily smoke, the stench of disease, and the thick choking tang of putrefaction.

Chuck felt the gagging taste of it coat the back of his throat. He wound up his window but the stench permeated through the cockpit and made his eyes water.

Just west of Avignon they drove slowly through the narrow cobblestoned streets of a small village, Chuck's head turning from one side to the other as each horror was revealed. The whole village seemed on fire, and there was blood stained across the road. The side streets were littered with bricks and broken glass. As they neared the outskirts, the roof of one building collapsed in upon itself sending a funnel of flames and sparks spiraling high into the sky.

"There's the bridge," Chuck pointed suddenly as the Fiat rounded a bend in the road and joined a four-lane straight stretch of tarmac. A kilometer ahead rose the hump of a bridge across the Rhône. Chuck dabbed his foot on the brakes.

Between the car and the bridge stood a roadblock.

The roadblock had been made from a barricade of steel drums, with a wide line of iron spikes laid across the tarmac twenty yards closer to the car. On either side of the drums were heavy sandbagged weapon emplacements. Chuck thought he could see the barrel of a machine gun between bags, the ugly long barrel pointing towards the sky.

An abandoned delivery van teetered on the verge of the road, the driver's door hanging open and the vehicle sagging to one side on shredded tires.

"What do we do?" Sherry spoke for the first time in almost three hours. Her voice sounded tiny and afraid.

"I think the roadblock has been abandoned. I don't see any soldiers, and there should be some."

"Can we ram the barrels?"

Chuck shook his head. "They're probably filled with concrete," he guessed, frowning and thinking hard. The little car coughed and surged again, wheezing for the last drops of gas like a man dying of thirst.

He crawled the car forward until they were just a few feet short of the iron spikes. He looked hard at the sandbag emplacements. The barrel of the machine gun had not moved.

"I need you to get out of the car and move the spikes," Chuck said softly.

Sherry looked straight at him. There was something fearful in her expression.

"And then what?"

"And then I'll try to move a few barrels aside so we can get the car through. It's either that, or walk the rest of the way."

For the first time, they peered through the car's grimy windshield to the view across the river. They could see the western wall of the ancient city behind a drifting haze of smoke. Closer, they saw boats that had lost their moorings, drifting downstream with the current. Two of the boats were on fire and two more had collided and become entangled. The river looked about seventy yards wide, its bottle-green color silted with mud from recent rains, and its banks padded with low shrubs and muddy reed banks.

"Chuck," Sherry felt the panic well up inside her. Blood drained from her face and the words came in sobs. "I don't want to get out of the car! I'm scared!"

"I am too," Chuck admitted.

Chuck left the motor running and climbed warily from the car. Sherry took a last sobbing, shudder of breath and pushed open the passenger door. The stench of burning smoke and corruption struck them like a wall. Chuck spat the taste out of his mouth, then masked his nose with the sleeve of his sweater. The stench smelled oily and over-sweet. It coated his tongue and the roof of his mouth.

Sherry gagged and dry retched on the tarmac. Tears streamed down her cheeks. She kept her mouth closed and covered her nose with her hand. She glanced at Chuck with one final look of appeal and fear.

The iron road spikes were seated into a long strip of thick rubber. Sherry dragged the obstacle to the side of the road and made the mistake of peering into the cabin of the disabled delivery van.

A man lay slumped over the steering wheel. He was dead.

Sherry stared aghast and felt her skin crawl.

The bloated corpse was still moving, seeming to heave slowly. Sherry took two steps closer and realized the dead man's flesh crawled with thousands of fat wriggling maggots. They had entered through the man's slashed throat, burrowing into the still-warm flesh to avoid the scavenger birds that had come swooping at dawn. The cabin of the van was fouled with feathers and droppings. The birds had plucked out the dead man's eyes, then pecked at the tender flesh of his lips and ears leaving half of his face eaten away and his mouth and jaw exposed in a hideous grinning rictus.

Sherry screamed.

Chuck had started wrestling with a steel barrel in the center of the abandoned roadblock, the sweat of his exertion breaking out across his brow. He had already moved two pieces of the barricade aside. He was gasping for breath, trying to breath shallowly in the sickening air when he heard Sherry scream. He looked up, suddenly filled with alarm.

He ran to where Sherry stood. Her bladder had voided. Her jeans were dark with the wet stains. She hunched doubled over with her hands clamped over her mouth as if to choke back her gorge. Chuck saw the dead, disfigured corpse in the front seat of the van and understood.

"Get back in the car," he took her by the shoulders and steered her back to the Fiat. She went numbly on rubber legs.

Chuck sprinted back to the steel drums. He was frantic, his eyes wild and alert.

A sudden new sound filled the air, building up to a far away roar, like the rushing waters of a flooding river.

From the broken ground about the burning village, distorted figures appeared through the wreaths of smoke. Chuck counted a dozen. Then that number grew to over a hundred. They sprang up from the long grass and appeared between the trees. They crawled and clambered up from the bushes along the riverbank and came running from the burning streets of the village.

"Oh my God!" Chuck whispered. He felt paralyzed. His legs suddenly felt filled with concrete, and steel bands of terror clamped his chest so that for a long moment he could not breathe.

Chuck ran. He ran back towards the car. He ran with

terror in his legs and strangling his breath. He ran with his heart pounding and his arms pumping.

The undead compressed into a solid horde as they reached the western approach to the bridge and came hunting towards the car. They filled the bridge from one side to the other, a howling, mutilated, terrifying throng that streamed forward like ants from a disturbed nest.

Chuck reached the car and threw himself behind the wheel. The engine was still running, but beginning to wheeze and splutter. He glanced over his shoulder and saw the undead closing, then stomped his foot on the gas pedal and the hire car howled as it lunged forward.

The gap Chuck had made between the steel barrels was precariously narrow. He lined the Fiat up and steered with one hand, reaching across the cabin to hold Sherry back in her seat, bracing for the impact.

One of the undead appeared suddenly. It had climbed up and over a bridge railing. It threw itself in front of the hatchback. The impact sounded like the heavy swing of an axe against a tree-trunk as the front of the car hit the ghoul and dragged it under the chassis. There was a jolting bump a split-second before the Fiat reached the narrow breach in the barricade. Chuck wrenched at the wheel, trying frantically to keep the nose of the car lined up with the precariously narrow gap.

He miscalculated.

As it shot the gap, the front left wheel of the Fiat caught the edge of one steel barrel and the car went cartwheeling over in a rending screech of metal, flung viciously into the air through a crunching revolution that flung the doors open, shattered every window into a storm of glass splinters, and wrenched the damaged wheel clear off the vehicle.

Chuck was catapulted clear of the car, shot out

173

through the shattered windscreen by the plunging force of the impact. He felt himself falling in a swirling vortex of space and then something cracked brutally into his ribs. The air thumped from his lungs. He had time to cry out a bellowing roar of pain before cold dark water enveloped him in a choking swirl of bubbles.

Sherry was trapped in the wreckage of the car as it lay on its crumpled roof, teetering against the steel guardrails of the bridge's center span. The sudden silence after the collision and howl of the car's engine seemed deafening. Sherry heard cooling metal pinking and a sound like hissing steam. She hung, pinned upside down, pressed into her seat by the crumpled front end of the car. She was bleeding badly, a piece of steel embedded in her chest. She cried out in weak dazed confusion, and then coughed. The car seemed to be filling with smoke.

It took twenty seconds before the undead swarmed over the vehicle. They tore the young woman's broken body from the wreckage of the Fiat and then savaged her to death. They fell upon her like a howling pack of wild wolves, using their teeth to sever each limb before eviscerating the torso.

Sherry Wilson died screaming and choking on her own blood.

* * *

Chuck Gudinski plunged forty feet into the icy depths of the Rhône River.

He struck the water hard, with his mouth open in an agonized scream of pain. The cold water smothered him and his heavy clothing dragged him deep below the surface.

His lungs caught fire. The cold seized his chest. He

thrashed madly at the water as panic overwhelmed him. He had heard people say that drowning was a peaceful death. He didn't believe it. Chuck kicked furiously with his legs and flailed in the water until he slowly began to rise. He felt himself choking and his lungs began to spasm. He had swallowed water and the pain of it was excruciating.

Above him he could see the rippling surface, glinting sunlight in bright shards. There were dead bodies there too; dark shadows like logs that drifted past, filled with gases and floating slowly downstream.

Chuck's head broke through the surface just as panic overwhelmed him. His limbs began to thrash in uncontrolled paroxysms. He made one last surge, beginning to feel himself blacking out. A sense of disorientation flooded through him and a moment of reckless, giddy abandon almost overwhelmed him.

He gulped greedy mouths full of fetid air, letting the meandering current carry him down past the pylons of the bridge before he began to strike out painfully for the western bank. Each time he stretched his arm to sidestroke closer to the muddy reeds along the water's edge, a fierce stab of pain seized his chest.

He reached the shore, gasping and exhausted, and lay face-down in the mud and slime of the reeds. He felt with trembling fingers down across his body, taking inventory of his injuries. He was bleeding. He could feel slow sticky blood spilling from between his fingers when he explored the left side of his torso. He held his breath and tried to probe the wound. White-hot pain struck like a knife. He stifled a groan and rolled onto his side.

He looked back to the span of the bridge fifty yards upstream. He couldn't spot the wrecked Fiat, but he could see the side of the abandoned delivery van. He could see too, dark swarming shapes roaming in packs along the nearest guard rail. They were moving towards Avignon.

Chuck knew Sherry was dead: she couldn't possibly have survived. The despair and heartache that overwhelmed him felt more painful than the bleeding injury. He wept, trembling and shaking with cold and fear. Every nerve in his body had stretched to snapping, and his fatigued, exhausted body threatened to fail him. He had to cling stubbornly to consciousness to avoid falling into oblivion.

Moving one careful, agonizing inch at a time, Chuck clawed his way deeper into the concealing reeds, and the only sound in his ears was the sawing noise of his own labored breathing and his soft whimpers of agony. The warm oiliness of his fear swirled in his stomach so that he shook uncontrollably.

The initial plan he had shared with Sherry had been to steal a boat and sail to safety. But all the boats were moored upstream of the bridge. He knew he didn't have the strength to swim back against the tug of the current. Instead he crawled into the reeds and lay in the wet mud on his stomach with his eyes fixed on the high stone walls of Avignon. There were people inside the city who were still alive. He could see men walking along the high battlements carrying weapons. He could see one of the city's wide gates barricaded by the overturned hulks of several buses. Then he noticed a small door set inside a stone gateway. The door had been boarded up, but a man stood guard on the nearby wall. Chuck made a quick calculation and guessed he was seventy yards from the small arched gate. To reach safety he would need to cross an open area of grass, then four lanes of road littered with crashed and crumpled cars. On the far side of the road stretched another narrow strip of grass.

If he stayed patient – and if he could stay alive until nightfall – he could make it.

* * *

The bleak decision made, Camille turned and re-crossed the road, running back towards the sanctuary of the Grande Hotel. Her senses were overwrought by her terror, so finely honed that every sight and smell seemed enhanced. She pushed the elderly tourists on ahead of her, herding them like cattle, and she ran with the icy hand of her fear clutching at her chest.

In the middle of the road she shouted for Eve's stranded group to follow her, then paused for the briefest moment over Eve's dead body. The corpse lay spattered in its own blood, the young woman's eyes wide open and staring in sightless surprise. Flies crawled over the flesh. They swarmed around the dark sticky bullet wound and crept inside the cavity of her gaping mouth.

Camille ran on, sobbing silently until a sudden roar of noise made her pause again on the sidewalk outside the hotel's glass doors. It was a sound like the rustle of a million locust wings, ominous and menacing. She turned wildly towards the river.

A hundred yards away, a howling shrieking tide of undead rounded the street corner and surged towards her, and the baying maddened shrilling in their throats was the most terrifying sound she had ever heard. She felt the hair on her forearms prickle, and her bowels turned to liquid.

The infected came on, pouring from over the bridge and then around the corner at the end of the block. The sight of fleeing people seemed to enrage them with wild lust. A growl came out of the throng, a beastly inhuman growl of bloodthirsty mayhem.

"Run!" Camille cried at the gaggle of elderly tourists, clustered and trembling around her like lost children. "Get back inside the hotel!"

They went through the doors screaming and sobbing. Camille stood at the rear of the group, watching the undead surge along the street. They were climbing over cars, howling and screeching. The stench of their rotting corruption made her gag. She had a glimpse of their grotesque faces; mouths open and gnashing teeth contorted in a cruel rictus, the wild insanity in their glazed eyes.

"Move!" Camille barked at the last of the elderly vacationers.

She sprinted for the door just as the nearest undead ghoul came racing towards her. Its face was bestial, consumed by the killing madness. Camille screamed a high shrill cry of dread and twisted away an instant before the ghoul's outstretched arm would have seized her. She felt a clawed finger hook into the thin cotton collar of her blouse. The fabric tore loose. Camille could hear pounding feet close behind her. She flung herself through the hotel door in a shuddering paroxysm of terror.

"Block the entrance!" she cried out, flat on her back in the foyer, her chest heaving, her heart about to explode through the cage of her ribs.

Several of the tourists reacted instinctively. They barricaded the entrance with pot plants, tables and stuffed sofa chairs until the jumble of furniture had been piled almost to the ceiling.

A mob of howling undead quickly gathered outside the hotel. They pounded their fists on the glass, smearing

**178**

blood and gore. They pressed their faces to the thick panes and their eyes rolled insanely in their bloodshot eyes. They snarled and hissed. Through the hammering horrifying madness on the street, Camille saw two men being dragged from an abandoned SUV. One of the men was a rotund figure in a rumbled suit and tie. The ghouls had him backed up against the side of the vehicle. One of the infected pinned the man by the throat and plunged its clawed fist into the man's bulging guts. The man shrieked a bloodcurdling cry of unimaginable pain, staring down at himself with a look of pure astonishment as his entrails bulged out through his shirt in long slippery ropes.

The second victim somehow managed to break free, and he ran blindly towards the hotel. His head was down, panic wrenched across his face. He howled with raw terror. He seemed to be moving in slow motion through the swirling skeins of smoke.

The terrified man reached the sidewalk and realized the undead were all around him. He slipped in a pool of blood but stayed on his feet. Then Camille heard the wicked retort of a gunshot and the man spun around, thrashing at the air with his arms. The bullet had struck him in the shoulder and he swayed like an artiste on a tightrope teetering for balance. The undead surged over him. He went down in a horror of snarls and high-pitched screams.

Camille stared in wide-eyed dismay, and shook her head as though trying to deny the horror of it all. Her hand clutched at her throat, fingers splayed. She caught a last gruesome glimpse of the man, soaked in his own gushing blood, as the infected began eating him alive.

"Get upstairs!" Camille shut out the gruesome sight and forced herself to think. The Grande Hotel was a six-story complex with twenty rooms on each floor, serviced by an elevator and connecting stairs. She knew it would be just a matter of moments before the glass doors or one of the windows exploded from the violent pounding fists. "Quickly!" Camille raised her voice. "Everyone up to the first floor!"

They ran.

Camille kicked off her shoes and used them to wedge the first-floor fire doors open. She stood at the end of a long carpeted corridor with rooms on either side. At the far end of the passage was a storage closet. The elderly hotel survivors had packed into the hallway, clinging to each other and weeping openly. Their faces looked like ghastly masks of fear.

"We need to barricade the stairwell that leads up from the foyer," Camille spoke urgently. "Bring everything you can find from each room; chairs, mattresses, suitcases – anything you can carry!"

They came back to the stairwell like wise men bearing gifts, their arms loaded with pillows, handbags and carrying bedside cabinets. Groups of elderly men appeared, staggering and sweating under the strain of corner tables and sofa chairs. Piece by piece the stairwell began to fill with a jumbled tumble of obstacles, while from somewhere below them there came a sudden sound like a gunshot.

"The hotel doors!" Camille gasped. "They've broken through. The undead are inside the building."

The realization put fresh panic into the terrified survivors. They banded together to heave single bed frames, televisions and small refrigerators down into the stairwell until it became as formidable an obstacle as a corridor of barbed wire.

Camille posted two hotel guests as guards with orders

to fetch her the moment the undead appeared, then went into the nearest hotel room that faced the street and Avignon's wall.

The room looked like it had been ransacked. Cosmetics and personal items were strewn across the floor. Every closet door had been flung open, and clothes lay in discarded piles. Camille strode across to the window and swept back the curtains.

Hotel safety regulations meant the window would only open a few inches. Camille snatched up a discarded boot from the litter and smashed the window to pieces with an almighty heave. Glass sprayed the street below and warm fetid air filled the room.

Camille leaned out through the window and stared in horror and the scene on the street below.

The undead numbered in their thousands, criss-crossing the wide street in running roaming packs. Crumpled bodies lay like broken toys in spattered puddles of gore, and the hotel next to the Grande billowed thick grey funnels of smoke and fire from several broken windows. Sirens and building alarms still wailed in the background, but it was the sound of the undulating wave of undead that was most chilling. It was the noise of a million bees and thousands of running, shuffling feet. It was the noise of shrieking, peppered by sporadic gunfire from the old city.

Camille snatched a rumpled bed sheet off the floor and sent one of the elderly guests to the storage closet. They came back clutching a thick black laundry marker.

Camille dropped to her knees and worked quickly, with the sheet spread out on the carpet, holding the marker pen in her fist like a knife. It capital letters she wrote:

*50 souls. Trapped. Send help!*

\* \* \*

"Christ!" Tremaine cursed with bitter futile frustration, riding the waves of his dismay. He did not need binoculars to read the message on the fluttering bed sheet draped from the hotel window, nor to recognize the slim figured woman who stared across the infested roadway with a pale white pleading face.

Camille had promised him over dinner the night before that she would not leave the old city. She had lied to him, and now she was trapped in the hotel, surrounded by thousands of undead.

"Damn it to hell!"

Tremaine raged silently around the top of the gatehouse like a caged lion, his hands clenching into futile fists, and then finally turned back to the gendarme Colonel, his face set, seemingly carved from stone. His eyes were ferocious and his jaw tightly clamped.

"We have to rescue them," Tremaine said.

"Monsieur?" LeCat looked startled.

Tremaine pointed at the white bed sheet, flapping from the hotel window. "There are fifty people stranded across the road. We have to rescue them."

"Why?" Colonel LeCat's own expression slowly hardened. His eyes turned flinty black.

"Why?" Tremaine looked astonished. "Because if we don't rescue them, they will be killed by the infected!"

LeCat shrugged. "We were all aware of the consequences for anyone left outside the old city's walls, Professor Tremaine," the Colonel's words were thickly accented and in his eyes there was an unsettling rigidity of purpose. "Indeed it was you who made that perfectly clear in the mayor's office yesterday."

182

Tremaine fumed. He knew damn well the French soldier was right, but he persisted stubbornly.

"Camille Pelletier is the mayor's daughter…"

"So?" LeCat remained devoid of emotion. "We have all lost loved ones in this apocalyptic nightmare, monsieur. My wife and son were in Paris when the infection swept through the city. I have not heard from them since. And corporal LeBouf," he pointed to one of the nearby gendarmes and shook his head sadly, "has a wife and baby daughter living just ten kilometers away. They too have not been heard from. This tragedy has destroyed millions of lives and killed millions of daughters. One more will count for little, I think."

"You cold-hearted son-of-a-bitch," Tremaine exploded, his voice rising indignantly. "You won't even try to rescue them?"

"Why? What makes the lives of these refugees any more valuable than the lives of the thousands who stood outside the Porte De La Republique gates just a short time ago, holding their babies in the air and throwing money over the wall as they begged for rescue?"

"It's Camille, damn it!"

"So what would you have me do?" LeCat spat fiercely. Behind the Colonel's hostile stare, Tremaine sensed some indefinable emotion in the soldier's eyes. It might have been regret, or sadness, or perhaps an unspoken guilt.

Tremaine shrugged his shoulders with exasperation. "You could send a heavily armed patrol of soldiers," he said impulsively. "We can cover their movements with machine guns from this gatehouse and put every spare man armed with an assault rifle along the wall."

"The undead are too many. The rescue party would all be killed. You know this, I think."

Tremaine pursed his lips until they were a pale bloodless line. "Then maybe there is another way," he said stiffly.

"Maybe," LeCat said, and let a glimmer of compassion soften his eyes. "I know you are fond of Camille," he leaned close and spoke in a confidential whisper. "But I cannot consider any plan that endangers the lives of anyone behind these city walls. Tens of thousands – maybe millions – have died today. It is the end of the world, professor. We must preserve every life we have already saved, and not risk them in a reckless gamble."

As if to reinforce the Colonel's cold warning, the undead horde suddenly seemed to surge around the smoldering gates directly below where the two men stood. They swarmed in their thousands. They could see the white-faced soldiers standing with their weapons on the battlements, and the tantalizing lure of living flesh sent them into frenzy. They tried to use the wreckage of the big truck to scale the barricades, but the sheer height of the escalade made it impossible. Gunshots rang out, and the infected were plucked from their precarious footholds and hurled back into the milling, seething mass below. The ancient fortifications were like a bulwark against the surging tide of grotesque bodies that moved in eddies and flows the same way a crowd at a musical concert rushes towards the stage when the band first appears.

LeCat leaned on the battlements and watched the undead gather until they crowded the surrounding streets for as far as he could see. He slapped his palm against the hard stone, satisfied.

"We are safe," he said, as much to himself as to Tremaine, allowing a moment of smug relief. "The undead cannot scale the walls, so we are safe. So long as these old fortifications stand, and as long as the barricaded buses remain fixed, monsieur, we have nothing more to fear from the infected undead."

Tremaine grunted miserably and stared past the Colonel to the bed sheet hanging from the hotel window.

Camille Pelletier had no walls and no weapons.

And there was nothing Tremaine could do to save her.

\* \* \*

It took almost two hours before the undead in the hotel foyer were able to smash down the heavy ground-floor fire doors and begin to clamber over the obstacles that barricaded the stairwell. They were frenzied with insane madness, driven wild by the nearness of flesh. They could smell the sweat and the fear of the living. They could hear their screams of fright and their quiet sobs of terror.

Camille abandoned the first floor, locking the doors behind her before retreating with the rest of the survivors to the second floor. A new barricade of furniture had to be built, but the elderly tourists were lethargic and exhausted. Camille, too, felt drained of resolve. Her throat scratched and she swayed sickly on her feet. She couldn't remember the last time she had eaten.

A dark fatalistic pall fell over the group as they moved numbly through the second-floor rooms, gathering furniture to barricade the next section of stairwell. Despair sapped the energy and urgency from them. It weighed on them like an insidious disease. Death, they began to realize, seemed inevitable. It would only be a matter of time.

**185**

An elderly Austrian couple sat down next to each other in the empty stairwell and refused to follow the rest of the group. Camille pleaded desperately with them.

"Leave us, please," the old man pleaded. His eyes were kindly.

"Help is coming from the city!" Camille crouched down close to the elderly husband and implored him. "The soldiers have seen the sign on the bed sheet. I know they have. We just have to wait for them to rescue us."

The man was in his eighties, with a face whose features had been ravaged and blurred into soft pouches of sagging flesh by fatigue and strain. He smiled benevolently into Camille's eyes, and then put his arm around his wife's shoulder in a tender embrace. They had been married for almost sixty years.

"Help is not coming," the old man spoke with a thick accent. He was not bitter. He was resigned. He spoke in a whisper so the rest of the group would not hear him. "You know that, my darling. And we are simply too old and too tired to go on fighting. We have had a wonderful life. Now we are ready to let it end."

"Help *will* come," Camille said with confidence she didn't truly feel. She took the old man's hand. It felt cold and had a texture like putty, the knuckles of each finger gnarled and swollen with arthritis. The elderly woman's eyes filled with soft glistening tears. She rested her head on her husband's shoulder like she was ready for eternal sleep.

"Leave us, dear," she spoke with quiet lethargy. "We've made up our minds. Do what you can to save the others."

\* \* \*

Tremaine stood at the battlements above the Porte Saint Roch gateway and swept the binoculars across the skyline.

Beyond the ancient walls of the old city, the outer suburbs of Avignon were burning.

It was dusk; the last rays of the day's light were fading in the west, but the view through the lenses of the binoculars was made stark by bright leaping flames. Tremaine could see thousands of grotesquely disfigured undead roaming the streets. They were moving in packs, agitated and restless. He tried to estimate their numbers but it was impossible. There were simply too many to count.

They ran through the flickering light and disappeared into dark shadows. They plunged into burning buildings, mindless with the insanity of their infection. They bickered and snarled, and turned savagely on each other like wild dogs, and they threw themselves at the high stone walls he stood behind, baying and howling for blood.

Tremaine heard glass shatter followed by the violent noise of an explosion. A fireball leaped into the darkening sky from the abandoned police station across the road.

Then a sound like someone being tortured cried out in the night. It was a shrill, agonized scream that climbed high and gasping into the smoke-filled darkness, screech upon wheezing, blubbering screech, and Tremaine felt himself cringe as he tried to imagine an unholy torment so vile that could give voice to that blood-chilling sound.

He felt himself shudder. The terrible cry came again, incoherent and high-pitched, becoming frantic and crazed. It sawed across Tremaine's nerves and brought a hot sickening flush to his cheeks. The agonized scream was followed by a roaring howl of triumph from a hundred inhuman throats that descended into snarling savagery.

The sudden silence came as a guilt-stricken relief. Tremaine took a deep breath, his hands still shaking, and focused the binoculars on the façade of the Grande Hotel.

The lower floors of the building were destroyed. Tremaine could see shattered glass and broken furniture tumbled onto the sidewalk. He saw smoke billowing from the lower floors, and then – from a smashed window on the third floor – he noticed another bed sheet with a desperate message scrawled on it.

*Help!*

Tremaine tried to focus the glasses into the open window, hoping to see Camille, but the entire hotel stood engulfed in ominous darkness. Shadows flitted through the room, but they were indistinguishable as individuals. Tremaine set the binoculars down and rubbed his eyes.

"There must be a way to save those people," he muttered.

He stared up into the night sky and saw a full moon rising behind ragged shreds of black smoke. The dark silhouettes of birds wheeled in the air.

Suddenly the hint of an idea came ghosting along Tremaine's spine, making the hairs on his forearms prickle. His brow puckered in a frown as he tried to block out the mayhem rising from the chaos all around him. He kept his head tilted back and watched a flock of birds fly low overhead. He could hear the great beat of their wings through the air...

The idea was there, stirring in his subconscious, but lurking just below the surface of his conscious mind, like the shadowy shape of something swimming up from the depths of the ocean. He closed his eyes and let his mind go blank.

"Christ!" he exclaimed, shouting so loudly that he startled two nervous gendarmes posted to the nearby section of wall. They snatched at their weapons in alarm, and a bright yellow flashlight beam swept across the gatehouse wall, looking for danger.

Tremaine apologized to the gendarmes with a sheepish, embarrassed smile. But new flashlight beams sliced through the darkness, criss-crossing in sweeping patterns over the city's southern fortifications as the alert was taken up. Barked orders were shouted and repeated. The men defending the battlements were exhausted and on edge. Tremaine cupped his hands to his mouth and shouted, "False alarm!" He heard men mutter darkly.

He went down the crumbling stone steps at a run with the idea still taking shape in his imagination. At the bottom of the ancient gatehouse, a sergeant stood by the open door of a P4 jeep, talking quietly on the radio. Tremaine thrust his face close to the soldier's, his expression worked into agitation and impatience.

"Where is Colonel LeCat?" Tremaine demanded. "I need to speak to him urgently. It's a matter of life and death."

\* \* \*

Pain roused Chuck Gudinski, and he woke with a gasp of confusion and a sickening, panicked lurch of his heart. He hadn't meant to sleep, and his first alarmed thought was for his safety. He blinked grit from his eyes, turning his head wildly. He lay on his stomach facing the walls of Avignon with his chest and torso amongst the

189

reeds, and his legs still immersed in the shallow water that lapped at the edge of the river. Masses of milling undead roamed the nearby road, hunting between the rows of abandoned cars. Dogs ran with them; mangy blood-spattered hounds with stiff bristled hair and tongues lolling dementedly from their mouths. Chuck stifled a sob of terror. The infected were grotesque silhouettes, flitting between shadows against a glowing firelight backdrop. Night had fallen and the entire world seemed to be burning.

Then the pain struck him and he had to bite down on the urge to cry out. He was stiff and cold, yet his chest felt like the flesh beneath his ribcage had been scorched by a blowtorch. The ferocity of the stabbing pain made him draw his knees to his chest, and sweat broke across his brow as nausea overwhelmed him.

He rode the waves of pain, clenching his jaw and panting short sharp breaths until the worst of it had passed, then dug his fingers into the muddy riverbank and clawed forward. He had lain unmoving, half-immersed in the icy water of the Rhône, all day. The cold had permeated his entire body so that even his bones ached, and spasms of shivering gripped him like the symptoms of high fever.

He dragged himself to the fringe of the reeds and paused, gasping and tight with cramp. The effort exhausted him and left a snaking trail of blood in his wake. From his new vantage point he could see the ground ahead more clearly.

There were bodies in the grass between the river and the road. Just a few paces to his left he saw the crumpled half-eaten remains of a woman, and nearer to the road slumped the shape of a man who had died sitting upright with his back propped against a tree. Two dogs growled

190

as they sniffed closer to the corpse. Chuck watched on in cringing horror and held his breath.

One of the hounds skulked close to the dead man, its head hanging, its shoulders bunched, and then suddenly bounded onto the body, straddling the cadaver's chest and latching its teeth into the flesh of the face. Chuck thought he heard the gruesome sound of the man's skin being ripped from one cheek. The dog growled and snarled, and the dead man's head jerked and twitched. The second dog went for one of the outstretched legs. The dogs savaged the body with gnashing jaws, then retreated into the deep shadows of the night, their mouths full.

Chuck gagged with a sickened shudder of revulsion and tore his eyes away.

Most of the infected were gathered outside the walls of the city. He could hear them howling. Flashlight beams swept the battlements and occasionally he heard a burst of furious gunfire that sounded like popping firecrackers.

Chuck took a deep breath and counted down from five, tensing every muscle, screwing his nerves tight. The grassy verge between the riverbank and the road seemed suddenly still. Nothing moved.

Chuck reached through the reeds and grabbed at a handful of grass, then dragged himself forward on his stomach, wriggling and straining like a maimed caterpillar.

* * *

"I have seen the face of God," Kane declared solemnly, and then paused to let the significance of his words sink in to the congregation gathered at abandoned warehouse.

The cavernous building was lit by a hundred burning candles that threw leaping shadows up the walls and cast everything in a golden glow.

Kane sat on the edge of the small platform that was his stage. The young girl sat obediently close beside him. Kane had his arm around her waist. Her face looked pale and serious.

"I have seen the face of God," Kane said again. "But I could not hear His words. He came to me in a moment of rapture, and beckoned me. He waits for the right time and place to reveal His plan to us."

He stood up then and lifted the girl to her feet. She seemed small and frail and fragile in the shadow of the preacher's huge bulk. She had changed into a fresh white dress and wore a blue sash of ribbon around her narrow waist. Her face and hair had been washed. She stood silent and serene. Kane clutched her to his side and discreetly let his hand drift down her back until he possessively cupped the firm round cheeks of her buttocks.

Kane faced the crowd standing tall above the glowing candles so the flickering flames lit his features from below, turning the deep cavities of his eyes into black caverns.

"God wants you to make your choice," the preacher kept his voice restrained, letting the words rumble from his throat as he addressed the gathering. "You can stay cowering and hidden from the Almighty's wrath, or you can walk in the divine sunshine of His love at my side. But the time to declare your heart is now." He paused dramatically and his listeners seemed to crane forward where they sat. The warehouse was eerily silent as they waited for more.

"Tonight we must place ourselves at His mercy and

192

into His service. Only those willing to accept our Lord will be saved."

He saw fear flash across the faces of those followers who were gathered closest to the stage, and he seized the moment.

"We are God's children! We live to serve His will. Each of us has been called, and I have personally felt the brush of His hand and the whisper of His breath. I have seen His magnificent countenance. I have been chosen as His messenger on earth, and you have been chosen as God's flock," he lashed the gathered congregation, his voice rising with the zeal of a prophet.

A soft sigh rose from the audience. They stirred like the leaves of a tree in a gentle breeze, captivated by Kane's compelling presence and the impassioned power of his voice. One of the women in the crowd nodded her head sagely and began to mutter prayers. Another man quietly clapped his hands then cried out, "Praise to God!"

The call was taken up by fifty other voices. Kane let the chorus ring around the room, his eyes glittering.

"But where?" Kane began again, his gestures rehearsed and stagey. "Where can we hear the exalted voice of God? Where can we perform a ceremony of such magnificence that God would be pleased and compelled to bless us with a clear message?"

It was a rhetorical question. Kane let his words hang in the air and the crowd leaned forward, quivering with anticipation.

"The Palace of the Popes!" Kane declared. "It was once the house of God and his most beloved messengers on earth. Tonight... tonight it will become that holy place again."

Kane fell dramatically silent and swept his eyes over

the faces that glowed in the firelight. He had them entranced, captivated.

"We must break into the palace and perform a ritual to connect me with the Almighty through the sacred vessel he delivered," Kane looked wolfishly down at the girl's face and drew a hiss of breath. "For only in the moment of rapture can the word of God be evoked, and only in a holy place can it be heard."

* * *

The ancient city was enveloped in the deep dark of night when Jacques Lejeune left his apartment and went creeping through the narrow cobbled streets of the western quarter. Electricity into Avignon had finally failed, and the only light came from four huge arc lamps standing at the edges of the town plaza, powered by military generators from the gendarmerie barracks.

The arc lamps seemed as bright as the sun, but their reach into the labyrinth of streets was limited. Jacques had no difficulty clinging to the shadows.

The military had imposed a curfew on all civilian movement throughout the old city after dark and the side roads were deserted. Police cars patrolled the main thoroughfares, and Jacques kept a careful, cautious watch for the sweep of their headlights.

When at last he reached the unlocked door and pushed it open, he was lathered in nervous sweat.

Candles burned in the cramped hallway, lighting threadbare carpet. The building had a musty airless smell, mingled with the odors of stale cooking and cigarette smoke. There were more candles on the staircase. He took the steps two-at-a-time, drawing deep breaths to settle his nerves. At the top of the stairs he turned right and then paused, suddenly overcome with anxiety, outside an apartment door.

He fumbled a cigarette from his pocket and lit it. A trickle of sweat ran down from his brow, over the unshaven stubble of his jowls, and dripped from his chin. He took three jerky steps back towards the stairs, then turned back with a sickness in the pit of his stomach and the sweat of his shame running down his sallow cheeks.

The door was faded blue, the paint peeling in flakes to expose leprous patches of another color underneath. He turned the worn knob and the unlocked door creaked open.

Jacques stepped into a room thick with incense smoke. The walls were covered with cheap posters in ugly frames, and in the corners were two stuffed, worn sofa chairs. There were two doors on the far side of the room and the floor was thick with a mish-mash of imitation oriental rugs.

Jacques went quietly across the floor towards a door that had a stained glass picture of an owl lead lighted into the top panel. The bird had been fashioned through a mix of transparent and brown segments of glass to represent the head and feathers, and a riot of bright colors to form the wings.

Jacques' hand shook. He tapped lightly on the door and then pressed his face close to one of the small clear glass panels to peer into the room beyond.

Jacques could see a bed, and there were burning candles on a chest of drawers nearby. They lit the walls with a soft muted glow so that it took him long puzzled seconds to interpret and understand what he was watching.

Amidst a mess of tangled sheets, a couple lay upon the mattress. The woman was on her back with her legs splayed wide apart, clutching at a naked man's hips between her knees. The man was thrusting in a wild erratic rhythm, grunting like a boar as his naked buttocks clenched and bunched with each new drive of his pelvis.

The woman lay gasping, speaking in husky breathless groans, urging the man above her to greater effort as she theatrically tossed her head from side to side and strained her body up to meet his.

Jacques felt an insane rush of hot jealousy and then an equally intense perverse voyeuristic fascination. He gulped in a ragged breath of air. His whole body shook with feverish thrill.

"Paulette!" he gasped, his voice bruised by a sense of betrayal.

He reached to push the door open, but timidity froze him. He stood, vacillating while the sounds from within the bedroom rose towards their inevitable crescendo.

Suddenly the other door into the waiting room opened and a slim blonde girl with a tender pale body appeared. She was naked. She saw Jacques and her expression became knowing. Her lipsticked lips curled into a whore's smile.

"Hello, monsieur," her voice was throaty. She stayed shamelessly in the doorway but changed her stance, shifting her weight onto one leg so that her hips tilted at an enchanting angle. Her smile became small and sly. She saw a flush of color bloom in Jacques' cheeks. "Can I be of service to you tonight? Are you lonely for companionship?"

Jacques felt his throat constrict. He flapped his hands.

"I have come to see Paulette," he choked the words out stiffly.

The blonde arched an eyebrow. It could have been a gesture of amusement, or perhaps a challenge. She pursed her lips and ran her eyes down Jacques body, letting her gaze linger when it reached the man's crotch. Jacques felt somehow violated by the brazen hunger in the woman's eyes, unaware that it was the skillfully rehearsed theatrics of her trade.

"That is a pity," the blonde fluttered her eyes and pouted like a spoilt child. "I could have been very, very good to you…"

Jacques shook his head with a jerk, and then turned, startled, as the door behind him was thrown open and a young man in a gendarme's uniform came into the waiting room, fumbling clumsily with his buttons. His face was flushed, his eyes glazed, and he grinned idiotically.

He muttered something unintelligible, then put his head down and made for the apartment door. A wash of stale cheap perfume and the aroma of sweat drifted into the room.

Paulette came from the bed with a cigarette clamped between her lips. She wore a black bra and panties.

"Hello, Paulette," Jacques called, his voice low and quivering.

Paulette stood at the foot of the bed. Her lipstick had been smeared and her hair tousled. A fine sheen of perspiration made her body glisten in the candlelight. She regarded Jacques with slanted eyes and gave him a petulant, dismissive huff of derision.

"What do you want, Jacques?" Paulette drew deeply on the cigarette and blew a thin feather of smoke at the ceiling.

"I wanted to see you," Jacques muttered. He felt acutely awkward and uncomfortable. He dabbed at the nervous sweat across his brow with the back of his hand.

Paulette grimaced a cold little smile and dismissed the

blonde with a flick of her eyes. The woman in the far bedroom doorway disappeared without another word.

"I know what you want, Jacques," Paulette thrust the glowing tip of the cigarette at him in accusation when they were alone.

Jacques' eyes were as black as coal, beady in their dark sunken sockets. He licked his lips guiltily – an involuntary reflex beyond his ability to control. Paulette straightened her stance and pushed her shoulders back so that her breasts were firm against the flimsy lace of her bra.

"I... I have money," Jacques thrust his hand into his pocket and brought out a fistful of crumpled banknotes. "Lots of money, Paulette. It's yours. You can have it all in exchange for one more night together..."

Paulette threw back her head and laughed. The sound was scornful and cruel. "Money?" she shrugged her shoulders dramatically. "What use is your money, Jacques? It is the end of the world! Money is worth nothing to me. I cannot buy the things I need. I cannot buy food or clothes. Keep your money!"

"But Paulette!" Jacques felt a flush of sudden panic, like a drug addict denied. "Just one more night..."

"Non," she shook her head, and the long tresses of her hair swished across her shoulders. "I am giving myself only to the brave soldiers who fight to defend us," her darting tongue flicked pink between her teeth. She stubbed the cigarette out into a brimming full ashtray and turned back to the bed to gather her discarded clothes, bending at the waist provocatively. Jacques felt his breath catch and a lump of lustful desire choked his throat. He averted his eyes guiltily.

"Paulette!" he wheezed.

She glanced over her shoulder, her eyes narrowed

into sly little slits, and pouted. "I said non, Jacques. I am only for the soldiers now. The brave boys deserve some pleasure in exchange for risking their lives."

"But I am a soldier too!" Jacques' voice rose to a squeak.

Paulette looked bemused. She laughed in a scornful, mocking tinkle. "You?"

"Oui," Jacques nodded his head earnestly. He came into the bedroom and reached for Paulette. She danced away, taunting and denying him. He went on, his voice wheedling. "I guard one of the small gates on the western wall. I am responsible for the security… and I have a gun."

Paulette stopped and scrutinized Jacques' face for long seconds. All men were liars, she knew, and they would say anything to a woman for sex. But there was something raw and desperate and utterly earnest in Jacques' expression that made her pause.

"Is this really true, Jacques?" she asked in a soft little breath.

"Oui," he nodded his head, sensing the change in Paulette's tone. "Look. I have the key on me," he produced an old brass key from his pocket as evidence. "And the gun is at my apartment."

"Which gate?"

"Poterne Raspail," Jacques named one of the narrow wicket gates built into the western wall. It was an arched stone gateway near one of the bridges over the Rhône, secured by a heavy wooden door. A path connected the gate to a pedestrian crossing. Paulette knew the gate well. In the summer months she often sat on a wooden bench near the Poterne Raspail gate to meet clients. "I am on duty from eleven o'clock tonight until sunrise."

Paulette glanced at the small clock on her bedside

table and made a quick calculation. A perverse devil's chill of mischief ran up her spine. She had not seen the infected; but the young gendarmes she comforted in her bed had told her gruesome, chilling stories of what they had witnessed from the walls. Paulette had become wickedly aroused by depraved, sadistic fantasies. Now she licked her lips with sudden elation. Her eyes slanted lasciviously and felt her own body overwhelmed by raw sexual arousal. Her fear mingled with her lust, and the brew of those emotions made her reckless.

"Very well," she could feel her heart trip and race, but her tone stayed contemptuous. "Then I will meet you at Poterne Raspail later tonight, Jacques."

Lejeune looked uncertain. "At the gate? But I want you, Paulette." He reached for her again but she stepped teasingly away from his groping hand.

"Not yet."

"But Paulette. I ache for you…"

"And you can have me, darling," she promised. She came into his arms at last and lifted her face to his. Jacques felt himself swell hard. Paulette melted in his embrace and he inhaled the musky sensual scent of her, his fingers hungry on her smooth, soft body. "You can have me until you're exhausted, Jacques… but first I want you to prove your bravery to me. I want to watch you shoot one of the infected."

\* \* \*

The undead broke through the fourth-floor fire door in the early hours of the morning. The hotel was blanketed in pitch darkness, but Camille had found a box of scented candles in a tourist's luggage. The survivors sat in the fifth-floor corridor clinging to their small flickering

200

lights, and listened to the infected ghouls in the stairwell below. The undead were trying to clamber up the internal staircase, past the ragged jumble of furniture that had been thrown in their way. Camille heard high blood-lusting howls amidst the nightmare sounds of furniture breaking. It was like listening, shivering in fear from an upstairs room, while burglars ransacked a home.

"They will be here soon," Camille said softly. She felt exhausted. Her hands trembled with fatigue and her face had been drained of all color by relentless hours of fear. Hopelessness had crushed the last of her resolve. Help was not coming – she realized that now. They had been abandoned by the soldiers in the city and left for dead.

It was just a matter of time.

She looked slowly at nearby faces. There was no more weeping. Everyone sat grim and fatalistic, hunched in forlorn little groups. No one spoke; they stared vacantly at the walls or at some point in space, lost in their own misery and despair while they waited for the gruesome inevitability of death.

"They will be here soon," Camille said again. No one even looked in her direction.

Camille flicked a glance at the heavy steel fire-doors the undead would soon burst through. She could see the faintest flicker of light from the gap between the carpet, and she wondered idly whether perhaps the hotel was on fire. Either way, death was inevitable, but she spent a few lethargic moments considering whether it would be better to burn to death.

She got wearily to her feet and clutched at a wall to stop her from swaying.

"We're moving up to the sixth floor," her throat rasped raw when she tried to raise her voice.

In ones and twos, the quiescent elderly tourists

staggered to their feet with bovine obedience, groaning and weak with vertigo. The oppressive dark was disorientating. One woman dropped her candle and cursed under her breath.

Some of the elderly had fallen asleep and had to be roused. Camille shook one man's shoulder, feeling the frail brittle bones beneath the fabric of his shirt. He was lying on his back, snoring softly with his mouth open and his hands twitching at his side. He came alert slowly, his eyes vague and unfocussed, and a tear squeezed from his eye and rolled down the withered parchment-like flesh of his cheek.

"Leave me," he said in a hoarse rasp. "I can't…"

Camille shook her head stubbornly and sniffed back the tears of her own misery. She wanted to lie down and die too. The weight of her despair felt like a heavy burden strapped to her back. It made her knees sag. She clung to the old man's hand and wouldn't let him go.

"Come on, Mr. Davis," she whispered. "I need you to be brave," she provoked him by appealing to his pride. "A lot of the ladies are very scared and they look up to you. If you give up, everyone else will too."

Their eyes met for a moment and silent understanding passed between them. Mr. Davis struggled to his feet and straightened his back. He was an Englishman who had been visiting family in Europe when the spreading undead infection had trapped him in France. He gave Camille a ghost of a smile and then lifted his voice above the desolate murmurs of the others.

"Follow me, ladies," the old man filled his voice with perky optimism and suddenly became as spritely as a London bus conductor. "Everyone to the stairwell, if you please."

Camille watched the elderly survivors limp and

202

struggle towards the stairs, then, when she was alone, let her tears come. They welled along the rims of her eyes and spilled over her lashes like glistening drops of morning dew. Her lips trembled, and she had to bite down hard to stop herself from being overcome. She sniffed, drew a deep shuddering breath, wiped her face with the back of her trembling hand, and pressed her ear to the fire door.

She could hear the horrible, hideous sounds of the undead just a few feet away from where she stood. They were mindless with the insanity of their infection. Camille heard throaty growls and sounds like demented giggling as they smashed and crashed their way higher up the stairs.

Camille turned and ran for the doors that lead to the top floor of the hotel.

* * *

Chuck Gudinski's world had telescoped down to the few feet of ground that lay directly before him. He lost all sense of time, suspended in a place of fear and pain. Every inch he crawled closer to the walls of Avignon cost him strength and blood and sanity.

The agony of his wound turned each movement into white-hot torture and he began to fret about blood loss. Twice in the open ground near the river he rolled onto his side and looked back between his legs. He could see a dark trail on the grass.

He crawled on, pausing every minute to put his head down and rest. His fingernails had been ripped from his fingers so his hands were a mess of raw bloody flesh, and his chest, through the tattered rags that remained of his shirt, was bruised and grazed by the coarse ground he

203

crawled over.

But it was his mind that worried Chuck the most. He could feel the threads of his sanity beginning to unravel, like a loose strand of yarn in a sweater being relentlessly pulled by the unimaginable fear of crawling through the undead horde.

The first ten yards had been easy, but as he crept closer to the shoulder of the four-lane road, the undead became more numerous. They staggered and skulked from one abandoned car to the other, tearing loose seats and smashing windows in their crazed lust for fresh blood. They crept in the night like stalking panthers and ran in maddened frenzied circles; they were unhinged with insanity and unpredictable. A dozen ghouls ran straight past Chuck as he lay, holding his breath and trembling. He felt spatters of blood and mud from the passing undead fall upon his head like rain. They were howling and snapping. One of them leaped onto the hood of a wrecked car. It had been a woman before infection. It was dressed in the tattered remains of a skirt and blouse. Its legs and arms were streaked with mud and the wiry tangle of hair on its head was falling out in clumps. The ghoul seemed to taste the air with its tongue, eyes rolling dementedly in the sunken sockets of its skull. Then it lifted its face to the dark sky and bayed like a dog. The ghoul had bite marks along the dead grey flesh of one arm, and around the injury were blisters of puss-weeping sores. Chuck pressed his head down into the gravel and lay still as a corpse.

The ghoul slithered off the hood of the car and dropped to its haunches, scratching feverishly at the ground just a few feet from where Chuck lay. All Chuck's senses were sharpened to compensate for his lack of sight in the darkness. He heard the sawing hiss of the ghoul's foul fetid breath and inhaled the oily sickening stench of its corruption. He felt the jagged little stones of the gravel stabbing into his flesh as he lay perfectly still while quailing fear squeezed his chest.

The ghoul suddenly threw itself down on the roadside and reached under the chassis of a car. It cried out an intelligible shriek of triumph and in its gnarled disfigured hand squirmed the black shape of a river-rat. The ghoul bit the vermin's head off and went scurrying away into the night, retching and screeching its triumph.

Chuck let out a slow careful breath. Then the shock hit him and he began to tremble like the victim of a car crash in the aftermath of an accident. His bloody mangled hands shook and the nerves along his legs jangled in uncontrollable spasms.

He gaped with incredulity. How had the ghoul not sensed him?

Carefully, an aching inch at a time, he rolled onto his side and stared back towards the dark clump of reeds by the riverbank. He frowned. Had the thick swampy mud he had lain in somehow concealed his scent?

He rolled back onto his stomach and braced himself for the next arduous challenge. Ahead of him were four wide lanes of blacktop, littered with wrecked cars, dead bodies, marauding ghouls.... and rats. He flexed the bloody stumps of his fingers and winced. He weighed up the hours of agony and fear that stretched before him against the blinding few seconds of gruesome torture that would accompany his detection and death. He could end it all right now, he knew, with a single scream. The infected would run him down and eat him alive before he could flee ten yards.

He drew a last shuddering breath to fill his lungs... and then crawled the next few inches forward onto the verge of the darkened road.

He wouldn't give up. He wouldn't surrender to death. He thought about Sherry and her memory galvanized him.

He lifted his head off the tarmac to get his bearings. Between the tangle of wrecked vehicles and the milling undead that surrounded the city, glowing flames and torchlight illuminated the façade of the Avignon wall. Directly ahead, and now less than fifty yards away, was the small arched gateway he had first noticed from the reed bank.

He could make it.

* * *

The wooden door was ancient, weather-worn, and unguarded. Kane put his shoulder to the timber and the door blew inwards on its hinges. He stood in the entrance for a long moment, letting his eyes adjust to the deeper darkness of the palace. He had a cigarette lighter in his hand. The glow from the tiny flame showed him a stone passage leading to a glass door. He kept his voice low and urgent.

"Follow me. Make not a sound."

There were twenty-two followers gathered around him in the shadows of the Palace of the Popes. They shuffled under the archway of the vast building and inhaled the cool dank air. Two of the men carried boxes in their arms. They followed the small glow of light, bumping into each other in the narrow passage. Kane paused.

The glass door before him was new and wired with an alarm. Kane took a hammer from one of the boxes and smashed in the glass. The alarm tripped but it had been wired to the electrical power. Apart from the jarring sound of shattering glass, the night stayed eerily silent.

Kane grunted with smug satisfaction.

They were out of view from the rest of the city. Kane took a flashlight from the box and swung its beam over the door. In the reflected light that bounced off the close stone walls, the faces of the people who followed the preacher were drawn and tight with tension.

"Do you remember the way?" Kane whispered. He saw grey faces nodding.

"Good. Then light your candles and gather in the great chapel of Clement VI. Mary and I will join you soon. Have everything ready," he hissed.

He reached his hand through the broken pane and unfastened the lock. This room – once part of the original palace – had been converted into the reception area for tourists who travelled from all parts of the world to marvel at the medieval home of Christianity. The Palace of the Popes was the town's most famous landmark, and on a nearby countertop were maps, brochures and a cash register.

The followers lit their candles and went like a solemn procession of feudal priests down the long labyrinth of dark passageways, light leaping along the walls and the sound of their footsteps scuffling on the smooth stone floor. Kane held Mary back until they were alone. He lit a candle, then took her by the hand. Tucked under his arm was one of the two boxes.

"Follow me," he led her through a different door and up a tight spiraling set of stone steps that had been worn down by thousands of feet over hundreds of years. At the top of the steps, the tiny flame from the candle showed the dark mouths of open archways on either side of a long stone passage. Their steps echoed in the cavernous silence as Kane hurried.

At the end of the passage they entered a room with a high vaulted ceiling the candlelight could not reach. Against one wall stood several life-size statues, and against the opposite wall was the stone effigy of a man in robes, stretched out on his death bed.

"This is the northern Sacristy of the palace," Kane explained in a thief's whisper. He pointed to the stone effigy. "That is the tomb of Philippe d'Alencon. He was vicar-general to Pope Urban VI. And that," he pointed across the room, "is the statue of Emperor Charles IV," Kane's voice was hushed with reverence and awe. He felt exalted in the presence of so much papal history. The Palace of the Popes had been an earthly conduit to God through the middle ages. He felt worthy; as though he belonged in such a revered place.

Through an arched doorway on his right he could hear his followers in the next room. They were moving furniture. He could hear their soft stifled grunts as they made their preparations.

Kane set the candle down and drew Mary close to him.

"You remember all I have told you?"

"Yes, preacher," the young girl said softly with dark solemn eyes.

"You understand your role, and you remember what you must say?"

"Yes," she said.

Kane nodded. He opened the box and took out a bottle of wine and a tall crystal glass. He filled it to the brim and handed it to the girl.

"This will sooth your nerves," he said.

She sipped at the wine. It was bitter on her tongue. She took another sip then coughed. Kane stroked her hair while he lulled her with his voice.

"You have been chosen as the sacred vessel…"

"It is your duty to God to be willing and wanting…"

"Your place in Heaven will be assured after tonight…"

A wondrous warm glow began to spread through Mary's body, tingling in her fingertips and blurring the sharp edges of her anxiety. She felt suddenly sleepy and her eyes became heavy. Kane set down the glass.

"Take off your clothes," he instructed.

Mary lifted the hem of her dress over her head and stood naked in the candlelight. Her body was slim, her skin smooth and flawless. Kane groaned aloud. He dropped his eyes, letting them roam over her body with intimate lingering appreciation, and then with gentle authority he began to fondle the girl until he saw her lips part and heard her breath quicken.

"Go into the other room and sit on the end of the altar," Kane's voice was tight and thick with his lust.

Mary went through the archway, guided by the glowing candles of the assembled followers. The rush of her own breathing sounded loud in her ears. The room was vast; she could not see the walls or the high ceiling. Kane's followers were standing gathered in circle around a long wooden table. They were wearing dark robes, and monk's cowls of the same dark cloth enveloped their heads. The candlelights they held seemed to float suspended in the black empty air.

Mary reached the fringe of the circle and the dark shapes parted for her. She stepped to the edge of the table, naked, yet unashamed. Her chin was lifted, her eyes focused on some gloomy space over the heads of the gathering.

From out of the dark a man suddenly began reciting

passages from the Old Testament. He had a deep serious voice and the sound in the huge room was like the rumble of far away thunder rolling across the sky.

Mary waited until she saw Kane appear in the sacristy doorway, holding the candle in his hand. The light lit his face with an eerie glow, accenting the wolfish glitter in his eyes.

"I am the sacred vessel," she announced in a clear firm voice, reciting the words exactly as preacher Kane had taught her. She lifted her arms over her head as if she might reach to Heaven. "I am the cup that holds the secret to the Almighty. Drink from me."

She let her arms fall to her side and slid her bottom onto the edge of the table. The polished wooden surface felt cool and smooth against the naked skin of her buttocks. She lay back with her hands clenched tight at her sides, aware of the unfamiliar tingling sensations of anticipation and fear that spread through her body. She felt she might suffocate, for her breathing choked tight in her chest.

Kane broke through the circle of followers and saw Mary laying on her back with her hair fanned out across the tabletop and her knees drawn up, her legs lewdly wide open.

Like a man in the grips of a trance, Kane moved towards her. The recitation from the bible stopped, replaced instead by soft chanting. The words where mumbled and unintelligible, becoming a hypnotic rhythm of sound that seemed to match the beat of his pounding heart.

Kane slipped his robes and stood naked in the flickering light. His gut hung heavy, his skin pale and pasty, his chest and back covered in thick pelts of whorling black hair. His voice rasped in his throat.

"I am God's messenger on earth," Kane intoned and the chanting became louder, the tempo more urgent. "I am the only one worthy to drink from the Lord's vessel and to hear His words."

\* \* \*

"Oh, my God!" Paulette moaned. "You are like an animal, my darling; a great hammering beast between my legs. Yes! Yes! More!" she gasped theatrically, tossing her head from side to side on the pillow and keeping a watchful eye on the time. It was almost eleven o'clock, and the young soldier rutting on top of her was hopelessly inexperienced.

She lay perfectly still and stifled a yawn, listening to the squeak of the bed. The soldier did not notice. His breath rasped in great foul belches of garlic, and his face turned swollen and coarse. In frustration and disgust, Paulette wrapped her arms around his waist and rolled him over.

"Let me," she said delicately, still carefully swooning her smile. She put the young man on his back and knelt over him, working skillfully with cunning touches of her hands, trying to curb her impatience. The soldier grunted, then sucked in a sharp breath.

Paulette hoped the young soldier was good with a gun, because he had no idea how to –

The gendarme grunted suddenly and made a sound in his throat like he was being strangled. A moment later it was over, and he lay gasping on the sweat-damp sheets like a runner at the end of a marathon.

Relieved, Paulette smiled coquettishly and kissed the soldier on the cheek. She dressed quickly.

Ten minutes later Paulette was scurrying through the

backstreets of Avignon with a black coat wrapped around her shoulders and her heels clutched in her hand to move quietly through the night. She felt breathless – not from exertion, but from tingling anticipation. While the young soldier had been losing his virginity in her bed, Paulette's mind had been a whirl of dark bestial fantasies that were so obscene and perverse, they startled even her weary soul.

The ancient city was dark and silent, and somehow broodingly hostile. She saw no burning candles through shuttered windows and heard no voices. Avignon was battened down for the night as if in dread the next day.

Paulette turned left, then right, then left again, pausing in the shadows of the final corner as a police car cruised through the intersection with its headlights on high beam and its blue lights flashing. There were two policemen in the vehicle, their faces lit by the pale ghostly glow of the dashboard and instruments. Paulette pressed her back to the brick wall of a building and waited until the car went past. She ran the rest of the way with her heart beating wildly in her chest and her breath fluttering in her throat.

"Jacques?" she whispered hoarsely when she reached a narrow laneway shadowed by the western wall. There were apartment buildings on the opposite side of the road with ornate second-floor balconies and iron grills over their windows.

Jacques Lejeune stepped out from the dark mouth of the gateway and signaled her with a brief flash of torchlight.

"I am here," he whispered, relieved that she had appeared.

Paulette crept like a teenager stealing from her parent's home in the dead of night. Jacques lit a cigarette, cupping his hand around the lighter to shield the small flame. Paulette used the glimmer of its glow to find him in the oppressive darkness.

"Do you have your gun?" Paulette stood close to Jacques, her eyes glittering like hard chips of diamond.

"Yes," Jacques said softly. Then his voice faltered with nerves. "But I have been thinking…" He stopped again, wrestling with the words and glad that he could not see the expression on the woman's face. "Perhaps this is too dangerous…"

Paulette crushed her finger to his mouth and the excuses died on Jacques' lips. With her other hand she ran skilled fingers down his body until she cupped his crotch. The resistance shriveled in Jacques throat as he surrendered himself to the tantalizing delight of her touch.

"This is not the time to think, lover," she enticed him breathlessly, crooning in his ear like a witch casting a spell. "This is the time for a brave man of action to win his woman's heart with a single heroic deed."

"But Paulette…" he wheedled.

"One shot, Jacques. Kill one infected ghoul. And in exchange for demonstrating your bravery, you can have as much of me as you can handle."

She crushed herself hard against him, flattening her jutting breasts and the secret hollows of her pelvis to his lanky, angular body. Jacques heard himself gasp. The ache for her was fierce. He gulped down a breath, his senses overwhelmed in a haze of cheap perfume and soft, intoxicating flesh.

"Very well," he abdicated. "If you want me to stand unflinching in the face of death to prove my love for you, then that is what I shall do," he said with valiant heroics to mask his trembling terror.

Jacques unlocked the door.

\* \* \*

"I've got an idea," Tremaine burst into Colonel LeCat's office. The door was open and the main barracks building deserted, although there were lights burning throughout the rest of the gendarmerie compound, powered by generators.

The French commander stood at his window in the soldier's stance with his shoulders squared, balanced on the balls of his feet, and both his hands clasped behind his back. He stared out through the office window at an uninspiring view of the base. Down on the parade ground, two mechanics in fatigues were working late into the night to repair one of the APC's.

LeCat turned. The white light through the window cast his face in a ghostly glow.

"Monsieur?"

"The people stranded in the Grande Hotel. I have an idea how we can rescue them."

LeCat looked weary. The strain of the past twenty-four hours showed in the deeply etched lines that anxiety and tension had chiseled into the flesh around his mouth and eyes.

"I have told you, professor," an edge of irritation came into the Frenchman's voice, "that I will not risk the lives of my men to save them. That includes Camille Pelletier."

"You don't have to," Tremaine's expression brimmed full of energy and agitation. "I have another idea."

LeCat sighed and regarded the American professor the same way weary parents indulge pestering children. He turned from the window and gave Tremaine his

214

attention. "What is this idea?"

Tremaine stopped in front of the Colonel's desk and leaned forward with his hands on the polished wood. A two-way radio lying on a pile of reports squawked with static and garbled voices. Tremaine ignored the distraction. "Grappling hooks," he said.

LeCat frowned. "You mean a grapnel?"

Tremaine shrugged irritably. The definition of the term didn't seem relevant. What mattered was the idea.

"Whatever you want to call it," he said dismissively, and then went on in a rush, the words bubbling up in a tide of enthusiasm. He was like an En plein air artist, working quickly to sketch the broad picture while it remained fresh in his mind. The relevant experts, he supposed, could thrash out the details, later.

"We fire grappling hooks from the wall or one of the gatehouses, and aim for the roof of the hotel. Maybe we can rig some kind of harness… I don't know… but the point is that the hotel is six stories high. The stranded people just need to hook something onto the line and hang on. Gravity will bring them across the road, and keep them out of reach of the infected."

LeCat sat perfectly still for long moments, like he had been carved from stone. He stared fixedly at Tremaine, but there was an opaque glaze over his eyes, as though his attention lay elsewhere. At last he drew a deep breath.

"World War Two," the Frenchman said softly.

Tremaine frowned, and wondered if he had misheard. "Excuse me?"

"During the Second World War, elite commando troops fired grapnel hooks from two-inch mortars," LeCat explained. "They used the idea to overcome difficult defenses, and during the D-Day landings…"

215

"Then it will work, right?"

LeCat said nothing. Tremaine's face became tortured in the fraught silence. He could smell his own stale body odor. He ran the palm of his hand over his jaw and it rasped with stubble.

"Will it work?" he tried again, his eyes boring into LeCat's.

"We have some small mortars," LeCat conceded carefully. "And we have plenty of grapnel hooks and rope..."

"Then it will work!" Tremaine enthused.

LeCat held up his hand. "Not so fast," he pushed himself out of the chair. First I must speak to my engineers and discover more... and second, we must wait until daybreak, professor. This cannot be attempted in the middle of the night. If there are still survivors in the hotel at dawn... we may be able to mount a rescue attempt."

\* \* \*

Kane stepped between Mary's splayed open legs and closed his eyes. He was trembling. Adrenalin coursed thick in his blood. The rapture of sexual and spiritual anticipation left his mind swirling and his body shaking. He thrust himself forward and savored the glorious ecstasy.

"Speak to me, Almighty God!" Kane threw back his head and lifted his eyes to the high ceiling. "Let your divine guidance be heard. Show us the path we must follow to exalt you."

Mary felt the press of him and she held her breath and arched her back off the table. She could smell him; the sweat of an unwashed body mingled with stale garlic

216

and cheap wine. She bit down on her lip and then her eyes flew wide open and a gasp like a groan was torn from her throat.

She heard Kane sigh and then felt the weight of him as he came over her. Mary whimpered and stifled a shuddering sob. A strange sense of sanctity overwhelmed her. She felt like a sacrifice spread out on an altar; an offering to God for mankind's salvation.

When it was over and Kane lay heavy upon her, his breath roaring in her ear and his heart beating like a drum, Mary stayed very still, breathing deeply.

The chanting from the circle of followers undulated around the vast empty space, the sound rising and falling as they waited expectantly to see what would happen next. The darkness settled over the chapel like a funeral pall. The silence became so intense and complete that it seemed to crush down on their voices with a physical weight until they were barely whispering.

At last Kane stood and straightened. He seemed somehow deflated; as if all the energy and vitality that made him such a towering, powerful presence had been drawn from him, leaving just a husk. His eyes were sad and blank, and on his face was an unfathomable expression that could have been remorse or regret... or guilt. He looked vaguely grotesque; an overweight middle-aged man standing naked and shriveled.

"I have seen the face of God," he spread his hands and pronounced solemnly, "and I have heard the Almighty's words."

There was an audible superstitious gasp from the dark circle of followers, and they craned forward, fearful of missing a single word from the preacher's mouth.

"He has spoken to me and told me again that I am His divine messenger."

"Did God tell you what we should do?" a voice asked.

"Yes," Kane said gravely, in a tone befitting someone who bore the heavy burden of mankind's survival on his shoulders. "God told me that His true believers are safe from the infection. We are shielded by His love. He told me that only by serving Him would we be assured our places in Heaven." In the flickering light his eyes suddenly glowed with the religious fanaticism of a zealot.

"Then we should leave the city and go amongst the infected to heal and tend to them?"

"Yes," Kane nodded. "And I shall lead you, just as Moses led his people out of the wilderness, so shall I walk with you amongst the sick to salve their disease."

There was a ripple of hushed excited murmurs around the circle.

Kane held up his hands in an appeal for silence.

"Tomorrow," he declared. "Tomorrow is the day we must save mankind with our love. Leave this place now and spend the rest of this night in prayer."

"But how do we get out of the city?" a woman asked, her voice brittle with anxiety. "The soldiers will not let us leave. They are soulless. They do not care for God's plan."

"Violence," Kane declared. "Through one act of violence we can nourish the entire world with love."

The answer seemed vague and cryptic. The followers lapsed into awkward confused hush, unsure whether the order to use violence was God's message or Kane's suggestion.

"How?" someone asked meekly.

There was a long troubled silence before suddenly – from out of the oppressive darkness – a new voice spoke, high-pitched and somehow disembodied.

"You must capture one of the blue tank cars that the

218

soldiers drive and ram the steel gate at the university."

Stretched out on the table, legs splayed and her eyes closed, Mary hadn't even realized she had spoken.

\* \* \*

Chuck Gudinski lay panting and shaken beneath the chassis of a Renault, and cursed bitterly.

He had crawled with infinite patience across four lanes of abandoned vehicles, worming forward inch by painstaking inch in the darkness until he had reached the far side of the road... and now he could go no further.

His face was a tight grimace of aching agony; his fingers were bare broken stumps of bloody flesh, and he felt lightheaded with blood loss. His arms and shoulders ached from the torture of clawing his bodyweight forward across the hard tarmac, and his chest and lungs burned with exertion.

The moon had risen high in the sky, beyond the skeins of the smoke-laden horizon, and now the nightmare world surrounding him was bathed in a soft pale glow.

Ahead, the ground between the roadside and the walls of Avignon was littered with a carnage of dead corpses and milling hordes of undead. The infected trampled the bodies underfoot, clamoring and snarling in mindless madness at a section of the high wall where two gendarmes were firing indiscriminately into the dark swarming mass beneath them. Flashlight beams probed the night and the sound of assault rifle fire ripped the dark apart.

Chuck lay perfectly still and cursed the gendarmes. He put his head down on the rough surface of the road and wept silent sobs of despair.

Away from the horde swarming around the wall there were other undead ghouls, moving in the ghostly moonlight. They were going like feral thieves amongst the bloated corpses, pausing on their haunches to gnaw at a pale arm, or to bite off stiff lifeless fingers with their teeth.

Chuck watched them from the corner of his eye, terrified that at any instant they might detect him. He cupped the bleeding mess of one hand over his mouth to muffle his wheezing breath.

The undead beneath the blazing gunfire numbered in their thousands he guessed. There was no way he could crawl the last thirty yards to the wall through that savage horror and survive. Despair and desolation wrapped around him like a funeral shroud.

He heard himself sob and blinked, startled at the realization he was weeping. The terror came back to him then on big beating wings; the nerve-shattering fear that he had held at bay through the endless hours of crawling now perched itself on his shoulders, pecking like a vulture at the last shreds of his sanity. He heard phantom sounds behind him and his body racked tight with dread.

"Please God!" he prayed. "Don't let me die. Not like this."

He had never believed in God and never attended church. He was too logical to believe the myth of the bible and its stories. He was a man of science... until death seemed suddenly inevitable. Now he prayed fervently and passionately.

"Please God!"

To keep a leash on his terror he distracted himself by thinking of Sherry. He remembered their first date, and the first time he had met her parents. Images came to him like snapshots; polaroids of perfect summer days and

220

winter nights in her bed.

He thought then about his parents and his sister back in Pennsylvania. Were they still alive? He doubted it, and the realization left him so overcome with sad bereavement that for long seconds he did not recognize the sudden far-away sound or understand its significance. It was only when the undead horde began to move, and the ground vibrated with thousands of stomping feet, that Chuck Gudinski looked up with sudden alarm.

The infected were leaping and howling like a vast herd of wild animals at hunt. He heard gunfire then; a continuous clamor of machine gun fire, muted by distance. He shot a searching glance along the wall and saw the bright spitting orange flame of a muzzle flash. It was coming from several hundred yards further north, and the harsh sound drew the undead towards it, whipping them up into a fresh stampeding frenzy.

Chuck waited. His lips were dried to white flakes and cracked through to raw flesh, his eyes gummed up with yellow clots of mucus and stinging with sweat. One by one the scavengers who had been picking through the bloated corpses nearby turned to follow the ripping sound of gunfire until suddenly the ground before him seemed deserted.

Chuck stared at the dark arched doorway directly ahead of him. He could see no soldiers on the nearby battlements and that bothered him. Had they gone? Would anyone hear his gasping cry for help before the infected savaged him?

He had no choice. He had to move now, or die where he lay.

He groped for a handful of soft green grass and hauled himself forward. The sound of his body dragging itself off the road was so loud in the sudden silence that he clenched his teeth and cringed. He was lathered in nervous sweat. He crawled over bodies and through blood and guts. He scrambled over severed limbs and startled scampering rats.

Ten yards from the small gateway he heard the sudden harsh sound of metal scraping against metal. He paused, wide-eyed and cocked his head to the side. The sound came again, chunky and vaguely familiar.

He waited, his breath jammed in his throat. He could hear his blood thumping at his temples. He felt himself gripped by a sudden swoop of dizzy vertigo and a moment of terrifying blackness. Then he heard a piercing screech and a blinding needle of white light stabbed into the night.

The wooden door within the gatehouse was opening. The torchlight jerked and shook erratically.

Chuck began to cry huge fat oily tears of relief. He was saved.

He lifted one aching arm and tried to call out for help. His voice croaked in his throat.

He was going to make it.

\* \* \*

Jacques Lejeune was sweating with fear; trembling under a cold clammy sense of terror that threatened to suffocate him. He thrust the torch out through the cracked open gateway and flashed the bright beam across the grass in front of the door. His hand shook so the light jerked erratically over the nightmarish scene of devastation.

The ground had been trampled to dirt and blood-soaked mud by thousands of rampaging feet. Dark grotesque lumps lay scattered in attitudes of horrific

222

torture. Flies buzzed in dark swarming clouds from the corpses. The stench of corruption coated his tongue and the back of his mouth with its oily, sickening tang. He heard himself gasp and choke back the urge to be physically ill.

"I... I cannot go out there!" He turned, pale-faced with horror.

"You must!" Paulette pouted. She stood close behind Jacques, her body pressed against his back. The heavy wooden door hung open just a few inches. She could not see past the man's skeletal frame.

"I cannot." Jacques shivered.

Paulette pulled the door open a few more inches. It screeched on rusted old hinges.

The beam of the flashlight caught on a body just a few yards to their left. It had been a woman. Her arms were very thin and pale, spattered with mud. One of her legs was missing and part of her face had been gnawed away. Paulette gasped and covered her mouth – then shivered deliciously. A hot rush of arousal washed through her, so intense that she swayed on her feet and had to clutch at Jacques to keep her balance. The sudden weight against him pushed Jacques forward – he tripped out of the doorway and into the fear-filled night.

The gun weighed heavy in his right hand. Jacques shivered spasmodically. He turned, silently pleading, back to the archway. Paulette stood wedged in the opening, her eyes wide and glittering with excitement.

"Shoot one of the infected, Jacques!" she whispered. She felt her blood quicken and her heart begin to pound.

Jacques' lips parted and another fit of trembling overtook him. Saliva dribbled down his chin. His jaw hung slack and unhinged.

Far away and lit by firelight he could see the

silhouettes of thousands of undead in a howling knot under the city's walls. Gunfire barked from the battlements and the sound of the clamor carried to him on waves of noise like surf breaking on a beach.

He swung the beam of the flashlight across the ground at his feet and let it fix on another mud-splattered corpse. The emaciated, skeletal frame was covered in loose baggy skin and shreds of a dark woolen suit. The old man had been disemboweled. Jacques could see the rack of the ribs and the half-eaten organs of his stomach.

Jacques took a faltering step closer to the maimed corpse and then froze. He had sensed movement somewhere close, not definite enough to pin-point and not so abrupt that he could be sure. It was a premonition that something lurked nearby in the dark. He choked on a breath and heard a sound like a wheeze of weak agony. A cold chill ran down his spine and his eyes flew wide. He slashed the torch from side to side in a frenzy of wild swatting strokes until it fixed on a figure laying on its stomach, about ten yards from the gate.

It was a man, Jacques saw. He was covered in mud and slime. His hair lay matted flat and stiff against the skull and his face was twisted into a tortured rictus of immense agony. But it was the eyes in the deep hollow cage of their sockets that struck fear into Jacques. They were wild and burning, filled with a look of insanity.

He heard himself gasp in fear and revulsion. He heard Paulette's sharp intake of breath from the doorway.

"It is one of the infected!" Paulette thrilled. "Shoot him, Jacques, my brave hero," her voice was husky with perverse erotic arousal. "Kill him for me!"

Jacques took a faltering step closer. The figure seemed to be maimed, trailing a long slick of dark blood in the grass.

Jacques lifted the gun and felt its dreadful weight, heavy as lead in his trembling hand.

"Shoot the ghoul!" Paulette squealed.

Chuck Gudinski made a supreme effort and gasped a desperate croak from between his bleeding lips. He reached up the bloody tattered stump of one hand in a beckoning plea for rescue.

"He's lunging for me!" Jacques cried out. Abject terror blinded him. He pulled the trigger and the gun hammered brutally in his grip, the recoil throwing his hand high in the air. The sound was an almighty roar that battered his ears and numbed his senses.

He dragged the gun down and fired again and again. He heard the meaty sound of bullets striking flesh.

When the echo of the sharp retorts had faded, Jacques stood over the dead body and let the violent thrill of the moment consume him. Savage emotion seemed to swell in his chest and turned his legs to trembling jelly.

"I killed one of the undead," the realization triggered some ruthless primal instinct, coarse and brutal, and he stared down at the corpse as if trying to burn the gory image into his mind. "I have killed."

Unseen from the darkness of the road, two undead ghouls emerged out of the night, moving towards the deafening sound of the gunshots like predatory panthers. One of then vaulted over the trunk of a wrecked car and came hunting towards Jacques, snarling ferociously.

The tall Frenchman saw the danger too late. His eyes flew wide and began to bulge. The blood drained from his face.

"My God!" he croaked. He turned to run back to the open doorway, his voice shrill and hysterical. "Save me!"

Mud flew from the heels of his shoes. He slipped and went over on his knees. The ghoul launched itself and landed on Jacques' back while the other infected beast charged at the open door where Paulette stood, suddenly white faced with horror.

Jacques heard himself screaming and icy blackness filled his head. The ghoul clawed at his face with its fingers, slashing his cheek and gouging out one of his eyes. Jacques had the sudden unbidden image of a zebra being caught in the jaws of a lion, thrashing its hooves feebly while the great cat ate it alive.

He felt the weight of the savage beast bear him down into the mud and then monstrous pain explode in pinwheels of color behind his eyes. He felt a sudden burning sensation and wondered if it was the spread of the infection through his bloodstream. He began to scream and died choking in his own blood.

Paulette had just a split second to react as the other undead ghoul bounded towards her. She started to force the great wooden door shut, screaming in fear, her hysterical terror echoing insanely in her own ears. The ghoul slammed into the closing door and the impact was so violent that it flung Paulette off her feet. She fell onto her back on the cold cobblestones of the laneway.

The ghoul threw itself at the door again. Paulette's legs were wedged in the opening. The infected beast slashed at her with its hands, slicing the flesh below her right knee open. Paulette cried out and clutched at the wound. Her fingers came away coated with sticky blood. She held them up before her eyes and screamed even louder, the sound becoming breathless and shrill as a steaming kettle.

Sixty yards away atop the wall, two gendarmes heard the wicked crack of three gunshots and came instantly alert. They ran along the parapet towards the source of the sound and then heard the high-pitched horrible

226

screaming. Flashlights criss-crossed the ground. Bodies lay everywhere in the mud. Then they heard the sickening savage growl of the infected and they stopped in their tracks, suddenly chilled with dread.

"Alarm! Alarm!" one of the gendarmes snatched the two-way radio from his webbing belt. He was breathless, his face pale and his hand shaking.

"The undead have broken into the city. They have broken through the Poterne Raspail gate."

\* \* \*

Colonel LeCat was dozing fitfully in his office chair when the two-way on his desk suddenly burst into frantic noise. He snapped instantly alert and seized the radio.

"Repeat!" he barked.

"Poterne Raspail!" the voice shouted through a hiss of static. "The infected have broken through the doorway."

"How many?"

"Unknown – " the reply was drowned out by a sharp burst of gunfire.

LeCat cursed. "Send the ready reserve!" he growled. "And hold your position. I am on my way."

\* \* \*

The two young gendarmes on duty had to sling their weapons and climb down ladders to get off the ramparts. They dropped to the cobblestoned ground and crouched side-by-side, their eyes wide with fear. The darkness was like a heavy blanket, but the sounds of the undead were unmistakable. The gendarmes could hear their ragged breathing, bubbling and hissing in their throats. One of the soldiers flicked on his flashlight and quartered the dark space around the gate.

The beam of bright blinding light fell on a hunched, obscene figure, squatting over a woman's body beside the open door. The ghoul was naked, its flesh grey, the cage of its ribs exposed through oozing bite marks and flaps of dead rotting skin that hung from the flank of its torso. It was a vile, disfigured creature with no hair, so wasted and gaunt that the knuckles of its spine and the bones of its shoulder blades showed clearly through tightly-stretched flesh.

The infected ghoul had its hands buried deep within the dead woman's chest, and there was fresh spattered blood on the beast's arms, all the way up to its elbows. Struck by the sudden light it looked up at the soldiers. The ghoul's eyes were enormous. It opened its mouth and snarled at them through broken teeth and purple swollen gums.

The soldiers opened fire from twenty yards, hitting the infected zombie full in the chest. The impact flung the ghoul down on its back. It lay, twisting and writhing, howling and thrashing at the ground. One of the soldiers came upright, weapon pressed into his shoulder, and went cautiously forward.

The sound of his footsteps scuffed on the cobblestones.

He was breathing hard, pumped full of adrenalin and raw fear. He could feel his trigger-finger trembling. The beam of light stayed fixed on the infected body.

The ghoul had been hit three times in the chest. Dark holes had been punched through the emaciated corpse. It still writhed on the ground, but now the movements were slow and drugged-like.

The soldier stopped three yards short of the body and aimed at the hideous, monstrous face. Almost drowned out by the sound of his own hoarse breathing in his ears he could hear the second gendarme shouting into his two-way radio while he tried to keep the ghoul within the beam of his flashlight.

"I think it is dead."

"Are you sure, Pierre?"

"I think so," the soldier standing close to the body squeaked. He had never seen combat action before. Sweat leaked into his eyes and his heart seemed to have swollen in his chest so each breath was an effort. "It's… it's stopped moving."

"Shoot it again to be sure." The second soldier came out of his crouch and ran forward, but before he could reach the open door another undead figure suddenly burst through the gatehouse and lunged at him.

Both soldiers turned and convulsed in terror. A burst of ragged gunfire buried itself in the ancient stonework of the wall. The second soldier went down under the weight of his attacker, flailing his fists and screaming.

The undead ghoul was frenzied with the madness of its infection. It clawed at the soldier with his hooked butchering hands and tore long ribbons of bloody flesh from the gendarme's cheek, then bit off his nose. The gendarme screamed a blood-curdling howl of agony. The sound seemed to enflame the zombie's instincts. It arched its back and flared up like a coiling cobra, poised to strike. The soldier underneath it squirmed and coughed. Blood filled the young man's mouth. The undead ghoul launched itself forward and latched its gaping jaws into the soft flesh of the writhing soldier's exposed throat. The gendarme died gurgling and screaming.

The men of the ready reserve saved the western wall. The two armored cars arrived in the laneway from different directions behind a blaze of blindingly bright spotlights and a roar of engine noises. They slewed the heavy armored vehicles to block the roads that ran like veins into the warren of nearby side streets, barricading the way forward for the undead.

"Fire!" one vehicle commander, crammed into the open cupola of the cockpit roared the order, and beside him, his gunner swung the vehicle's machine gun onto the wild frenzy of struggling shapes in the doorway.

A long flickering tongue of flame leaped from the mouth of the weapon and the sound in the little laneway juddered and echoed against the walls of the surrounding buildings.

Colonel LeCat arrived in a P4 jeep and came running past one of the APC's just as the armed gendarmes were spilling out of the back doors of the vehicle.

"Soldiers! Soldiers!" he shouted the word.

He ran straight for the gateway. "Soldiers!" The men of the ready reserve were the most experienced troops from the barracks, veteran fighters who had seen active duty in many of the world's trouble spots. "Soldiers!"

LeCat snatched the sidearm on his hip from its holster and stared, fuming. How had the undead breached the doorway? A burst of assault rifle fire from behind his shoulder joined the hammering batter of the APC's machine guns. LeCat could see just a jumble of thrashing bodies under the door's stone arch, but he recognized figures in blood-soaked uniforms and understood that soldiers had been attacked and infected. He put that thought out of his mind an instant after it registered. His task, and the task of the ready reserve, was to contain the infected before they could wreck havoc in the nearby streets, and to close the open door before more of the undead could surge through the breach.

LeCat saw an obscene pale figure in the midst of the

scrambling melee suddenly break free of the struggling knot in the doorway and come in a scampering charge towards him. The ghoul looked like a starved wretch from the horrors of a nightmare. Its skin was sickly grey, oozing puss from a dozen open wounds, and the flesh of its hairless head had shrunk and shriveled tight over the skull.

LeCat ran forward to meet the attack, snarling a challenge. "Follow me!"

He sprinted into the laneway, boots echoing loud on the ancient cobblestones, and fired at the charging ghoul on the run. The pistol kicked in his hand, the recoil pulsing all the way up his shoulder, and the sound of its retort loud in his ears. The shot struck the ghoul between the eyes and a perfect round hole appeared in the withered ugly flesh. The ghoul was flung on its back by the close-range impact and didn't move again.

"Get to the door!" LeCat shouted at two of the gendarmes who had followed him across the narrow lane. There were other men close behind, but in the confined space there was little room to move and no way that the support troops could find open fields of fire. It was up to LeCat and the men beside him to clear a path to the door.

LeCat ran on, careless of the danger. He saw the ruin of a woman's body lying on the ground. Her clothes had been shredded and her chest ripped open. Blood and guts ran across the cobblestones, slippery as oil. Beside the woman's corpse he saw the thrashing boots of a young soldier. He had been flung onto his back. His throat had been ripped out. The gaping wound in the soldier's neck was gruesome.

A snarling figure suddenly turned and leaped at LeCat from beneath the stone arch of the gateway. It had been half-hidden from the APC's bright search lights. Now it pounced out of the shadows like a wild animal.

It had once been a middle-aged man; now it was a disfigured creature in a blood-spattered shirt that hung down over a swollen gut. The front of its ragged trousers were stained with gore and stank of stale urine. It howled fiercely at the soldiers. Thick brown blood bubbled in its throat and spilled from the slash of its rotting mouth.

It lashed out at LeCat with its hooked hand. LeCat deflected the attack with his forearm and the soldier running at the Colonel's shoulder was clawed across the face. The man dropped his gun and spun away with a high shriek of terror. He was not badly wounded and the cry was not of pain. But shock and black unholy fear tore the terror from his throat in a shrill scream.

The soldier sank down on his knees, sobbing and gasping. "I have been infected!" the soldier gasped. The zombie pounced on the fallen man and bit his ear off before another gendarme following close behind shot the ghoul in the head.

LeCat lunged desperately for the heavy open door. Through the open archway he could hear the thunder of approaching footsteps pounding through mud like the sound of racehorses as they turn into the finishing straight of a race. The ground seemed to tremble and the black night shook.

Along the battlements overhead, gunfire erupted and the noise of ten thousand maddened voices suddenly rose to a frenzied crescendo. The undead had been drawn to the heavy fusillades of machine gun fire around the gateway. They were out there, LeCat knew, and rushing towards the open door.

He threw his weight against the heavy door and it

groaned on rusted hinges. The ground was slick with blood and someone's guts. He couldn't get purchase for his feet.

Three undead figures swarmed in through the closing doorway. They were snarling, savage beasts. The insanity of their infection made them mindless. They lunged at the closest soldiers and knocked them tumbling from their feet. Behind the shield of the door, LeCat screwed his face tight with effort and dug the toes of his boots into the slippery stone cobbles. The door gave a last groan of rusted resistance, and then closed. LeCat threw his weight against the door and wrestled with the first bolt. His hands were slippery with sweat. On the other side of the door the first of the undead flung themselves against the barrier. The door kicked and bucked.

"Soldiers!" LeCat barked. "Soldiers to me!"

The fight in the laneway was close to getting out of hand. The three undead were wrecking havoc. LeCat could smell the stench of their rotting corpses and their foul fetid breath. He could smell the fear of his men and he sensed the fight was on the verge of being lost. The undead were mindless killing machines and the close confines of the lane gave his men no space.

"Soldiers!" Two men were down on the ground, clutching at savage wounds and coughing, but one gendarme forced his way through the frantic madness and reached the doorway. He threw his shoulder against the rough wood and rammed home the ancient steel bolt. There was another bolt at the bottom of the door. The gendarme stomped at it with his boot.

"Stay here!" LeCat shouted to the man. Then he turned and understood instantly that Avignon was on the brink of falling.

A ghoul lunged at a gendarme and the man reeled

back and fell over. The undead beast screamed like a banshee and clawed at the fallen soldier's face. Another gendarme fired a snap shot that struck the infected ghoul in the arm and spun it around. The battle had degenerated into a brawling street-fight. Assault rifles were useless in the cramped space and the undead had the advantage.

"Kill them!" LeCat came out of the darkened doorway with his pistol in his hand, gasping, his chest heaving for air. His eyes were cold and flat and merciless. He threw up the weapon to fire at one of the mud-spattered creatures but had to abort the shot for fear of hitting his own man. He swung his heavy boot at the ghoul instead and felt the weight of the impact smash in ribs and break bones. Automatic fire exploded close to his ear and he turned to see a nearby gendarme going to ground. Another of the infected was wrestling with the man, snapping at him with gaping jaws. LeCat put the muzzle of the pistol to the back of the zombie's head and blew its brains out in a cloud of grey custard content.

There were two still of the undead loose in the laneway and the gendarmes were falling back. The ghouls were like enraged bulls, maddened by their infection and their eyes filled with insanity.

The cobblestones were slick with blood and the lane filled with the screams of the dying. Another gendarme went down as a ghoul lunged for him. The zombie latched on to the man's leg and bit through the stuff of his uniform like a savaging dog. The soldier threw back his head and screamed in agony. There was naked terror in his eyes. He turned, pleading for help. The men around him shrank away, knowing he was doomed.

"Behind the APC's!" LeCat shouted over the madness and mayhem of the melee. "Withdraw!"

The soldiers turned and ran, and the ghouls went bounding after them.

LeCat filled his lungs, then called to the machine gunners aboard the armored vehicles.

"Fire!"

A straggling gendarme got caught in the blaze of fire that erupted from the two vehicles. His body was torn to shreds. Another man staggered from a bullet wound before he got clear. LeCat threw himself flat on the blood-soaked cobblestones and the flail of gunfire swept over him. It went on for thirty hammering seconds and then the guns fell suddenly and dramatically silent.

LeCat lifted his face slowly. Smoke hung in the air and his ears were ringing from the heavy percussion. The two ghouls lay under the bright beams of the spotlights. One had been dismembered by the brutal fusillade. The corpse lay in broken pieces of bone and gore. The other had taken so many hits it no longer bore any resemblance to the man it had once been; it had been butchered by gunfire.

When LeCat got to his feet, he felt a sudden rush of vertigo and relief. He glanced back at the door and saw it was still locked. The man he had posted there was pressed against the wall and grim-faced.

LeCat let his gaze sweep slowly around the lane. His features fixed in a tight grimace, and his eyes narrowed to slits. There were a dozen dead bodies, sprawled on the cobblestones in tortured blood-soaked attitudes of death. Most of them were gendarmes.

"Head shot them all," his voice sounded raw and scratchy as he gave the order to the ready reserve's Captain. His heart raced as if he had run a long way, but his face was stony. "We cannot take the chance that some who died are infected and will come back to life.

Then I want all the corpses and remains burned."

* * *

The dawn's light was still just a sickly pale glow on the horizon when Tremaine climbed to the top of the Porte Saint Roch gatehouse. Without a breeze to stir it, the air was oppressive; a miasma of rotting festering smells that rose from the undead hordes and hung like a languid blanket over the city. Tremaine wrinkled his nose and felt his eyes begin to water.

Colonel LeCat was already standing at the battlements. He had a handkerchief knotted over his mouth and nose. The soldiers around him were subdued and bleary-eyed. On the ground between them sat a small modified mortar, several long coils of thick rope, and four steel grapnel hooks. The hooks looked to Tremaine like boat anchors. Each had four sharp claws. The mortar was set on a square base-plate weighted down with sandbags and elevated by a bi-pod. It had been aimed towards the Grande Hotel.

LeCat handed the binoculars to Tremaine. The Colonel's uniform was rumpled and stained with dark spots of blood. "There are no signs of life in the hotel," the Frenchman said.

Tremaine lifted the glasses to his eyes and ran them slowly over the façade of the building across the wide road. The lower floor windows were scorched and blackened, but the upper floors seemed undamaged. Tremaine scanned every window on the fourth and fifth floor, looking for telltale signs of movement. He saw nothing and a heavy sense of despair made his shoulders sag.

"They might still be alive," he handed the binoculars

back to the Colonel. "They could be hiding in one of the rooms on the opposite side of the building."

LeCat shrugged. "We will soon find out," he said grimly.

One of the gendarmes came forward with a bullhorn. LeCat snatched the handkerchief from his mouth.

"Camille Pelletier!" the sound from the speaker was monstrous in the still morning air. "Camille Pelletier, this is Colonel LeCat. Can you hear me?"

For a long moment there was still silence. LeCat raised the bullhorn again. "Camille Pelletier!"

Suddenly a window on the sixth floor blew outwards in an explosion of flying glass, followed by the dark bulk of a chair. A pale, exhausted face appeared in the jagged space and Tremaine felt his spirits lift with sudden relief.

Under the magnification of the binoculars, Camille looked haggard with fatigue. Her blonde hair hung lank against her skull and her eyes had receded in her face, underscored by dark bruises. Her cheeks looked hollow and her skin had a tired waxen cast. She called out at the top of her voice but the words were drowned by the rumbling growls from the undead that filled the street below.

LeCat nodded his own secret relief. Tremaine saw the ghost of a smile on the Colonel's forbidding face.

"You must go to the roof!" LeCat shouted into the bullhorn to carry his voice. "We are going to send ropes across."

Camille was leaning on the frame of the window, and there was something desperate and yearning in her posture. She waved her hand to signal her understanding, then disappeared from the window.

LeCat threw down the bullhorn and turned to his mortar crew. "Do it now!"

The three-man crew had been at the gatehouse battlements for an hour before daybreak, and had test-fired the pneumatic weapon three times at the barracks the night before. They fitted the first grappling hook into the narrow tube and after a long moment of preparation, fired.

There was a sharp sound like a cough, and the hook shot from the barrel of the weapon and sailed high into the air on a steep parabola, whistling as it flew. The attached rope trailed like a gossamer thread. Tremaine watched with his heart in his mouth. The hook arched higher until it reached the zenith of its climb and then began to fall. The trailing rope whirred from its coil.

For a sinking moment, it looked like the hook might overshoot the hotel completely. Tremaine held his breath. The hook dropped like a falling star across the sky and landed on the hotel's roof in a cloud of dust.

A ragged cheer went up from the men at the battlements.

LeCat turned. His expression had not changed. "Now it is up to the survivors," he said to Tremaine without emotion.

* * *

The roof of the Grande Hotel was a flat concrete maze of pipes and rusting air conditioning boxes that could be accessed from room 612 on the sixth floor. The room was on the opposite side of the building with a view across Avignon's sprawling outer suburbs. Outside the room's window hung a steel ladder, bolted to the building's wall.

Camille gathered the remaining survivors about her in the sixth-floor hallway. They were drooping with fatigue

238

and nervous exhaustion, grey and ashen figures that seemed to have shrunk during the long torturous hours.

"The army has sent rope across from the city walls," Camille explained. Her voice croaked and rasped. She felt shaky. Her skin looked pale and felt tight as a drum across her cheeks.

"Are they sending men across to rescue us somehow?" an elderly woman asked.

"It's not possible," Camille said. "But it means we still have a fighting chance to survive."

"How?"

"We will have to zip-line," Camille said, then explained. As she spoke she saw the last lights of hope fade from the eyes of people around her. They were old and frail, and on the brink of collapsing with exhaustion. The idea of clinging to a rope or a leather belt to ride down a line to the city's walls was physically impossible.

"I would never make it," a woman from the back of the group shook her head forlornly. Others close by nodded. There was no outrage; no frustration – just a weary bovine acceptance that their last chance to survive was no chance at all.

In small disconsolate groups the survivors began to drift away. Some disappeared into nearby rooms where they sank down on the floor to rest. Others went to the end of the corridor and stood before the fire-doors as if expecting the undead to break through the final barricaded stairwell. Old Mr. Davis spoke up.

He came from out of the dwindling crowd on stork-like legs and stood at Camille's shoulder. He had a devilish twinkle in his eye. He gave a dapper little smile.

"There is a way…" he lifted his voice so that it reached into the closest rooms. "We can tie a Swiss set rappel harness."

239

Camille blinked. "Monsieur?"

The Englishman brushed at his moustache with the tip of his finger. "I spent some time in the Royal Navy back in the fifties, my darling. Learned some fancy rope tricks along the way, what?" his accent was a fraud of jaunty upper-class breeding.

"What is this rope harness?" Camille became intrigued. From the corner of her eye she saw some of the survivors drift curiously back from the end of the corridor.

"It's a kind of seat, my love," Mr. Davis still had the energy for a flirty wink. "All we need is enough rope and something to cut it with."

A pocket-knife was found amongst the ransacked luggage. Camille went running along the corridor into room 612. The window had been screwed down. Camille hurled a chair through the tinted glass.

"I will go first," she turned back to the others. "Do what I do, and put your feet in the same places I put mine."

She climbed carefully out onto the windowsill, then reached for a rung of the ladder with her hand. When she had a firm grip, she swung herself across and felt for a foothold. Camille was flushed in the face and shaking. She had a fear of heights. She caught a quick view of the ground between her feet and gasped with a sudden attack of vertigo.

"Don't look down!" she admonished herself.

The climb to the roof was easy. At the top there were iron handholds. She swung her leg over the waist high wall that surrounded the rooftop and stood panting and trembling. Her hair hung into her eyes. She swept it away with a brusque flick of her fingers, and then saw the line of rope attached to a steel hook. One of the barbed prongs had snagged on the cage of an air-conditioning box. The box was the shape and size of a large refrigerator laid on its side, with wire vents that covered fan blades.

Camille sagged with relief. She untied the line from the hook and went running back to the ladder. None of the other survivors were poised in the window. She frowned and called loudly. Mr. Davis thrust his head through the opening.

"On my way," he said brightly, but his face looked hectic with agitation.

While Camille waited for the elderly Englishman to climb up the ladder she walked a slow circuit of the hotel's roof, gasping as each new horror was revealed. For as far as she could see the world was shrouded in the smoke of a thousand fires, turning the rising sun into a blood-red fireball. She had seen this phenomenon before during the summer months when vast tracts of forest had burned and the TV news cameras showed firefighters battling the spreading blazes. There was something doom-laden and eerie about the image that gave her chills of foreboding.

She reached the far side of the roof and stared at the walls of Avignon. Camille could see a knot of men standing on the Porte Saint Roch gatehouse. She wondered if one of them was the American professor.

The wide road between the two buildings was a writhing, heaving sea of undead bodies. They moved like water around the battered and burnt-out carcasses of abandoned cars, and they howled like wild animals. The putrid stench of death and corruption rose up from ground level and made Camille's eyes water. She reeled away from the stench as if she had been punched with an uppercut, smothering her mouth with her hand.

241

Mr. Davis came stepping across the roof.

"Where are the others?" Camille frowned.

"Still down in room 612," he said casually.

"Why. They must come up to the roof."

"Yes," he agreed. "But we all had a vote, you see. And everyone decided that you should be the first to test the line, Camille. You're the lightest and the fittest. And when you make it across, you can ask the soldiers to send over extra rope. We'll need more to harness everybody."

Camille felt herself bridle. There was something offensive about the Englishman's reasoning. It might have been her sense of chivalry, or perhaps her sense of duty. The elderly and frail should be the first ones saved. If the hotel had been a sinking ship, it would have been women and children first…

"Mrs. Witterstein is a small woman. She would be lighter than me. She should go first. And then Mrs. Hartigan…"

Mr. Davis looked pained with embarrassment. "I agree," he said diplomatically. "And they're the next two ladies coming up the ladder. But they're old and scared, Camille. They want to see this rope harness first. I told them I would fit it to you."

Camille stayed tense, her expression dubious. She stared into the elderly Englishman's eyes and saw nothing but polite innocence. Camille nodded her head.

Mr. Davis drew the line from the gatehouse taut and tied it off around a six-inch steel pipe. He hacked the remaining rope free with the knife.

Camille stood with her legs apart and her arms stretched wide. Mr. Davis looped the rope around her narrow waist and tied two half-hitch knots in front of her belt buckle. He let the loose ends drop to the ground then fed them between her legs and tied each piece to the loop around her waist. When he was finished, the harness was a pattern of knots across the front of her body and looped securely under both her buttocks. The Englishman looped the remaining rope over the zip-line and tied it off securely.

He stood back admiring his work. Camille felt tightly trussed. Mr. Davis tugged on the knots, looking pleased.

"What do you think?" he propped his bony hands on his hips. His trousers and shirt were rumpled and sweat stained.

Camille tried to bend at the knees. The rope that looped the zip-line was too short. Mr. Davis led her to the edge of the roof and sat her sidesaddle on the low wall.

"Okay," he stepped back. "Can you wait for a few minutes until I fetch Mrs. Witterstein? I'm sure once she sees the harness, she'll be confident it will hold her for the crossing."

Camille nodded. She had her bottom resting on the low wall and her feet dangled. Instinctively, one hand clutched the rope that tethered the rig to the zip line.

"Quickly," Camille said. "Soon the infected will break through to the sixth floor."

The old man smiled sadly and suddenly his whole demeanor changed. Gone was the spritely step and the sparkling jaunty eyes, and in there place stood a tired, exhausted old man. Something heartbreakingly tender crept into his expression. A shadow of deep regret passed across his eyes, and then Camille saw them fill with glistening tears. Emotion seemed to twist the shape of Mr. Davis' mouth.

"They already did," the elderly man whispered.

"What?"

"The infected broke through the last fire doors,

Camille. They're in the corridors now. They're on the sixth floor."

"Non!" Camille's voice was a hoarse croak. She shook her head slowly in a gesture of numb denial and incomprehension. Her lips parted and began to quiver. Grief welled up within her, and she felt the world lurch giddily. "But… we have heard nothing. No screams…"

The elderly Englishman began weeping unashamedly. His lower lip trembled and his hands fluttered at his side like trapped birds. "They broke through a moment after you reached the roof. We agreed we would hold them off and die without crying out because we wanted to give you the chance at life you deserved. Your bravery kept us all alive, sweet Camille. We decided we wanted to save you in return."

"Non!" Camille cried again. Now she understood why the Englishman had taken so long to reach the roof. The rest of the survivors had gone to their death without screaming their terror so she might have a chance to survive. The enormity of their sacrifice struck her. She reached up impulsively to untangle the tight knots of rope.

Mr. Davis made a face of tender compassion and farewell – then pushed Camille off the roof.

Camille felt a sensation of falling for a split-second, and then there was just the wind in her face and a cry of wild exhilarating panic in her throat as she slid down the zip-line.

The rope sagged under her weight as she plunged towards the wall suspended by just the makeshift tether. She felt herself beginning to swing from side to side. She started to scream her panic. The undead saw her and a ravenous howl went up. Camille flashed across the road and hurtled towards the Avignon battlements. She lifted

244

her feet instinctively, still clinging to the rope. Momentum carried her over the gatehouse wall and straight into the arms of the three burly gendarmes who had fired the mortar.

* * *

"I oughta kick your silly, sneaky ass!" Steven Tremaine raged at Camille.

She sat slumped against a stone battlement atop the gatehouse; her face flushed crimson red and her whole body trembling from a maelstrom of emotions. She had her knees drawn up to her chin, and her mouth hung open, lips quivering. She was on the verge of tears.

"I'm sorry…" she apologized in a small whisper.

"You lied to me." Tremaine heard the berating harshness in his own voice. Anger and relief gave his words the scornful tone used by a parent to a child who has stepped into a road full of traffic. "You promised me you wouldn't leave the old city."

"I'm sorry," Camille muttered again. Her chagrin brought big glistening tears to her eyes. Her shoulders heaved and she began to cry.

Tremaine's anger evaporated into a sense of dismay. He clamped down on his lip, aware that the horror of Camille's experience and her sudden humiliation under the lash of his tongue had pushed her over the edge… and alienated her. He clawed his hands through his hair and paced a slow circuit of the gatehouse.

Colonel LeCat stood with the binoculars pressed to his face, staring at the roof of the hotel. An elderly man was waving. It was a sad, listless gesture; the wave of someone fare welling a friend they will never see again.

"Where are the other survivors, Miss Pelletier?" the

245

Colonel kept the glasses to his eyes and the elderly man in focus.

Camille drew a deep shuddering breath. Her face was slick with tears.

"There will be no others, Colonel," she said softly. "They sacrificed themselves to save me. By now they will all be dead."

LeCat said nothing. The elderly man on the rooftop stopped waving to look urgently over his shoulder. The Colonel kept the binoculars focused on the man's face. He saw shock, then weary resignation register on the gaunt wasted features. The old man climbed stiffly onto the hotel's ledge and settled himself on the precarious platform like a high diver. Undead appeared on the roof behind the man. They were howling with savage triumph. They lunged for the man, clawing at his arms and back. He teetered for an instant, then launched himself into space and plunged to his death.

LeCat set the binoculars down and ordered the rope zip-line untied.

Tremaine lowered himself down on the ground beside Camille. She looked very small and frail, crushed by her sadness and the trauma of the long hours of desperate survival. He could only imagine the horrors she had seen.

Tremaine felt a sudden awkward wave of compassion wash over him. He put his arm around her shoulder like a shield, and Camille collapsed against him with her eyes closed. He groped for the words of an apology but before he found them, he heard her break down into shuddering sobs of grief. Tremaine squeezed her shoulder and stared sightlessly into the smoke hazed distance, not daring to speak. It would be too easy to say the wrong thing now, and so he held her in his arms and let her tears wash away her pain.

246

It was Camille who spoke first. She turned to face Tremaine and lifted her eyes to his, fortifying herself with a determined act of courage. The movement of her head loosed a tear from her eyes; it trickled down her cheek.

"I am sorry."

Tremaine let out a long breath. He was too tired to be angry any longer. "Forget it. The most important thing is that you're alive and safe."

"All those people…" Camille broke off, thinking again about the elderly tourists who had sacrificed themselves for her. When she closed her eyes, she saw their faces and a fresh wave of grief overwhelmed her.

"You kept them alive for almost twenty-four hours. You gave them hope. Without you they would have died in the first moments of the attack."

It was cold comfort, but it was all Tremaine could offer.

Camille sniffed back fresh forlorn tears and was about to say more when a sudden garble of panicked voices on LeCat's two-way radio broke the melancholy sadness.

The Colonel seized the radio and clamped it to his ear. There were multiple voices, urgent and frantic, reporting over the net in breathless rushes of French that Tremaine could not understand.

\* \* \*

Kane left the men in the patisserie's storage room at the rear of the building and crept stealthily through the shop front's shadowed doorway. He stared up at the sky, watching the day's new light spread slowly behind the building façade on the opposite side of Rue De La Republique. He sucked his teeth and peered carefully down the length of the long straight road. It was empty.

He went back to the storage room. One of the waiting men was standing in the rear doorway urinating noisily into the service laneway behind the shop. He came back into the little room zipping the fly of his jeans and yawning.

"I am changing the plan," Kane announced.

The six men in the room became wary. The one who had come in from the laneway narrowed his eyes.

"Preacher, we have spent all night working on this plan. The men are in place in the upstairs windows."

"I know," Kane said irritably. He had chosen the firing positions himself when they had broken down the back door of the shop.

"The patrol will come along soon. There is no time to make new arrangements."

"There is – if we act quickly," Kane insisted.

"But why would you change a good plan?"

"Because I don't want Mary hurt," Kane growled, "and those fools upstairs are not experienced with their guns. Mary could be caught in the crossfire if the soldiers resist."

"Mary is one of us, Preacher," the man said with respect that was edged by fatigue and irritation. He had been one of the robed followers who attended the ritual in the Pope's Palace and he had not slept since. "She would gladly give her life to serve the Almighty, as we all have committed to do. Her life is no more special than any of our lives. We all work in the name of the Lord, and we all sacrifice ourselves for His greater glory."

Kane's face worked with agitation and then turned into a look of such burning malevolence that it struck fear into the man who had dared challenge him. Kane's lips clamped tightly together and a rush of merciless cruelty flared in his eyes. It lasted for just a terrifying instant – and then Kane choked down his temper and nodded his head. It *was* a good plan, and it *was* too late to make changes.

Mary's fate – like his own and the rest of his followers – rested in God's hands now.

Kane began to pray…

\* \* \*

Sergeant Bitou ordered his driver to stop the APC as it passed the imposing grand façade of the Post Office. The driver swerved into the carpark at the bus terminal and left the big diesel engine running.

Bitou unfastened the hatch overhead and stood up behind the vehicle's machine gun to survey the length of Rue De La Republique with binoculars.

The sun's first light painted the buildings that lined the thoroughfare with eerie light, but the boulevard itself remained hunched in deep shadow.

They were coming to the end of their patrol – making one final circuit of the ancient city before returning to barracks. Bitou yawned, and then choked on a lungful of thick smoky air. He was impatient, but too rigidly disciplined to take shortcuts. He finished his routine scan of the street ahead, then slid back down into the seat beside the driver.

"Forward," he ordered.

The interior of the armored personnel carrier sounded like being trapped inside a big empty drum. In a combat situation the vehicle was capable of carrying ten fully-armed soldiers in its elongated rear compartment. Without those troops it became a noisy hollow shell full of nothing but engine noise and rattles. The driver crunched the vehicle into gear and turned the corner, trundling down the wide empty street at fifteen kilometers per hour.

Bitou stifled another yawn and glanced at the darkened shops that lined the sidewalk. There were black bags of rubbish piled beside some of the doorways and glittering chips of broken glass in the gutter. The heavy-lugged tires jolted through a pothole and the whole vehicle rattled.

Then sudden movement caught the corner of the French sergeant's eyes and he turned his head frowning. From the darkness of a doorway a figure suddenly appeared, running diagonally into the empty road, waving its arms desperately.

Bitou made a chopping motion with his hand, waving the driver to slow.

"Merde!" the sergeant swore. It was a young woman. She had long hair and wore a pink nightdress. The garment clung tight around the slender body and was torn around the collar, revealing tantalizing flashes of the naked flesh beneath as she ran closer. Her mouth gaped open and her eyes looked hunted. Bitou felt himself tense with the first stirrings of alarm.

The driver braked to a halt and let the diesel engine idle. The girl reached the middle of the road and stood, gasping for breath, in the beams of the APC's headlights. Her hair hung in wild disarray and she was barefooted. As Bitou looked on, the girl suddenly sagged and dropped to her knees in the middle of the blacktop.

Bitou heaved himself up through the overhead cupola and called out.

"What happened to you?"

The girl looked up. Her chest heaved. "A man attacked me," she sounded close to tears. "He tried to rape me. I ran from him but he chased me."

"Where is he now?"

The girl looked over her shoulder, then back to the soldier. "I don't know. I am scared."

Bitou's face became a scowl. He dropped back inside the vehicle's cockpit to wrench open the heavy passenger-side door. Lawlessness became inevitable in a siege situation. People turned desperate, and pretty young women became prey for brutes.

He jumped down onto the roadway. His heavy boots crunched on a sprinkle of broken glass. The girl in the glare of the headlights pressed her hands to her face and her shoulders began to heave. Sergeant Bitou's frown deepened. The girl looked about eighteen; a pretty slim thing wearing nothing but the threadbare nightdress. The sergeant had a niece about the same age. He bent to offer a helping hand to the girl – and felt the sudden cold steel of a gun's barrel press hard against the back of his neck.

"Do not move, or do anything to raise an alarm," the man's voice in his ear sounded harsh as gravel.

"What is this?" Bitou turned. "Who are you?"

He heard a scuffle of sound and a short cry of pain that was cut off abruptly. Two dark shadows appeared over his shoulder and there were other men, moving urgently towards the APC on the periphery of his vision. He heard the engine note of the APC suddenly change.

The armed man in front of him thrust his pistol under the sergeant's chin. He wore a crude mask, fashioned from some kind of paper shopping bag. Through the two eye-holes, Bitou saw the glittering gaze of a fanatic.

"What do you want?" the sergeant lowered his voice. Two other armed men dragged his driver into the middle of the road. The young soldier had his hands trussed tight behind his back and his head lolled drunkenly on his shoulders. His face was awash with fresh dripping blood.

"We're taking the vehicle," the masked attacker said. "You will come to no harm."

Sergeant Bitou's face screwed up into an expression of derision. He spat his contempt. He heard quick steps behind him and then a searing white explosion of pain detonated in his back. He cried out and his legs buckled beneath him. He fell to the ground and felt a heavy foot between his shoulder blades.

"Tie him," Kane's voice behind the mask rasped, hoarse with urgency. He called Mary to him and hoisted her through the passenger door of the APC, then stood in the arc of the headlights and waved his arms. The men positioned in the upstairs windows of the patisserie shop abandoned their posts and came running out into the street. "Get in the back," Kane gestured.

He was gasping for breath when he settled himself behind the vehicle's steering wheel. He snatched the paper bag off his head and jammed his foot down on the gas pedal. The APC leaped forward with a sudden jolt, the engine bellowing like a wounded bull and belching black oily exhaust into the morning sky.

Kane shivered, his body pumped full of adrenalin. His features were swollen and flushed with triumph. He flicked a glance sideways at Mary. The girl smiled back at him.

The heart of the ancient city was the plaza adjoining the Town Hall, but the roads radiating out from Place De L'Horloge were a warren of lanes so narrow that the Council had barricaded them to all vehicle traffic. Kane reached the next intersection and turned right, jouncing the heavy armored vehicle over a pedestrian sidewalk and past a church to find a connecting road. The APC picked up speed down a gradual incline, its engine snarling loudly along a built-up street of old apartment blocks and gift shops. Ahead lay a sharp jinking turn and a sign for the university.

Kane changed down through the gears and put the big vehicle to the turn. It seemed to sway on its suspension then righted itself. Kane drew a deep breath. At the end of the street he could see a wire mesh fence and a white gatehouse that marked vehicle access to the university. Kane tightened his grip on the steering wheel and crushed the gas pedal under his foot.

The APC charged towards the fence.

Kane thrust out his jaw aggressively and braced himself for the impact. "Hold on!" he shouted over his shoulder to the men seated in the back of the vehicle.

The APC blew through the flimsy wire-mesh fence at forty kilometers per hour, swaying from side to side like a boat on an ocean as it mounted a curbed footpath and ploughed towards the steel-barred gate on the far side of the campus. Small trees were flattened under the huge heavy tires, and a plume of dust and dirt billowed into the new morning sky.

Kane wrestled with the steering wheel and lined the front of the heavy vehicle up with the approaching gate.

"Brace yourselves!" he roared. He felt wildly alive with exhilaration, and giddy with righteous virtue. His faith made him fearless; he was God's messenger on earth, shielded by His love. In the rear of the APC he could hear the men from the ambush team fervently singing.

There was a solid crowd of infected pressed against the grille of the gates. Kane could see their tortured rotting faces and their hideous disfigurements. It was the first time he had seen the undead. They were gruesome beyond his wildest imaginings. Kane felt his heart quail with a tremor of uncertainty. They were howling; he couldn't hear them above the rattling noise of the vehicle, but he could see their gaping mouths and the insanity in their eyes. He felt a cold chill of doubt, and the first premonition of doom crept icily down his spine.

Kane started to pray, mouthing memorized words as they raced towards the ancient stone gatehouse. His eyes grew wide and fear draped itself around his shoulders. Blind panic overwhelmed him. He started to scream with fear and wrenched the wheel to the right.

It was too late.

The APC struck the steel bars of the gate and tore the huge grill from its chains and fixtures. The sound of the collision was calamitous. Beside Kane, Mary screamed shrilly.

The vehicle hit the gate at an angle, swerving violently as it cannoned into the stone side of the tower and ricocheting on, out of control. The steel bars bent then folded under the impact, wrenching Kane's hands from the steering wheel and hurling him sideways against the door. A shower of bright sparks plumed like a comet's tail as metal crashed against metal. The APC bucked like a wild creature, rearing up on its back wheels then plunging down, the engine still roaring.

Momentum carried the APC clear through the barred gateway and out onto the sidewalk beyond the walls, crushing dozens of infected ghouls under the chassis in a spreading oil-slick of blood and gore. The vehicle slewed wildly across the tarmac and one of the huge front wheels blew out, hurling chunks of shredded rubber through the air like shrapnel.

The APC crashed into the trunk of a fallen tree and came to a sickening juddering halt. Kane sat stunned, hunched over the steering wheel. His ears were ringing, and he could taste the coppery tang of blood in his mouth. He blinked bleary eyes until they focused on Mary. He groaned in shock and pain.

Mary had been thrown head-first into the armored glass of the APC's windscreen. Her skull had been crushed, and there were lurid smears of blood and tufts of hair stuck to the thick, cracked glass. Kane reached out for her. Her head lolled loose on her broken neck. Mercifully her face was turned away from him, towards the passenger side window, so that he could not see the dreadful damage the collision had done to her beautiful features at the horrific instant of her death.

Kane cried out in grief and confusion, but the roar of the undead that had surrounded the vehicle drowned out his appalled croak. They hammered their hands against the steel and smeared blood in streaks down the glass. They pressed their rotting hideous faces to the windows and howled. The sound inside the armored car became the maddened beating of a thousand drums, rising louder and louder – until the door was wrenched open and clawing hands reached for him.

Kane screamed.

The APC rocked violently on its remaining three wheels. In the back of the vehicle other men were screeching. Kane heard a gunshot and then a savage howl. He thrashed at the hands that reached for him, and lifted his arms to the heavens.

"God!" he cried out, with his face lifted to the smoke-scarred sky. "Give me the power you promised. Let me walk safe amongst the sick and infected so that I may do your work on earth."

Something seized his leg and dragged him bodily from the armored car.

Kane hit the ground and scrambled onto his hands and knees. One of his followers from the rear compartment of the APC lay nearby on the sidewalk. The man writhed in a pool of his own blood. He looked like some savage beast had mauled him. His left arm had been torn from its shoulder and one of his legs was missing below the knee. His eyes were wide open, staring bewildered at the sky.

Kane screamed again. His other followers were squirming in the dust of the footpath, surrounded by heaving knots of undead. Kane heard the gruesome howls and the ragged gasping pleas for mercy. It blurred into one unholy sound of frenzied savage terror.

Kane died hard. The undead tore at his body, flensing the skin from his legs and arms, then slashing at the soft fatty flesh of his stomach until it unzipped like a purse and the content of his guts spilled over the footpath. They mauled his throat until his long beard became thick with blood, and then fought over the delicacies of his eyes, tongue and heart.

The last thing his conscious mind registered was not the voice of God; it was a wail of fear and panic that rose up around the ancient city of Avignon as the undead poured in through the open gateway and buildings began to burn.

It was the sound of mankind in its death throes.

\* \* \*

LeCat, Tremaine and Camille bundled into a jeep and the Colonel raced to the gendarmerie barracks on Boulevard Raspail. As he drove, putting the vehicle to the corners without slowing, he shouted above the buffeting wind.

256

"The gate at the university has been broken down," LeCat snapped. "Insurgents seized the vehicle and rammed it into the gatehouse. The infected are in the city."

Tremaine felt the shock of it like a punch to the heart. "Christ!" he swore. Avignon was doomed. An enemy from within had betrayed them. "Can they be stopped?"

LeCat said nothing.

They reached the barracks and LeCat slewed the P4 across the road. Gendarmes were running from the buildings carrying their assault rifles. An alarm wailed in the background, high and piercing. One of the APC's rumbled down the driveway and lurched out into the street. A man standing in the passenger side cupola swung the machine gun round and aimed it at the intersection a hundred yards away.

LeCat was on the two-way barking instructions. The replies over the net were garbled and panic-stricken. He had just fifty men in a defensive perimeter around the front of the barracks. He sent five of them with a machine gun to the opposite side of the road where a laneway littered with drifting piles of autumn leaves intersected the boulevard. Three more men were positioned behind sandbags in the middle of the roadway facing west to warn of an unexpected attack from behind his position. The rest of the gendarmes faced east, from where LeCat felt certain the undead attack would come.

He knew he didn't have enough men.

"Take Miss Pelletier inside," LeCat told Tremaine. "You can use my office. Barricade the doors behind you with furniture."

Tremaine shook his head. "Camille can go if she wants, but I'll stay here."

LeCat flashed him a sharp look of admonishment.

257

The Frenchman was not accustomed to having his orders ignored. He looked utterly baleful.

Tremaine narrowed his eyes and set his jaw stubbornly. "Nowhere is safe, Colonel. This is as good a place as any to make a stand."

"I'll stay here too," Camille said in a small but defiant voice.

LeCat nodded bleakly and drew his pistol. Across the old city, gradually coming closer, he could hear the sounds of panicked gunfire and terrified shrilling screams. Oily black columns of smoke rose into the sky and blotted out the sun.

LeCat issued his last instructions, walking amongst the frightened young soldiers. He had them fanned out across the middle of the road with the P4 and the armored car side-by-side as a barricade. They were nervous. He could see the anxiety in their faces and smell their sweating fear. He spoke calmly, as though they were on an urban warfare exercise.

"When they come around that corner," he gestured with his pistol towards the intersection, "do not conserve your ammunition. This will be the last fight. We must hold them here, or not at all."

\* \* \*

The undead surged through the battered-down gateway and wreaked havoc throughout the university. Gendarmes who had been posted to safeguard the city's horded food and water supplies were overpowered within minutes. Thousands of infected spilled through the breach, like a vast tide of filthy water that had broken down the walls of a dam.

Buildings on the east side of the old city quickly

caught on fire and people ran screaming into the streets.

The undead were driven to roaring, howling insanity by the lure of fresh flesh. They rampaged, unchecked, like violent rioters, and the cobblestoned roads began to run with blood.

The quiet streets surrounding the university precinct were overrun first. Doors were battered down, windows smashed and people killed in their beds. On Rue Muguet, a narrow laneway that bordered the campus grounds, a baby was taken screaming from its cot and carried out into the street like a trophy. The infant's parents were still alive, drowning slowly in their own blood, as the child was seized by both feet and swung head-first against the wall of the building. The baby's tender skull cracked open like an egg and the howling undead roared their voracious hunger. They snapped and snarled for the oozing contents of the dead child's skull, scooping the spattered custard-colored contents up in their rotting fingers.

The soldiers manning the battlements were trapped and unable to flee. The undead came swarming up the ladders and over the worn stone steps. The gendarmes and the civilians who bore weapons fought back, flailing the undead on the narrow ramparts with determined fire that plucked them off the precarious ledge and threw them back into the roiling horde below.

Four gendarmes formed a tight knot on top of the gatehouse and fought bravely, but it was only a matter of time before their ammunition ran out. The undead came at them from both sides of the wall and ran into a frantic hellish chorus of assault rifle fire. Still the ghouls came on, now forced to clamber over a tangled blockade of their own mutilated. The gendarmes fought for their lives, firing together, and the hail of lead cut down their attackers in swathes. The voracious undead were thrown back and the steps became slick with gore. They attacked again, scrambling over the mound of rotting corpses, berserkers driven to madness by the insanity of their infection. The second growling assault was beaten back, but the infected would not be denied. The third wave struck from both sides of the gatehouse simultaneously and the gendarmes were overrun. One soldier shot a ghoul from point-blank range. The bullet hit the zombie in the temple as it turned, howling. The ghoul's head distorted, swelling and bursting. Its wild snarl became a hideous rubbery grimace for a split-second and then its body was slammed back onto the ground by the awesome force of the impact. The gendarme fired again at another of the undead but the weapon in his hands fell on an empty chamber. The soldier cried out in fear, then turned and hurled himself off the wall to his death.

The other three gendarmes went down under the sheer overwhelming weight of their attackers. One of them screamed in agony. The undead eviscerated the bodies and gorged themselves on the slices of bleeding flesh until all that remained of the corpses was bone and gristle.

The undead ran howling and barking through the streets. The apartments all had their doors bolted, the ground-floor windows covered by shutters or iron barred grilles. The citizens of Avignon cowered in the shadows and hid in their closets.

Others ran, terrified, to the nearest church and pummeled their fists on the huge wooden doors, crying out for refuge and sanctuary. The undead threw themselves into the masses of wailing bodies and tore them to shreds until the closed and bolted church doors were splattered with blood and the stone steps became sticky with gore.

Mangy wild-eyed dogs ran barking through the dark laneways, foraging through overturned garbage bags and gnawing at the gristle of freshly severed limbs. Children squatted on the ground next to their dead parents, sobbing with unimaginable terror until they too were savaged by the infected. A row of old houses caught fire and burned furiously. The trapped, terrified people inside the buildings burned alive, or flung themselves from the second-story windows.

The alleyways stank of blood, death and the corruption of rotting flesh. Bodies lay in dark puddles and as the screams grew louder and more terrified, the sounds of gunfire gradually diminished. A man stood sobbing and bloodied in the main plaza, wandering in a daze until he was driven to the ground by one of the infected. Another ghoul pounced on the body and the two undead fought like rabid dogs, squabbling over the scraps of his flesh. A teenage girl ran screaming with icy black terror from a ghoul and tripped through a plate glass window. A nun, clutching her rosary beads to her chest, made not a sound as the undead surrounded her and threw her to the ground. She lay with her eyes closed and her mouth working in frantic prayer while the undead gnawed the flesh from her legs and then tore out her throat.

Black smoke roiled into the sky and raucous birds and swarms of flies feasted on the splattered remains. The sun rose into the morning sky, shrouded by a thick pall of haze.

Henri Pelletier's apartment overlooked one of the long wide roads that ran like an artery between the outer city walls and the central plaza. Frantic gunfire had dragged him, scrambling and alarmed from his bed. Now

261

he stood at his kitchen window, gaping with horror, his shoulders hunched, his face baggy as a bloodhound's with sadness. He heard sporadic rifle fire and the sounds of doors and windows breaking. Through the glass he could hear screaming. He watched as a woman in her nightdress ran into the street below him, her face a mask of terror. She was being hunted by three of the undead. One of them lunged for her and hooked a bony hand into the collar of her clothing. It tore open and the terrified woman spun naked. The undead howled then leapt on her. Bright arterial blood fountained into the sky as they dismembered the thrashing body.

Taking the numbed, drugged steps of a condemned man, Henri Pelletier went to wake his wife for the last time.

* * *

"You have been the love of my life," Henri Pelletier said in a sad little voice. "From the moment I met you, I knew we were meant to be together, and you have made me a happy man."

His wife said nothing. Henri smiled lovingly. "And look at all we have accomplished," he spread his arms wide in a gesture that seemed to encapsulate both their neat apartment and the city itself. "I became mayor, and I served Avignon proudly…"

His voice trailed off, interrupted by the sharp retort of a rifle somewhere in the street beyond their building. Henri knew his time was running short. He shambled lethargically around the room, touching a photo frame that showed a picture of himself in his ceremonial mayoral robes, and then ran his hand gently over the smooth polish of the piano. He sighed, overcome by a profound melancholy of despair.

He picked up the pistol from the kitchen table and reloaded it. His hands were shaking. He glanced over his shoulder. His wife sat in the big stuffed armchair that faced the television wearing her dressing gown. There was a plastic bag filled with knitting at her feet. The bullet hole between her eyes was the size of a small coin, but there was very little blood – and Henri was thankful for that. His wife's eyes were staring and vacant.

He thought about his daughter Camille then. He wondered if she was still alive. He doubted it. He wondered then if she had died at the hands of the infected… or if she had also chosen the swift mercy of suicide.

A sudden terrified scream slashed across his thoughts and Henri's attention snapped to the locked apartment door. The sound had come from somewhere in the passageway, shrill and chilling. He heard running, pounding footsteps and a cold blade of dread ran down his spine.

Suddenly the pistol felt heavy in his shaking hand. He carried it across the room and leaned carefully over his dead wife. He kissed her cheek. The skin against his lips felt cool and waxen.

"Vive la France," Henri muttered, and then opened his mouth and thrust the barrel of the gun between his lips. He could taste oil.

He closed his eyes, drew a deep last breath.

And pulled the trigger.

\* \* \*

The long minutes of fretful waiting shredded the resolve of the soldiers huddled outside the gendarmerie barracks on Boulevard Raspail. Most of the troops who had been left at the barracks were raw recruits that had never seen combat. They were young and inexperienced. The nightmare sounds of approaching horror plucked along the strings of their nerves so they stood at their positions, their faces pinched and terrified.

A young soldier crouched next to LeCat behind the steel bulk of the APC cursed softly each time a shrilling scream cut through the clamor of rioting, gnawing on his soft slack lips to stop himself from crying out.

"Merde!"

He had the barrel of his assault rifle braced on the steel prow of the vehicle, but still the weapon trembled in his white-knuckled hands.

"Merde!" he swore again as a blood-curdling shriek of terror slashed across the growling chaos that crept relentlessly closer.

"Is your weapon loaded, soldier?" LeCat asked the young gendarme.

The pale-faced boy blinked, then nodded. "Yes, sir."

"Is this your first action?"

"Yes, sir."

"How long have you been a gendarme?"

"Nine months, Colonel," the boy's voice squeaked. His belly felt full of oily fear. The sour taste of it coated the back of his throat. "My uncle served in the Congo."

"Aah!" LeCat seemed genuinely intrigued. "So soldiering runs in your blood, yes?"

The young man blushed bright red. He was uncomfortable and awkward. "Yes, Colonel."

"Good!" LeCat said. He stared ahead at the intersection, with his eyes narrowed. A thick haze of grey smoke blanketed the end of the road, cutting visibility. "Then I can count on you?"

"Sir," the gendarme stiffened with pride.

"Good. Then keep your eyes on that smoke," he gestured with the pistol in his hand. "And notify me when the enemy appear. Understand?"

"Yes, sir."

LeCat straightened and holstered his weapon. He had a frown on his face as though suddenly distracted by a vexing problem that proved difficult to solve. He wandered away from the shelter of the APC and strolled across the road with his hands clasped behind his back and his head down, deep in thought.

"They're coming," Colonel LeCat muttered from the corner of his mouth as he drew level with the American hunched behind the P4 jeep. Tremaine's skin crawled with the insects of his fear.

"Are you sure?"

"Oui." The Colonel said. He continued walking without pause to the Captain he had delegated to command the machine gun post on the opposite corner of the road.

"They will soon be here, Captain Falviur," he said conversationally.

The Captain stood leaning against the wall of a building with his weapon aimed into the distant bank of smoke. Two of his men lay behind the machine gun that had been set up on the footpath, and two more were kneeling in the shade of a small roadside tree with steel boxes of spare ammunition.

"Do not open fire until I order you," LeCat kept the tone of his voice calm and casual. "Let the machine gun on the APC do its work first."

"Sir," Falviur nodded. There was nothing more to say.

LeCat turned on his heel and now he had the look of

265

a man enjoying a summer's morning stroll, knowing that all eyes were surreptitiously upon him, and that under such anxious scrutiny he must maintain the pretense of confident assuredness. In the face of terror and almost certain death he had to set an example to the frightened young gendarmes around him.

A high-pitched squeak of sound broke the spell. LeCat turned. It was the young gendarme. His face looked white as bone china, his mouth open wide, slack jawed and lips quivering. He pointed with a shaking hand.

"There they are, Colonel."

LeCat turned and stared into the obscuring bank of smoke that shrouded the intersection.

The road lay blanketed in a thick haze, and the air seemed to vibrate with the sounds of rioting and horror, rising to a chaotic crescendo. Dark swirling shapes emerged within the veils of smoke and then, dramatically, the wind stripped the haze away. A horde of growling undead erupted into the crossroads. Their wild frenzied roar rattled the air.

LeCat filled his lungs to bark orders to the nervous gendarmes around him. "Stand to your guns! Stand to your guns!"

There was a fidget of final movement and the mechanical clatter of weapons being checked and loaded.

"Fire!" LeCat roared.

The length of the boulevard erupted in a juddering roaring maelstrom of noise and howls. The machine gun mounted atop the APC proved lethal, cutting a swathe through the front running ranks of the undead and piling the bodies across the road. The gendarmes on either side of the armored vehicle added their weapons to the deafening chorus as bullets twitched through the smoke, and the vast tide of infected lost momentum. They milled

266

in the middle of the road, trapped in a quagmire of hideously rotted bodies and dismembered limbs. The hail of concentrated fire being thrown down the narrow road churned the infected undead into shattered pulp.

But after fifteen seconds of furious fire, the tempo of resistance lost its unified voice and degenerated into a broken staccato of noise as individual soldiers stopped to reload. Relentlessly the undead pushed closer, driven by their insatiable blood-lust and the weight of the undead bodies still spilling into the street, pushing them on to the guns.

The carnage became gruesome. Broken bodies, flailed and flensed of their flesh, lay like discarded litter on the blacktop. The gutters ran thick with gore and brown oozing blood. A blue haze descended over the troops behind the barricade and the world became a numbed, deafening nightmare of noise and savage shrieks.

Many of the undead were thrown to the ground writhing and twisting. They crawled away from the crushing weight of the horde to the sidewalks, bones shattered and rotting flesh punctured by multiple wounds.

LeCat leaped up onto the top of the APC and surveyed the battleground. From his elevated position he could see that the massed column of undead reached all the way to the end of the street; thousands upon thousands of infected funneling into the narrow boulevard, as endless as the ocean. He slitted his eyes.

"Aim higher!" he punched the machine gunner's shoulder to get the gendarme's attention. The shuddering roar of the weapon overwhelmed his shouted voice. He stabbed his finger at the side of his head and fixed the gunner with a baleful stare. "Head shots!" LeCat shouted.

The machine gunner seemed to understand. He traversed the weapon in a slow sweep of the boulevard, elevating the barrel just an inch or so. A soft pink mist hung in the air as a burst of well-aimed fire decapitated three of the undead and turned their skulls to pulp.

LeCat grinned fierce appreciation. His face had been grimed with sooty dust, and his eyes made bloodshot by the smoky haze. He tapped the gunner on the helmeted head to signal his approval and leaped from the top of the vehicle to the road. Tremaine stood there, hunched behind the broad bulk of the vehicle and staring wide-eyed at the gruesome carnage.

He saw a gendarme track a charging figure that emerged from out of the smoke and then heard a bark of gunfire. The ghoul had been a teenage girl. One of the bullets caught the zombie in its open, snarling mouth. The contents of its head blew out through the back of the skull. It dropped to the ground and got trampled beneath the feet of the rushing stampede.

"They're getting closer," Tremaine shouted at LeCat. The Colonel nodded grimly. The sheer weight of numbers would overrun the defenders eventually.

In a normal combat situation, such heavy losses would have a devastating effect on morale. If the undead were a regular army they would have fallen back, broken by the guns. But the undead were made mindless and blood-thirsty by their infection. They would not retreat.

"It is inevitable," LeCat said. "Unless we can kill them all, we cannot hope to survive."

The battle became a series of moments for Tremaine, like frozen images captured by a camera. He saw two of the undead stagger, punched full of bullet holes, to the gutter then drag themselves back to their feet. A moment later they went down again, this time fatally as the sweep of the machine gun took off the top of one ghoul's head and severed the other undead beast's head from its neck. The contents of their skulls splashed against a window and dripped down the glass like thick sauce.

He heard men calling for ammunition, and noticed Camille hunched on the ground with her back against the jeep. A soldier standing beside her stumbled and his gunfire went wild, accidentally shooting another gendarme in the back. The shot soldier fell forward, his arms cartwheeling in the air. He slumped, dead on the blacktop in a bright puddle of his own blood, limbs thrown wide and his trunk twitching convulsively.

"Christ!" Tremaine swore. He scampered to the body and snatched up the dead gendarme's assault rifle. He didn't know how to fire the weapon. He aimed it at the surging wall of undead and it bucked ferociously against his shoulder. The shots went wide and then the weapon clicked on an empty chamber. He had no idea how to reload. He threw the weapon down and saw Camille scramble for it.

"It ran out of bullets," Tremaine shouted lamely.

Camille fumbled a magazine from the dead soldier's webbing and reloaded with deft skill. Tremaine looked on, stunned. Camille handed him the weapon back, but Tremaine shook his head. Camille shoved herself into the line of men behind the jeep and opened fire. Tremaine scuttled across the road and saw a trenching spade and an axe clamped to the side of the APC behind steel brackets. He knocked the lugs aside with his palm and seized the axe. He felt better with a weapon. The weight of the crude blade in his hands was reassuring.

The undead pressed closer to the guns, like a relentless tide. There were so many dismembered rotting corpses on the ground now their broken bodies formed a gruesome wall that the following horde were forced to clamber over. Still they pressed forward.

LeCat drew his sidearm and fired into the swarming torrent of hideous rotting creatures, aiming at a zombie who had once been an old man. The ghoul opened its mouth to howl, but before the sound came from the rotting hole of its throat, it was punched backwards, flung down as if from an invisible fist. LeCat's bullet had blown through the ghoul's eye socket and torn off the back of its skull. The ghoul fell to the ground into an oily pool of guts and vomit.

"Now!" the Colonel gave the order, roaring to make himself heard above the staccato of deafening gunfire. Captain Falviur had been waiting impatiently for the command. He kicked the boot of the machine gunner lying prone on the sidewalk beside him, and the street erupted in a fresh hell of deafening fire.

The second machine gun caught the undead in a thunderous crossfire and they edged away from the threat, piling bodies deeper and narrowing the front of their attack. The nearest ghouls were within forty feet; close enough to see the mutilated faces, close enough to see the insane frenzy burning in their eyes, to see the flaps of rotting flesh and gruesome open wounds, to see open howling mouths of black rotting teeth, to see the bite marks and the strike of each bullet. The undead tide began to stall and falter, though still they seethed and snarled like wild animals.

"Keep firing!" LeCat could sense the pendulum of momentum swinging slowly in favor of the defenders. The mound of bodies strewn across the street reached head high, piled like hideous rotting garbage. Bullets tugged and plucked at the smoky haze and then for a brief moment, the battlefield seemed eerily silent. Both machine guns needed reloading and the men behind the APC were running low on ammunition. The gunfire became halting and sporadic. LeCat knew the fight for survival teetered on the next few seconds.

He clambered up the side of the APC and stood squinting into the haze. The horror spread before the barricade caught him in the chest like the punch from a fist. The mounds of undead were skeletal rotting tangles of stringy grey flesh and gore, slaughtered in their hundreds and thrown down in careless tangles of limbs and bones. The carnage was holocaustic, and the putrid stench overwhelming.

In the no-man's land space between the piled wall of bodies and the barricade, some of the infected still crawled, clawing themselves closer to the soldiers with bony bloodied hands, trailing stinking slicks of brown blood. Their tongues lolled maniacally from the sides of their mouths, and their jaws snapped on broken jagged teeth. They were barely recognizable as once being human, so withered was their dead flesh. They barked and grunted, and the flies swarmed over their rotting corpses, feasting on the corruption.

LeCat shot the closest ghoul as it lifted its head to roar, while behind the barricade men scrambled for fresh magazines of ammunition.

The illusory lull lasted just a few moments – and then the next wave of infected came pouring over the mountain of bodies.

They came clambering over the broken corpses like WWI soldiers springing from their Somme trenches, howling and roaring and flailing their arms in wild madness. The clamor became deafening, rising on the air like furious surf on a storm-lashed beach. LeCat felt his blood chill in the face of the fresh relentless horror.

"Fire!"

The machine gun on the corner juddered a furious blaze of enfilade fire, tearing into the horde as it crested the hideous wall of bodies, but shots went high, flailing the building opposite and biting off chunks of debris. It added to the dust and smoke so that the field of battle became a swirling haze.

"Fire!" LeCat's voice rose above the maelstrom. He shot one of the running ghouls between the eyes, then swung the pistol onto another hideous figure jinking diagonally across the face of the barricade towards the street corner. LeCat's bullet took off the top of the ghoul's head and flung him down on the blacktop.

Tremaine watched on in growing horror, his hands flexing and clenching at the handle of the axe with rising apprehension. It seemed the tide of undead would surge to overwhelm them at any moment. He turned to look for Camille and saw her still behind the jeep. She had thrown down the assault rifle when it had run out of ammunition. There were no more magazines to spare. Tremaine started to run towards her when something caught in the periphery of his vision.

He spun round and felt his guts seem to drop from his body.

At the opposite end of the boulevard a second phalanx of undead appeared through the tendrils of hazy smoke, like monstrous apparitions drenched in blood. Tremaine felt himself sag in defeat and despair.

The three gendarmes posted behind the makeshift wall of sandbags opened fire but the sound of their defiant fusillade sounded puny compared to the triumphant savage howl of the undead throng. LeCat somehow sensed the new threat and turned to see the shape of the second attack. He threw his head back and roared his frustration, as though furious with God. Across the smoke and chaos of the street, Tremaine locked eyes with LeCat and watched the French Colonel shake his head in mute surrender.

The last shreds of resistance went from the gendarmes. They saw their imminent death through a bowel-churning blur of smoke. Only LeCat refused to give in the fight. He bellowed over the fury of noise defiantly.

"Captain Falviur!"

"Sir?" the officer on the far side of the road looked up. His face had been caked with dust and grime.

"You will shoot the first man who takes a backward step!"

The Captain blanched but nodded. "Yes, sir!"

Satisfied, LeCat drew himself erect and reloaded his pistol. He climbed unhurriedly over the APC and stood in front of the barricade. Only the relentless hail of fire from the two machine guns pinned back the surging tide of undead. LeCat turned to face his men. He stood in an inch deep layer of thick sticky blood and guts. He raised one arm into the air and looked along the ragged line of young faces that stared back at him. They were sweating and pale with fear.

"Men of the French gendarmerie. We are going to charge," LeCat declared. "One final charge for the glory of France. Who is with me? Who will fight to the death alongside their Colonel?"

An insane, reckless and ragged cheer went up from a dozen hoarse parched throats. Men began clambering over the barricade.

"Then follow me!" LeCat cried.

He turned to face the horde of undead and charged into the swarming mass of bodies. Behind him, the

273

gendarmes followed in a ragged line, firing from the hip as they ran. The undead seemed to melt before them as the French soldiers cleaved a pocket of space into the front ranks of the infected. The defiance lasted just a few glorious seconds. The zombies surrounded the gendarmes and they went down, still firing, their valiant shouts turning to breathless, desperate screams of unimaginable torture. They vanished from Tremaine's sight like drowning men disappearing beneath the surface of a plunging storm-tossed sea.

"Run!" Camille Pelletier seized Tremaine by the arms and dragged him to the APC. They had just seconds before the undead tide overwhelmed them. The gendarme behind the machine gun kept firing, tragic tears streaming down his cheeks, cutting runnels in the grime that caked his face. Camille threw herself in the driver's side door and the big engine howled to life in a black belch of exhaust. Tremaine crammed himself in the small space beside the gunner's booted legs.

"Can you drive this thing?"

Camille was sweating. Her hair hung in lank tendrils down over her forehead. Her brow puckered in a frown of fierce concentration. She slammed the APC into reverse and rammed the jeep aside.

"Yes." She said.

A ghoul flung itself against the vehicle, slamming bloody hands against the passenger-side window. The noise inside the closed APC was a deafening drum until the machine gun fell suddenly silent, the last of the ammunition spent. Tremaine seized the soldier roughly by the belt and tugged him down into the cockpit. The cupola hatch slammed shut. Camille put the APC into low gear and it leaped forward.

"Where are we going?" Tremaine had to shout. The

undead were pounding on the steel walls of the vehicle with their fists, drumming their fury and frustration. One of them threw itself onto the long nose of the armored car and clung there, snarling and snapping at them through the glass. Camille pushed the gas pedal to the floor, and the APC lunged forward like a steel battering ram. The undead fell beneath the chassis, ploughed under by the vehicle's weight. The armored car jounced and rocked, swaying from side to side. Camille gripped the wheel with bleak resolve. Her face was flushed, her eyes enormous with fear and fierce concentration.

"Where are we going?" Tremaine shouted again as Camille changed gear. The big diesel engine bellowed and the undead were battered aside by the APC's momentum. Broken bodies crunched under the huge, heavily-lugged tires. Later on, Tremaine understood, there would be time for remorse; to ponder his survival and to regret that he had never said farewell or thanked LeCat for his dour bravery. But that time was not now, for survival still seemed far from assured.

"I know a place," Camille said urgently, then wrenched hard on the wheel to turn the corner. "A place we can defend and survive."

"Where?" Tremaine had to shout past the gendarme who sat squeezed between them. He was a young soldier, barely old enough to shave. His pale face dripped with sweat under the heavy weight of his helmet. His eyebrows had been singed away, giving his face a bland, startled look. He gaped at the phalanx of undead beyond the windscreen.

"Fort Saint-Andre," Camille said.

* * *

275

"The only way out of the city is through the same gate the undead broke in," Tremaine found he had to shout to make himself heard above the rattling cacophony of noise inside the APC. "There's no chance we can push one of the barricaded buses aside at any of the other gates."

"I know," Camille kept her eyes fixed on the road ahead, wrestling with the vehicle's steering wheel. The armored car broke through the wall of infected that had overwhelmed the gendarmes and rumbled along Rue De La Republique. Hundreds of zombies crowded the ancient city's main thoroughfare; Camille ran them down and crushed the ghouls under the huge tires. The windscreen splattered with gore and guts.

"But you're going the wrong way," Tremaine's voice betrayed his confusion and alarm. "This isn't the way to the university."

"We can cut the corner when we reach the plaza," Camille said, inadvertently taking the same route that Kane had driven the stolen APC filled with his religious followers.

Tremaine sat back. Camille knew the city; she had lived in Avignon all her life, and he trusted her judgment. But that didn't stop him frowning his concern as the APC reached the city's cobblestoned plaza and then jounced over the guttering to turn right. He clung to a hand-hold and everything loose in the steel cabin rattled.

Behind the APC followed a trail of running undead, drawn by the loud revving diesel engines like rats behind the Pied Piper. They came howling from buildings and crashed through glass windows. They crawled from litter bins and staggered from the shadows. Camille put her foot down on the gas pedal and let the speed build up to distance them.

Suddenly she swung hard left, catching Tremaine and the young gendarme off guard. Tremaine was thrown against the steel door as the APC rounded the corner like a boat in rough seas. Camille cried out and wrenched hard at the wheel. The armored car responded slowly, leaping the sidewalk then crashing down again. Tremaine braced himself for the impact.

"Christ!" he flinched. "What are you doing?"

"My parents," Camille shot him a glance. Her lips were pressed into a thin bloodless line. Tremaine saw the stubborn resolve in her eyes. "They live in an apartment on this street."

She slammed on the brakes and the APC juddered to a halt in front of a three-story building beside an old church. The stone façade of the apartment block had been spattered in blood. Behind grilled iron bars, the ground floor windows were all smashed, and the front double-doors hung broken on their hinges. On the footpath was sprawled a naked woman's body. She lay on her stomach in a pool of blood. Her back had been ripped open so the ribs showed like a row of jagged white teeth through shredded flesh. A swarm of black flies rose into the air for a moment and then re-settled over the body like a blanket, crawling across the dead flesh and laying eggs in the wet warm cavities of her bloating corpse. The street was deserted but strewn with a debris of loose stones and broken glass. Camille kept the armored car's engine running and threw her shoulder against the door.

"Wait!" Tremaine grimaced. His face filled with alarm and consternation. "Let us go instead," he groaned. "Just keep the engine running."

Camille nodded. "Apartment 107, on the first floor," she said.

Tremaine and the gendarme scrambled out of the APC and stood wary and tense on the sidewalk, listening for threats. There were screams and shrieks of agony and terror, but they sounded far away. Tremaine scanned the street in both directions then went through the broken doors into the building at a run.

The foyer was shrouded in musty gloom. Tremaine saw a crazy pattern of blood spatters on the carpet. He took the steps two-at-a-time. At the top of the landing he turned back to the gendarme and whispered, "Stand guard here. Shout if you see anything."

Tremaine crept along the passageway. Doors on both sides of the corridor had been broken down and were smeared with streaks of blood. A litter of papers and rubbish lay strewn on the carpet. Rats scampered into the shadows.

The door to apartment 107 hung wide open. Tremaine felt a sudden sickening lurch of foreboding squeeze his guts.

"Henri?" Tremaine stood in the open doorway and whispered. All his senses were heightened to straining. His breath sawed in his throat and his blood sang in his ears. He licked dry, cracked lips and called out again.

"Henri? It's Tremaine," he called hoarsely.

Nothing.

Tremaine drew a deep breath. He felt vulnerable and exposed without a weapon.

He took two steps through the open door and froze.

The apartment was in semi-darkness and he hesitated long enough to let his eyes adjust, aware that above the eerie silence was a low hum of noise that made his skin prickle.

"Henri?" Tremaine took three more steps around a teak wood display cabinet and into the living area. The hum of noise became a buzz of disturbed sound, and then an odor jagged like broken glass in the back of his throat. It was the stench of death, now so familiar that it no longer made him choke or gag. He went to the nearest window and drew back the curtains.

Henri Pelletier lay on the living room floor, and if it had not been for the gruesome spatters of blood splashed against the wall and the dark brown stain around his head, Tremaine might have thought him asleep. His face looked peaceful, his eyes closed, his body stretched out, but somehow serene and composed. Flies crawled over the corpse in a black swarm of buzzing noise, dipping and feasting delightedly in the shattered contents of the man's skull.

Sitting in a chair beside the mayor's body slumped a middle-aged woman in a crumpled dressing gown. She had been shot in the head. A rivulet of blood trickled from a hole between her eyes, down her sagging face.

Tremaine stood, unmoving for long seconds. A pistol lay on the carpet beside Henri's dead body. The mayor had evidently shot his wife, and then committed suicide. Tremaine felt no grief; he barely knew the man and had never met his wife – but he felt an unaccountable sadness for Camille.

"Shit," he muttered.

He went through to the bedroom and stripped the blankets off the mattress. The room smelled of perfumes and powders. He draped the blankets over both bodies and stepped back into the corridor. The young gendarme stood anxiously on the top step of the landing. His face was white.

He pointed at another open apartment door. "I... I think I heard something."

A chill ran down Tremaine's spine. He crept like a cat

burglar to the landing, holding his breath, with his eyes fixed on the threatening door. The gendarme hopped anxiously from foot to foot, impatient to flee. Under one of his boots a floorboard creaked.

The sound slashed across the silence. Tremaine froze in mid stride. The gendarme sobbed a startled gasp.

Suddenly the door across the corridor flew back and a hideous blood-drenched ghoul stood growling in the threshold. It had once been a middle-aged man. The shreds of a tie still hung around its neck, and the scraps of a white business shirt draped in tatters off its rotting, decomposing skeleton. The ghoul's grey greasy flesh was covered in a disease of livid swollen blisters and from its jaw and throat dripped drooling blood. The zombie saw the two men. Its face turned ugly and enraged, its mouth a dark pit as it snarled.

"Run!" Tremaine cried. The word barely escaped his lips before the zombie lunged. It exploded across the narrow passageway in a howl of noise, seizing the gendarme by the throat. The young soldier lost his balance and the two bodies crashed and tumbled down the flight of stairs. Tremaine heard the gendarme scream in agony. The infected ghoul had the soldier on his back, pinned and helpless. Its clawed hands were tight around the gendarme's throat. Tremaine started down the stairs and kicked his foot into the ghoul's ribs. It had no effect. The zombie reared back and then lunged for the gendarme's face. Its jaws latched onto the soldier's face and bit through his chin, growling like a dog until it tore off a bleeding chunk of the soldier's flesh. Blood spattered Tremaine's legs and sprayed across the staircase. The ghoul turned its head, spat the mouthful of warm flesh onto the ground, and lunged again, biting off the soldier's nose. One of the gendarme's eyeballs popped from its socket and dangled on his bloody cheek from the end of its nerve stem.

Tremaine fled through the doors and into the bright sunlight, sweating and shaking with fear. The APC was where he expected it to be. Camille sat hunched behind the wheel, staring impatiently. Tremaine sprinted to the passenger door and threw himself inside.

"Drive!" Tremaine cried in alarm.

"Where are my parents?" Camille instinctively put the armored car in gear and began to pick up speed. "And where is the gendarme?"

"The soldier was attacked by a ghoul. He's infected."

Camille's eyes widened. She noticed the fresh wet blood on Tremaine's pants. "And my parents? My mother and father?"

"They weren't there," Tremaine told a compassionate lie. His heart was racing. He could feel his hands shake. A hot flush of blood burned on his cheeks.

"They escaped?"

"It seems that way," Tremaine could not bring himself to tell Camille the terrible truth.

Camille went very quiet for a long moment, frowning with concentration until she steered the APC onto the wide road that would take them to the university. Finally she said softly, "My father told me there were secret tunnels under the Palace of the Popes that ran beneath the old city walls," she muttered. "I never believed him." She gave a wry shake of her head. "But that must have been how they escaped to safety, right?" When she turned her eyes to Tremaine's he saw the desperate silent appeal in her gaze.

He nodded his head. "Right," he said. "They're probably miles and miles away from here now. They might even have found a boat…" He was about to say more when a sudden noise startled him. He jumped with fright. It sounded close by.

"Christ!" his nerves jangled. He heard voices. He shot a glance out through the blood-smeared windows and saw nothing, then turned and peered over his shoulder. In the rear compartment of the APC he saw two white-faced grubby children and half-a-dozen cowering adults.

"Who are they?" he heard himself shouting.

"They are refugees and survivors, just like us," Camille said reasonably. "I saw them run from the church. They're coming with us."

\* \* \*

The undead roamed in the thousands across Avignon, wandering in packs as they hunted down the last of the city's survivors. When the APC bumped over the broken wire fence that bordered the university campus, there were still hundreds of the infected milling on the grounds.

Camille steered the armored car straight for the gatehouse. She could see that the ancient stone fortification had been damaged; the structure had a precarious lean to one side and several of the great stone blocks had been gouged by heavy impact. The steel gate that once held back the undead now lay folded and broken on top of crushed, mutilated bodies.

Camille shot a quick sideways glance at Tremaine. He sat hunched forward, peering through the blood-smudged armored glass of the windscreen, gripping tightly at a hand-hold to brace himself for impact.

"Don't slow down!" Tremaine sensed Camille's eyes upon him and the question they contained. "You have to keep the speed up. If you slow down and the undead overwhelm the vehicle, we'll never make it."

In response, the engine note of the APC changed and became a determined throaty growl. A plume of dust rose up from behind the big tires. Camille wrestled with the steering wheel until the vehicle was lined up with the open gate. Beyond the wide arched opening she could see the shape of another armored car, slewed across the footpath with its doors open and the blue paint splattered in blood.

The surrounding undead spilled from the university buildings and came at a frenzied run, drawn by the roaring noise of the diesel engine. Camille stole a glance through the driver's side window and saw one of the infected throw itself at the APC as it rumbled past. The ghoul had its face pressed to the glass, howling at her. Its face so disfigured by lacerations and the awful ravages of decomposition that it hardly looked human. She swung the steering wheel and the APC began to swerve and slalom.

"Concentrate!" Tremaine barked.

The APC shot through the stone arch and then jounced over the crumpled steel gate. Inside the vehicle, everyone screamed in alarm as the armored car rose up on its offside wheels and the world tilted for a long sickening moment. The vehicle swerved, out of control, then righted itself. Camille cried out in fear and snatched at the wheel.

"Lookout!" Tremaine thrust a finger ahead.

The other armored car had crashed into a felled tree trunk and was slewed across the footpath, broadside to the road. Camille watched in horror as the vehicle filled the windscreen. At the last second the steering responded. The APC's nose clipped the rear side of the other armored car in a screeching jolt of steel on steel

283

and a feather of grinding sparks. Camille was thrown forward by the impact, and her foot came off the gas pedal. The vehicle rocked from side to side and the view through the windscreen lurched drunkenly.

"Keep going!" Tremaine shouted. "Keep going!"

In front of them stretched the wide road that ringed the old city walls; a wasteland strewn with abandoned burned-out cars and debris. Camille could see no way through. She swerved hard to the right and the armored car responded sluggishly. The steering felt suddenly heavy.

The APC mounted the curb and the big wheels churned at the blood-soaked grass beneath the walls. Behind her she heard the baying howls of the undead, following like a pack of hunting dogs.

She reached the Porte De La Republique gates. Thousands of dead bodies littered the ground, scattered across the grass and the sidewalk in mounds. It looked like the gruesome aftermath of a battlefield. The dead lay, swollen and bloated, staring up at the sun while the scavenger birds perched on their corpses and pecked at the flesh. For some reason they did not understand, these victims of the undead had not caught the contagion. They had been slaughtered but had not turned.

"What do I do?" Camille balked. The road was jammed with cars. She could see no way through.

"Drive over them," Tremaine said flatly.

Camille had never heard that tone in his voice before. She snatched her horrified gaze from the gruesome spectacle and saw the fixed, stern expression on his face. His jaw was clenched, his eyes black and terrible.

"I… I can't!" Camille quailed. Her foot came off the accelerator and the APC began to lose momentum. Behind the vehicle, the horde of undead quickly closed.

"They're not infected. They were murdered."

Tremaine reached across the cabin of the APC and seized Camille by the arm. His face was swollen, his voice brutal as he shook her, burying his fingers deep into her flesh.

"Do it!" he snarled. "Do it or we will die too. Do it or else every life that has been sacrificed will have been wasted for nothing."

Camille's grip stiffened on the steering wheel and her face drained of all color. She heard herself gasping short sharp pants of breath. The APC rolled forward and then hit a bump. Camille heard the big tires breaking bones and crushing bodies. The sound coming up through the vehicle's steel hull was gruesome. She began to sob, steering over the piled corpses through tear-misted eyes. The APC lurched and jolted.

"Keep going," Tremaine's tone became crooning and sympathetic. He could hear undead howls coming closer. He licked his lips, judging the corpse-strewn distance still to cover and then stealing a glance through the vehicle's side mirror, still attached to the door. The undead were a solid wall of looming horror, bearing down on them like the onrushing malevolence of an avalanche.

"Just a little longer," Tremaine coaxed Camille. "Keep your foot on the gas. Don't slow down."

The fastest, most ferocious zombies reached the armored car and pounded their fists against the steel walls of the vehicle. Someone in the rear compartment screamed with shrill fear.

"Faster!" Tremaine's voice became edged. "You're almost through."

A rotting, hideous face slammed itself against the side window of the APC and he flinched in shock. Half the ghoul's face had been torn away, and the jaw hung slack over exposed bone and bare gums. Its dead flesh had begun decomposing: the empty eye-socket crawled with fat white maggots. The ghoul snarled at Tremaine, then retched across the windscreen.

"Faster!"

Finally the ground ahead of the APC cleared of bodies and the vehicle gathered speed. Ahead, Camille could see the burned out remains of the Grande Hotel, still smoldering on the far side of the wreckage-strewn road. A rush of traumatic memories overwhelmed her. She remembered the horror of defending the stairwells, and then a vision of Eve's dead body flashed across her mind. She remembered Mr. Goldstein's murder and the sight of his frail broken body on the grass. Tears rolled unashamedly down her cheek. When she reached the southwest corner of the wall, her lips were quivering and she sobbed.

Camille turned right, following the road along the bank of the Rhône, swerving onto the footpaths and grassy verges to avoid abandoned cars. Street signs drifted by, and on the river she saw the charred remains of boats tied to their moorings, burned down to the waterline. A bridge loomed in the distance behind wandering packs of undead. The ghouls emerged from the carparks and the riverbank and ran screaming towards the APC. Camille stared fixedly ahead and did not slow down again. The undead thumped and bumped beneath the chassis as the big tires ran them over.

She turned left onto the arch of a bridge and changed down to low gear. Away in the distance, and smudged by a haze of drifting smoke, Tremaine caught his first glimpse of Fort Saint-Andre. The ancient stone battlements sat perched high atop a hill.

"How much further?" he leaned across the cabin and

asked Camille. It was the first time they had spoken in several minutes. Tremaine stole a surreptitious glance at the APC's fuel gauge. The needle showed half-full.

"Just a few minutes," Camille spoke without taking her eyes off the road. The bridge was an obstacle course of burned out cars. One hatchback hung precariously over the steel guard rail. They reached the middle of the bridge and saw a roadblock ahead. Camille felt a sudden chill of apprehension.

She flicked a glance at Tremaine.

He checked the rear view mirror. Undead were following but had been left behind by the APC's steady speed. He guessed a horde of over a hundred ghouls had massed on the threshold of the bridge and were gradually closing. He focused on the roadblock.

It was a barricade of steel drums, with sandbag emplacements on either side. Two of the barrels had been rolled aside, and a third lay, knocked down like a tenpin. The APC would not fit through the narrow breach.

Tremaine made his decision.

"Stop!"

He flung open the heavy door and dropped down to the blacktop. He glanced over his shoulder and figured he had just thirty seconds before the undead would be upon them. He sprinted to the barricade and threw his weight against the barrel lying on its side. It had been filled with concrete. He braced himself and began to push. Suddenly there were three more men around him; a teenage boy, maybe seventeen years old, and two middle-aged men. One of them had a pistol tucked inside the waistband of his torn and stained trousers. They had come from the rear compartment of the APC. Together, Tremaine and the youngster rolled the barrel aside while the other two men grunted and strained to move another drum clear.

Tremaine's brow blistered with beads of sweat. He heard the strained rasp of his own breath. The undead were closing quickly; a dozen of the ghouls had streaked ahead of the pack, baying and snarling. He heard Camille gun the big engine in rising panic.

With another drum rolled aside, the gap had been made wide enough for the APC. Tremaine ran back to the armored car with the others following. Camille sat hunched at the wheel, her gaze fixed on the rear-view mirror. The undead were close enough that she could hear their ragged snarls and see the fierce frenzy in their hideous expressions.

"Quick!" she cried out. Tremaine's fingers fumbled for the door handle. He saw the rear doors of the APC swing wide. The teenage boy and one of the men scrambled into the back of the troop carrier, but the man with the gun stood facing the undead with the pistol drawn.

"Get in!" Tremaine saw the drama unfolding in the mirror. He doubted the shooter could even hear him. He was an overweight man with a short stubble of beard and a fleshy round face. He stood side on to the undead like an old-fashioned duelist, with one hand propped on his hip and his feet a shoulder's width apart.

Tremaine cried out in rising horror.

The retort of the gun sounded deafeningly loud. The shooter's hand was thrown high into the air by the recoil. One of the stampeding undead went down in a hideous tangle of limbs and three more ghouls following close behind stumbled and fell over the corpse. The respite lasted just seconds. The rest of the undead reached the shooter and overwhelmed him. Tremaine heard terrified pitiful screams from the back of the APC. The rest of the survivors could only watch on in impotent horror as the man was brought down like a buffalo being attacked by a pride of lions. He went down on his haunches, screaming. The gun fired again, but Tremaine guessed the shot went wild. The shooter died in a flurry of howls and blood.

"Drive!" he pounded his fist against the side of the door in frustration, then stared over his shoulder and watched the teenage boy lean far out of the rolling vehicle to pull the two swinging rear doors shut.

The APC shot the breach in the barricade with inches to spare on either side. Camille let out a sigh of relieved breath she had been holding throughout the tense seconds of the attack. Tremaine stared fixedly ahead. On the far side of the bridge were the burned out remains of a village. Black puddles of dried blood criss-crossed the road. A street sign at an intersection showed a route north to the left. Camille turned right onto a narrow secondary road and the ground beneath the big wheels began to slowly rise.

Tremaine wrenched himself around in his seat and peered hard at the white shocked faces of the passengers in the back of the vehicle. Apart from the two children, the teenager and the man who had survived the attack at the barricade, there were four women huddled close together along one of the long bench seats dressed in ragged blood-spattered clothes. They were aged in their twenties and thirties, their faces powdered white with soot ash and dust. They stared blankly with unseeing eyes, underscored with the heavy dark bruising of grief.

"Does anyone have a gun?" Tremaine asked. "Any personal weapon at all?"

The middle-aged man who had survived the attack

289

turned his head slowly. He looked like the victim of a ravaging terminal disease. His face was very pale and gaunt, the features indefinite and blurred. His mouth hung slack and spittle rolled from the corner of his mouth.

"I have a gun," he said softly. To Tremaine's ear the man's accent sounded vaguely Italian. He touched at a bulge in his pocket but did not reveal the weapon. Tremaine nodded. He regretted throwing down the axe when they had fled the gendarmerie barracks.

A sudden abrupt change of course brought his attention back to the road. Camille had turned again and the APC began cruising through the burned out shell of another village. Many of the buildings were stone. Their roofs had collapsed and internal walls had tumbled down. Their broken windows looked like black vacant eyes as the armored car growled along the narrow street. At the end of the road was a round-about with signs. Camille turned right again and changed down to low gear.

"This road takes us up to the fort," she said. "But I don't know how far we will get. We may have to run the final kilometer."

Tremaine stared stupidly through the windscreen. The road was narrow and winding, rising at a steep gradient. Along the shoulder of the road were waist-high stone walls. There was nowhere to maneuver. He felt a new surge of panic well up from deep inside him and it took all his will to crush down on the fear and keep his voice calm. He had seen the fort and knew it sat high on a hill that overlooked the surrounding countryside... but he had never considered the possibility that the fort could not comfortably be reached in the APC. Now the reality struck him and tied knots in his guts.

"Go as far as you can," he said. He started to search the sides of the road as each new twisting bend leaped out at them. There were houses here, but they had been built into the face of the rising promontory. The scene was dramatic and eerie. The hillside looked utterly desolate.

The incline up the hill grew steeper and the road narrowed. The APC slowed to a crawling pace as the engine came under strain. At the next tight twisting bend, the side of the vehicle scraped harshly against a rock barrier – and stuck fast.

"Christ!"

Camille killed the engine and everyone clambered out of the armored car. Tremaine had to exit through the cupola because his door had wedged tight against the wall. He paused for a moment on top of the steel beast and turned in a slow circle. Fort Saint-Andre stood at the crest of the hill, almost a kilometer further up the steep incline. Tremaine could not see the road beyond the next bend because it was shrouded by a small stand of trees. He looked back along the narrow path they had driven up. From this height he could see over the village they had passed through, all the way to the bridge and beyond. Avignon lay hidden behind a billowing pyre of black smoke that columned high into the sky.

He jumped down to the ground. Camille had herded the small knot of survivors into a group. They set out on the narrow path towards the summit.

The gradient became so steep that they had to lean forward into it. The road was dusted with loose stones and drifting dirt. Tremaine felt himself break out in fresh blisters of sweat. One of the women began to lag behind, limping heavily. Tremaine's head was never still, turning and twisting like a fighter pilot looking for threats.

291

They smelled it first; a cloying over-ripe stench that hung heavy on the air and painted the back of their throats. It was the sickening odor of putrefaction. Tremaine felt himself stiffen with tension. He stopped in mid-stride and turned with a wide-eyed warning of alarm to the rest of the group.

The gaunt man with the gun went into a crouch and fumbled in his pocket for his pistol. It looked like a relic from the last World War.

Tremaine and the man locked eyes and silent understanding passed between them. Together they crept warily forward to the next bend.

Fifty yards away, two figures were squatted on their haunches at the side of the road. Between them, lying prone on its back, twitched the corpse of a woman. The creatures were naked and covered in filth. One of them reached into the cavity of the dead body's guts and rummaged around for a handful of bloody organs. The man beside Tremaine gasped his revulsion – and the undead heads turned in malevolent unison.

The man with the gun stood rooted to the spot. He raised the weapon, extending both his arms. The ghouls came to their feet and hissed. One of them clambered over the wall and began to circle through the nearby stand of trees. It was small; in life it had been a child. It moved like a wraith in the shadows, snarling through bleeding lips.

The taller of the two ghouls charged, driven by instinct and blood-lust. Tremaine felt his guts turn to hot liquid.

"Shoot!" he shouted at the man beside him. "Shoot the bastard!"

The ghoul was a ferocious apparition of blood and fury. It howled in screeching madness.

"Shoot!" Tremaine could hear the rising panic in his own voice. "Shoot!"

The gun roared in a deafening explosion of violent noise and blue smoke. The recoil caught the man off guard and flung him backwards so he staggered to keep his balance. Tremaine's ears were ringing. His heart leaped into his throat and threatened to choke him.

When the haze cleared, the ghoul lay sprawled on its back in the middle of the narrow lane, the top of its head blown away and the contents of its infected skull flung across the asphalt. Its heels drummed on the blacktop. Its fingers twitched then stopped.

Tremaine let out a gasp of breath and turned back to where Camille stood watching in alarm.

"Quickly!" Tremaine shouted, throwing the last vestiges of caution to the wind. "There is another one somewhere in the trees. Run for it!"

A panicked sound like a wailing moan went up. The group began to run for their lives.

Tremaine led the way. His legs burned and his chest heaved like a bellows. The gradient became steeper and the loose dusty gravel beneath his feet more precarious. He slipped and threw out his hands to break his fall. He felt giddy with fatigue and exhaustion.

The teenage boy reached the top of the rise first and stood breathing deeply with his hands on his hips. The rest of the group had strung out like the peloton of a bicycle race. The man with the gun had lost ground. His face was twisted in pain.

Camille and Tremaine ran side by side. Camille's steps were still light while Tremaine labored. Behind them the limping woman suddenly hobbled and swayed heavily. She cried out in anguish and panic. Her tattered clothes clung damp with sweat to her body and her hair hung in ratty tangles over her face. Her mouth hung open, gasping for air, and there was a helpless, desperate appeal in her tortured eyes.

The undead ghoul sprang from the shadow of the trees and knocked the woman off her feet.

Tremaine saw the ghoul attack and knew he could do nothing to save the woman. She went down with a cry of terror choked in her throat. The zombie rolled her onto her back and went for her face. The woman screamed hysterically. She flailed with her fists and kicked her legs. The ghoul was like a savage dog, snapping and snarling. It lunged for her neck and buried its teeth into the soft pale flesh. The woman gave a last hoarse gasp and then went very still. Tremaine reeled away, trembling and seized Camille by the arm.

"We can't help her," he croaked. "Run!"

The woman was still conscious, still breathing shallowly as the ghoul gnawed its way up from her mauled throat and feasted on the delicacy of her eyes. Her hands fluttered weakly and she tried to gasp for help. No sound came. For long gruesome seconds she was alert and aware that she was being eaten alive, cringing in unaccountable agony but paralyzed by the weight of the beast that squatted on her chest and the debilitating trauma of her injuries.

She died in a slow, excruciating nightmare of pain.

Tremaine and Camille reached the top of the rise. Fort Saint-Andre stood at the end of the road. It was a vast imposing bastion; two huge round stone towers crowned with battlements and between them the yawning dark hole of an open gatehouse. The western wall stood over thirty feet high and ended in another stone tower. Tremaine swayed, breathless and gaping in wonder, while Camille and the others ran on. The fort was a preserved medieval masterpiece.

"Keep going!" Tremaine shouted. He felt the first faint stirrings of renewed hope and it put fresh strength into his legs. He ran along the path with the breath sawing in his ears, getting louder and louder until he realized it was not the sound of his strained breathing, but something more sinister.

The knot of survivors were fifty yards away from the gatehouse, with Camille leading the group, still running comfortably despite the taxing incline. The rest of the survivors were swaying and stumbling with fatigue. Tremaine had fallen behind. Now he sensed his own vulnerability. He flashed a look over his shoulder and saw nothing until he turned back towards the fort and sensed movement to his right.

There were houses hidden from the path by a high row of trees. The homes had been built facing a view across the river to Avignon. All Tremaine could see were rooftops. He stared, fretting anxiously. The noise in his ears grew louder and took on a menacing tone.

"Christ!" he swore.

He started to run.

A dozen undead burst through the dense line of trees, drawn by the sounds of pounding footsteps and Tremaine's shouted voice. They were newly infected, he realized; their clothes were blood-spattered and their bodies ravaged with gruesome wounds, but the flesh had not turned grey, had not begun to rot. They came howling like beasts and ran to intercept him.

Ahead, Camille and the others passed suddenly into the deep shadow of the fort's gatehouse entrance. Tremaine ran on with sweat streaming into his eyes and a stabbing stitch of pain cramping his side.

The nearest undead ghoul sprinted ahead of the

baying pack. It lunged for Tremaine when he was just seconds away from safety. Tremaine felt his legs ripped from underneath him. He went down in the dust with the ghoul clawing at one of his feet. Tremaine rolled onto his back, screaming in fear and blind panic. He kicked out with his free foot and connected with the ghoul's blood-streaked face. Tremaine lay sprawled across the gatehouse entrance. The following undead saw him go down and a triumphant howl of anticipation snarled in their throats.

The ghoul clawing at his leg howled ferociously. Tremaine dragged himself into the shadows of the great gatehouse on his elbows, still kicking out and cursing. Frantic shots rang out. The man with the gun knocked down two of the ghouls and then the weapon fell silent.

Standing in the deep shade of the archway, Camille lunged for the safety latch that raised and lowered the fort's gate. A thick loop of chain tethered to a hook hung by her head. She slipped the chain free of the hook and the vast gate plunged down from its holding rail within the stone wall. It dropped like a guillotine blade.

The gate was a latticework of thick tempered steel bars. It fell with a deafening rattle of chain, like a warship's anchor as it spills through the hawsehole. The gate crashed to the ground and crushed the ghoul's skull under their massive weight.

Tremaine stared wild-eyed with fright. He was panting for breath, lathered in sweat and trembling like a man in the grips of fever.

But he was alive.

And they were safe inside the fort.

# Epilogue:

The moon rose slowly over the far horizon, and creeping nightfall painted out the horrors of the world.

Sitting pensively atop the battlements of Fort Saint-Andre, Tremaine stared down across the valley and tried to count the fires. He felt impossibly tired; overwrought with tension and fatigue.

The fort was impregnable; defended on three sides by high walls and on the western side by sheer cliffs that rose above swampy marshland, and in the abandoned caretaker's residence they had found food, water and the beginnings of a small vegetable garden.

They were safe; a handful of survivors who had endured the apocalypse. Tremaine felt no relief. The days ahead would be filled with hardship.

Camille came quietly up the stone steps and sat beside him. She stayed very quiet and thoughtful, watching the fires in the valley with exaggerated attention. She did not look at Tremaine, but it was impossible for her not to be aware of him.

"We found buckets and set them to catch any rainwater," she said at last. "And there were cans of soft drink in the room they used as a visitor's center."

Tremaine grunted. Food and water; they would be the next two great challenges. Tomorrow, he would extend the caretaker's vegetable patch and search the residence for tools – and weapons.

*But at least there would be a tomorrow.*

"Do you think we're the last people alive in the world?" Camille's voice sounded small in the darkness.

"No," Tremaine said, and believed it. "There will be others, Camille. There are other places like Avignon across Europe and there will be people hidden in underground bunkers and high in the mountains – individuals and small groups like us."

"Then we're not alone?"

"Only temporarily," Tremaine tried to sound optimistic. "But one day the infection will burn itself out and the world will be wiped clean. Then we can leave here and look for them. Mankind will survive. Tonight is a night for remembering loved ones and remorse. Tomorrow morning, we start afresh."

Camille's thigh casually brushed Tremaine's as they sat close together, alone in the night. She made no move to pull away.

In the valley far below, under a blanket of smoky haze, the ancient city of Avignon continued to burn.

Printed in Great Britain
by Amazon